THE CELESTIAL ISLES
BOOK ONE

THE

ELECTRICAL MENAGERIE

MOLLIE E. REEDER
© MMXVIII

THE ELECTRICAL MENAGERIE
Copyright © 2018 by Mollie E. Reeder.

For information contact :
info@writeratops.com

Revolver artwork provided by Vecteezy.com
Special thanks to Artisticco

ISBN: 978-0-692-12428-4
First Edition: June 2018

for my collaborators,
my co-producers,
and my friends:

those past,
those present,
and those to come.

35 YEARS AGO

Sylvester had a book about birds, and the book said that the bones of birds were all hollow.

Watching starlings from the window, he considered the diagrams and envied the concept. Birds went freely, in their lightness somehow stronger than any forces that wanted to pull them down. Tethered — flightless — he remained trapped behind the high and imposing arched window of his second-story bedroom.

The view from that window was like a map. Beneath him, the unchangingly green estate rolled away to wooded parish, its colors fading as darkness set. There was the pale gravel path that wrapped around the house and then curved away, headed to the high road, and there was the hill far beyond the woods where lambs made white dots against the grass.

Looking through the window, he liked to imagine that he was there — on the hilltop with the lambs, or walking bravely through the wood even though it was very dark, or following the road away from home.

From his window, he had learned the secret names of the lambs, and he had discovered the creature that lived in the wood, and he had charted a hundred expeditions down the driveway, past the gate and onward to something new.

Just now, none of those games held any interest. As twilight set over the garden, his sisters played with hobby horses, galloping through the rosebushes. Their laughter, clear and bright, reached him through the window glass, and he wanted to call down to them.

Fumbling with the brass latch on the pane, he wrested the window open. A sweet and bracing evening air greeted him, his sisters' voices carrying high and away. He opened his mouth to call out.

"Sylvester!" Mother interrupted him, and crossed the room. "You'll catch your death!"

His hands shook from the effort of undoing the latch. He lowered them, resting against the cool pages of the book splayed open in his lap.

Mother leaned out and called the girls indoors for bed, then she shut the window up and locked it. Just above, the Stars were barely agleam in a milky purple sky. Sylvester stared up at them until she drew the curtains and blotted them out.

Taking his wheelchair, Mother turned him away from the window and wheeled him to bed.

He looked down at the book he was reading. A pop-up paper castle rose as he turned the page, every line of its architecture carefully reconstructed with many parapets and bricks drawn in dark ink.

"Do you know what I learned today?" he asked her.

"The royal palace on Celestia has four hundred rooms. Can you imagine? Four *hundred* rooms?"

It didn't seem like there were four hundred rooms in the whole world. His world consisted almost entirely of this one. The high window with heavy panes. The deep rug that sank, miring the wheels of the chair, grasping his feet when he tried to walk. The rocking horse he'd outgrown years ago. The many too-soft quilts on the bed, and the railing on the side in case he rolled over in his sleep.

Everything frozen exactly the way it had been before he got sick — except him. Mother took him under the arms and lifted him onto the bed, but he was almost too big for her to do that anymore. An unchanging world was not enough to keep him unchanged himself.

"How fascinating," she said.

"Every room is connected by a secret passageway," he went on. "All four hundred of them. And — there's a whole room of nowt but swords!"

"Sounds dangerous." Mother took the book from his lap.

"I'd like to see that," he said.

"What a pleasant dream," she answered, and blew out the lamp by his bedside. "Perhaps you will. Goodnight, Sylvester."

She returned the book to the shelf and shut the door behind her.

What a pleasant dream.

Mother was talking about the kind of dream that took hold of you while you slept. The kind that whisked you away. The kind that didn't often make much sense, and didn't stick around with daylight. There was nothing wrong with that kind of dream, but he wasn't ready to sleep. When her footsteps receded down the hallway, he yanked the covers from his legs.

There was another kind of dream. The kind you took hold of when you were awake — the kind contained in books, daydreams, and new inventions. And he thought that kind was even better.

He looked for his chair, but she'd pushed it to the other side of the room. Sitting up, he put his legs over the edge of the bed and reached for the crutches at his bedside.

Grasping the crutches with feeble fingers, he eased off the bed until his bare feet touched the wood below. It was a relief to feel anything in his feet and legs, even the cold flatness of the floor. There were days when he couldn't. He steeled himself with a sharp breath, then leaned forward, drawing himself out of bed and onto the crutches.

Halfway to the bookcase, he gritted his teeth to suppress a cry of frustration as his leg twisted up beneath him. Tears pricked at the corners of his eyes, the angry kind, which were the only kind he knew how to cry anymore. His doctor said that if he stayed indoors, he might get better. But with every day spent behind the window, outgrowing the room more by the minute, he felt worse — and not just in his legs.

He meant what he said. He desperately wanted to see that palace on Celestia, and its room full of swords — but it was so far away, so far beyond his small world. Even this gap between the bookcase and bed was an impossible distance.

He looked toward the wall, to the animal menagerie painted in silhouette.

"I'll never make it," he whispered to them. He had named them all, and knew each of them.

You will, they whispered back.

He tightened his grip on the crutches until his fists burned with pain and took another step toward the bookcase. The book he had been reading, the one about the palace, was sitting right there on the end. Its gold lettering flashed against a navy blue spine, beckoning.

Staggering the last few steps, he buckled against the bookcase with a heavy thump. Taking the book in his hands, he cast his crutches aside and slid down to the floor with the bookcase at his back. The curtain was just within grasp, and he used his last ounce of strength to pull it aside, opening the room to the clear and resplendent starlight.

Holding the book in his lap, Sylvester turned another page and continued to dream.

2

THE ELECTRICAL MENAGERIE

Tabatha wanted to see the electrical.

"Two tickets," said her father, thumbing through his pocketbook. Beside him, she stood on her toes to peer over the worn wooden shelf of the ticket-taker's booth.

"Two tickets," repeated the electrical ticket-taker, then its mechanical brains hummed as it counted the change. There were not many electricals on Carpathia Isle, and the only ones Tabatha had ever seen were for labor and service, dull gray with lifeless voices. This electrical was a pale blue-green, chipping around the back of the head, with a bright voice and a friendly face. It raised an arm to wave goodbye, joints whirring. "Thank you! Enjoy the show."

Bursting into a smile, she stood higher on her toes to wave back.

"Get along," said her father, and pushed her forward with a hand on her back.

The big tent stood under a towering black sky, and all the Stars watched. The tent was blue, sashed with gold, and a shaft of warm light spilled out of its open doorway.

From inside, there was the discordant hum of musical instruments beginning to warm up.

A crowd moved from the ticket booth toward the yawning tent. Some people had the long brown trousers of the tenant farmers, like Tabatha and her father; others were ladies and gentlemen in gowns and coattails.

Feeling sort of fancy herself, Tabatha skipped ahead of her father, but he halted her with a shout before she got too far. Taking his hand, Tabatha walked with him through the doorway and into the tent.

It was the biggest tent ever, with bench seating that faced a painted ring in the center. Tabatha and her father climbed the steps to find their seats, but she was too excited to sit down, and stayed standing.

To one side, an electrical marching band began to play — a yellow electrical with long fingers, who played the trumpet, a tall green electrical who banged a drum, and a round blue electrical who played the fiddle. Delighted, she clapped for them.

"Daddy," she said, noticing that his hands were still in his lap. "Clap for them!"

"They're electricals," he said. "They don't know the difference. Sit down."

She sat down and folded her hands in her lap, heart sinking.

Nothing had been the same since that day two winters ago, when Mama fell down in the field and never got back up. Daddy never laughed anymore. Neither of them did.

For a moment, Tabatha became overwhelmed by a

sadness so powerful that it muted the sounds around her and turned the rich blue ceiling to gray.

Then the lights went out completely.

A single spotlight illuminated the center of the ring, and the green electrical started to roll his drum. A disembodied voice pealed like thunder out of the darkness. *"Ladies and Gentlemen..."*

Twin spotlights turned on the crowd, roving, as if searching for someone.

"Children and electricals..."

The spotlight bounced over Tabatha and her father, momentarily lighting them, and her sadness fell away to anticipation. She gripped Daddy's arm, excited, and leaned forward to see better.

"Traveling across the farthest reaches of the Celestial Isles to perform for you tonight..." From backstage, glinting in the darkness, paraded the shapes of fantastic mechanical people and creatures.

A single light flared in the center of the ring. A pair of electricals pulled a dark cloth away to reveal a looking glass. Tabatha took in a breath. There was a *man* inside the mirror! He put his hands against the glass, trapped, feeling for some seam by which he might escape. The electricals turned the mirror around to show that it was ordinary — nothing hidden on its backside.

The man, desperate, banged on the glass from its inverse side. Once, twice — and then his fist emerged from the mirror. The crowd shouted, and a lady even screamed. He pulled his hand back into the mirror and held it up to quiet the crowd.

The crowd hushed. Tabatha didn't breathe.

Then the man leapt out of the mirror.

There was a thundering crash and a brilliant flash of pink smoke and blinding light, and the lights all came back on. He stood in the flesh at the center of the ring, air around him plumed with neon smoke and still faintly sizzling with sparks. The shattered glass glittered in pieces at his feet. The frame of it was hollow and empty behind him.

"S.F. Carthage and his Electrical Menagerie!" that disembodied voice boomed.

Mr. Carthage was a human, not an electrical, with dark, tousled hair, sideburns that followed his jawline to meet in a mustache, and a blue coat with tails. His arms were flung wide in a gesture of greeting, a velvet hat in one hand. A broad smile made small creases at the corners of his eyes.

The fantastic Mr. Carthage looked across the crowd, and by chance, his gaze landed on Tabatha. They locked eyes, and she had never felt so *seen* in all her life.

For a moment she felt they were standing in the ring together. That she was an actual part of the show — part of something bigger and more fantastical than her mud-splattered life in the tenant fields. Something that wasn't filled with grief and fear.

Something like a dream.

In just an hour, the show contained more amazing things than Tabatha had seen in a whole lifetime. An hour was too fleeting, and — far too soon — it was over.

Daddy took her by the hand and pulled her out of her

seat and down the steps to leave. Sawdust sank under her shoes, then turned to hard-packed dirt as they exited the tent into the clear and cold night.

Another farmer called out a greeting, and when the two men stopped together to talk about the drought, Daddy released her hand. The smells of popcorn and sugar clung to her nose, stronger than the juniper and sagebrush of the field. The air was hazy with lingering smoke, and the back of her throat tingled. She turned toward the emptying tent, yearning to see it all over again.

Daddy wasn't paying attention when she glanced up at him, so she walked away, back toward the big top.

CARTHAGE STOOD IN the empty big top and inhaled, tasting the metallic sizzle of lingering stardust burn at the back of his throat. He wanted just one more moment here before they tore it down and left for another stop on the tour. The transient nature of touring entertainment meant he would never stand on exactly the same stage again.

He was tired. He wasn't as young as he had been in the days when he lived hand-to-mouth doing card tricks on the streets of the Central Isles, and this — *this* was harder. The Electrical Menagerie was going on its sixth month touring, an itinerary that took them across two dozen isles and twice as many different rail depots.

He never struggled to perform. Performance was electrifying. Standing under a spotlight had a sensation for him like currents of energy bolting up and down his body. But when the show was over, he was a frayed wire. Still live and sparking, but shorted.

Sensing somebody at his back, he turned with a slight start.

A small face, peering into the tent between two parted flaps, pulled back. The wee girl seemed startled to have been caught lurking, and there was a moment of indecision — was that even fear? Not wanting to scare her off, he called out in a strong but gentle voice.

"Are you looking for something?"

There was a pause as she mustered the courage. "I just wanted to see if you would do something else."

He chuckled to himself. "Like what?"

The girl, seeming confident now that he wasn't going to be angry at her for intruding, squeezed through the part and entered the tent with him. She shrugged to his question.

He put his hat back on. The show was not over. Feeling the energy return to him, he crossed the distance, stopping just inside the ring. She stood just outside.

"I was wondering," she said, "how you made it seem like you escaped the looking glass?"

He looked down at her. She was a very clever girl. She wasn't very old, and many young children simply took his illusions for what they appeared to be: magic. The fact that she understood there was some gimmick to it filled him with both pride and pity.

"How do you think I did it?"

She pressed a finger to her mouth, thinking. "Projectors, I think."

"That's not it," he said, impressed. "But that's a very clever idea."

"Well," she said, and stepped up on the edge of the ring to gain the few inches of height. "How then?"

"I have a better question." He bent at the waist, meeting her in the middle so they were eye to eye. "What's this doing there?"

He produced a foil-wrapped chocolate coin from behind her ear and held it up. Her ponderous look fell away, the furrowed brow giving way to a bright smile of wonder. The first trick he had ever learned, the simplest one he knew. But as she took the coin, she looked at him like nobody had ever done anything so amazing.

He smiled back.

"Tabatha!" a harsh voice sliced through the holy silence of the empty big top. A man in a baggy brown coat stormed into the tent and grabbed the little girl by the arm. "How many times have I told you not to wander off?"

Carthage straightened and opened his mouth to ask the father about the show. But the father didn't even acknowledge him. Instead, he yanked his daughter, too sharply, away. Carthage frowned.

As she was pulled back outside, the little girl turned one last time to look over her shoulder. Carthage gave a small wave and earned one final smile before his audience of one was taken away.

Exiting into the crisp night air, Carthage coughed lightly to clear his lungs. His bulky, black-painted electrical stagehands were already flurrying to strike the camp, and the smaller backstage tent collapsed as someone pulled the final stake. He heard his name called, but chose to ignore it, and started walking toward the nearby rail line, where the train was parked.

"Carthage? Carthage!" Huxley chased Carthage down and fell into step with him. "Didn't you hear me calling you?"

Arbrook Huxley was something about twenty-five, with stylishly trimmed wheat-colored hair and an obnoxiously strong Fallsbright accent that reminded Carthage of a typewriter hammering letters.

"How was the show tonight, Huxley?"

"Abysmal."

"The dangerbeast's timing is off, I—"

Carthage came up short as it sank in. He turned. "Did you say *abysmal*?"

"It was a terrible audience," answered Huxley.

Carthage had been heckled more than once, and this was hardly what he qualified as a terrible audience. A little lackluster, perhaps, a little sleepy, but that was rural towns for you. "It wasn't *that* bad."

"*Starsfall*, Carthage—"

"Mind your mouth, Huxley— "

Huxley thrust a hand back toward the show. "It was half empty!"

Carthage looked at Huxley and almost laughed, the frustrated kind. As usual, they were talking about two different things.

They first met on a street corner on Astoria Isle where Carthage was busking. Huxley had been the worst kind of onlooker, the type that stood there for thirty minutes, arms folded, staring at your hands. It was called a *burn* — when a person was so intent on "beating" the effect that they refused your misdirection and simply stared. Finally, when the crowd dispersed, Huxley approached Carthage and told him how the trick worked.

He was wrong.

When Carthage told him he was wrong, Huxley surprised him by laughing. Pleased, instead of frustrated, that he had been fooled. That laugh warmed Carthage immediately.

In his young life, Huxley had been a bank clerk and then a Sixes dealer, but over coffee, he introduced himself as a producer, sermonizing show business with the fervor of a door-to-door salesman. He said Carthage was talented, and could be a star, and didn't need to be playing for tips on a sidewalk.

Listening, Carthage found himself believing it. A partnership felt like an opportunity he'd been waiting his whole life for. Together, they went in and bought a train, 50/50, named themselves The Electrical Menagerie, and set out with their roadshow.

But everything appealing about Huxley turned out to have fine print. He was smart — *so* smart that he always knew a "better" way of doing things. Full of youthful stamina — meaning he could continue an argument indefinitely. Intensely focused — which was a polite way of saying neurotic. And, as Carthage learned *after* they went in together, his new "producer" knew literally nothing about stage magic or even the theater when they met.

Silver-tongued, perhaps, but not exactly sterling.

Although Huxley's varnish had come off, Carthage didn't regret striking out on tour. This was what he lived for — the thrill of a live audience, the heat of the lights and the always-changing view outside his window. Didn't Huxley have any passion? What they were doing meant more than a bottom line.

"Why are you always so worried about money?" he asked.

"When we went into business together, you said, verbatim, 'I want you to worry about the money.'"

"Well, I didn't expect you to take it so literally." They started walking again, and Carthage reached the gangway of the train's freight car. "What was the take?"

"We spent a hundred and twenty dollars," Huxley said.

Carthage turned again, certain he misheard. His ears were still ringing from standing too close to the pyrotechnic blast caps and the electrical band. "We only made one hundred and twenty dollars?"

"No, no. We *spent* one hundred and twenty dollars. As in, we *lost* money."

Carthage came back down the ramp. "We *lost* money? How did that happen?"

Huxley ran a hand over the gold watch chain strung across his waistcoat. "Uh, well... do you want the thorough answer or the short one?"

"Thorough."

"Local permits. Location fees. The isle imposes its

own taxes on public gatherings larger than fifty people, and there was a fifteen-dollar fee attached to the—"

Carthage waved off. "Alright. The short answer."

"Advertising," said Huxley. "We desperately need advertising. We have to fill sixty percent of the seats just to break even — and by that, I mean break even on production expenses. Not counting our salaries. If we don't sell out the next three shows, we'll be forced to cancel the tour."

"Sell out...?" Carthage stared at Huxley. It felt like someone had severed his power completely.

He'd never sold out a show in his life.

Huxley didn't seem to want to say it twice.

Carthage was silent for a moment, staring off as the the last of their patrons dispersed across the field, headed home. When he looked back, Huxley had a raw look, one that was almost frightened.

"Listen," said Huxley. "I know it hasn't all been easy. But neither of us wants to see it end like this."

To be young and afraid — that was a feeling Sylvester Carthage knew too well. "It won't," said Carthage, feeling a sudden compassion. "We'll come out of this."

The trouble was *how*.

★

IN THE MORNING, the train found its next stop.

Carthage stood on the steps of the train where she was parked in the depot and rubbed his hands together until they were warm. The train, blue with gold flourishes, stood out among heavy black freighters and pale silver passenger trains, and the sight of her had already drawn attention on the platform.

He left the train and headed across the depot to the newspaper stand. He was old enough to remember when you could linger in front of the stand and read the headlines, but these days all the papers were blank until you bought them.

"How long are they good for?" he asked the vendor.

"Six weeks of news," the man replied.

Six weeks! That was a good deal. A holopaper purchased in the Central Isles was usually only good for a week's worth of news before it expired. Maybe being way out here in the backwaters of the Southern Isles had its advantages.

Carthage slapped down a sterling dollar and picked up the nearest paper. It flickered as he picked it up, print appearing across the page.

"Keep the change," he told the vendor, unfurling the paper as he walked away.

Locating a bench nearby, he sat down and opened to the classifieds. He hadn't slept at all, lying awake in his compartment trying to think of a way to save his show. Sometimes rich people placed requests in the paper for private performances. He didn't particularly enjoy them — he enjoyed playing to the public. But he'd done more than a few private engagements as a young illusionist, and they were a good source of income.

He patted himself down, but couldn't find his reading glasses, and conceded to reading the paper at arm's length. The classifieds were mostly as expected. A baron on Astoria Isle searching for a nine-string player for his impending wedding. An acting troupe holding open call auditions for actresses, training in the classical works preferred. Another casting call, summoning all young people with interest in performing as moving picture talent, which Carthage suspected was a scam.

Finding nothing in the classifieds, he turned the paper over to its last page. The paper jittered for a moment, and he shook it to clarify the text. On the bottom, a half-page ad appeared. It had scrollwork corners, large type, and the seal of the Crown.

He stared at it for a moment, then held the paper abreast again to make sure he was seeing the fine print correctly, then read it all over again.

He had contracted sweeps at just six years old. At that time, what caused the illness was still contested, and the doctors recommended that stricken children remain indoors, bed-rested in isolation.

Of course, it was advice that was later reversed, but he was part of that ravaged generation that suffered its toll. The next fifteen years of his life were spent in that second-story room, feeble legs wasting from disuse, trapped behind the windowpanes and watching the world go by without him. His friends grew up, their games went on, and their narratives erased him. He wasn't dead, but everyone treated him like he was, even his parents, who talked about him as if he wasn't there.

His solace was his library. For a boy whose view never changed, hardly even with the seasons, books did more to alleviate his pain than any doctor ever could. Fiction, and nonfiction, encyclopedias! Even stories with pictures and no words. Books were wonderful, fantastical things. Carthage loved books. But books didn't satisfy him.

They awakened him.

It was now understood that in most children, sweeps showed remission during adolescence, and usually disappeared entirely before adulthood. But not always. Carthage was already a young man by the time the grasp of his childhood illness faded.

Although he taught himself to walk without a limp over time, he continued to feel out of step. He once thought that by regaining his health he would finally be free, but he remained confined, just in different ways. This time, it was a crippled heart.

Where was that grand world, the one he read about, the one full of heroism and adventure? His childhood acquaintances were all adults, and had given up on that world a long time ago. His family told him to be sensible, and to settle down — refusing to understand that he'd done enough *settling* for a lifetime.

Bones were miserable anchors.

Not just ailing bones.

Yes, also the healthy ones.

He still stood sometimes and watched the starlings, thinking of that book and its diagrams about birds' bones. Starlings were greedy, capricious little birds, clamoring with other birds at the feeders and the baths, but still he envied them. If the birds were given hollow bones, why did God bind men to the ground?

Although Carthage's body was tethered by gravity,

powerless against the natural forces of living, his *thoughts* were birds. The real world was nothing like what he thought it should be. But with imagination — and a little sleight of hand — he could create something *better* than the real world.

As the words of the advertisement finally clarified in his heart, he surged to his feet.

This was not just an audition notice. This was the audition notice of a *lifetime* — a royal talent competition with the ultimate prize.

A single chance to burn like the celestial bodies.

There were two kinds of dream — the kind you had while sleeping, and the kind that came true when you were awake.

This was the second kind, but the second kind could be cruel. The second kind had to be seized upon before it slipped away. It didn't just give, it *took* — took every ounce of courage and effort you had.

And perhaps every penny.

He looked at his train, and the motley crowd assembled to admire it. They were freight workers and flower-peddlers, station inspectors and foot messengers. The kind of people with glum shoulders and tired eyes. People who worked the dim, stale depot every day and never saw anything different.

Sylvester Carthage would never settle again. He would never watch life pass by from behind a pane of glass.

And he would *never* be written out of the story.

He would write his own.

Breath rattling as he exhaled, he looked down at the fine print one last time:

Winner of the contest will perform onstage at the Royal Palace on Celestia.

3

A TELEGRAM & AN ADVERTISMENT

The telegram contained just four words:

WE ARE FINE TOO.

Arbrook Huxley stared at it for a long moment.

"Do you want to send a message back?"

"No," he said, and, not wanting the telegraph operator to notice how upset he was, changed the subject. "Where can I buy holopaper around here?"

The telegraph operator looked disappointed. No doubt. It was expensive, sending messages all the way out to Fallsbright, and Huxley was sure the operator hoped he'd send a few more.

Instead, Huxley went down the street to the print shop right away. He preferred to print the advertisements on holopaper, instead of with regular ink, because then they could change the details at every stop, sparing the expense of waste. But it took him half an hour to haggle the printer down to a reasonable price on a ream of paper. Maybe it was the tailored blue morning coat Huxley was wearing, or maybe it was his dialect, or his age. But he recognized that the printer was trying to take advantage of him. He'd learned quickly, dealing at a Sixes table on Astoria Isle, to recognize when somebody thought you were stupid. At last, maybe just to get rid of him, the printer compromised and they reached an agreement. Huxley shook his hand, but the grasp was cold.

Cold, just like everything else on this starsfelled isle. Leaving the shop with a parcel of paper tucked under one arm, Huxley braced himself against the frigid air.

Carpathia Isle was mountainous and gray, steeply stacked with jagged alleys and stony plazas. It couldn't exactly be called architecture. It looked more like somebody had piled a bunch of rocks up and called it a city — then, for decoration, rubbed it all with charcoal.

The worst part was that there were no horizons. The city was too tall and too twisting, tenement housing leering overhead, and even the sky was obscured by laundry lines and electric light bulbs when Huxley looked up. He felt like he'd taken a deep breath the moment he stepped off the train, and still hadn't let it out.

There was a restaurant in the depot, paneled with dark wood and brown upholstery. Huxley chose to sit outside, which really meant sitting at a small patio table right on the platform as trains hissed sharp breaths and freight workers hollered over the noise.

He'd skipped breakfast, and his stomach complained that it was almost lunch. He was looking forward to a hot meal — bacon and fried eggs, sourdough with strawberry jam, strong coffee, hotcakes and blackberries and fresh cream on the side...

"What's the chef got on for brunch?" he asked the electrical waiter.

"Kippers and toast."

Huxley's empty stomach did a roll. "I think I'll stick with the toast."

He sat alone for a moment, heart aching, and took the telegram out of his pocket. He had crumpled it up, but now he regretted that and smoothed it back out.

Something in him pined for more than just a home-cooked meal. He was sick for sprawling acres of green, warm sunshine and the smell of oranges on the trees. Flat roads, grassy hilltops, trees with spreading limbs that afforded pleasant shade, and looking up to find that comforting line where earth met sky.

He'd written a letter to say he was healthy, and to share a few stories about things he'd seen. He said he was doing well, lied that business was booming, and earnestly requested an update on how things fared on Fallsbright.

We are fine too.

He crumpled it up again, but this time sank it in the pitcher at his left hand so that he wouldn't be tempted to unfold it and read it again.

Somebody slapped a holopaper down on the table. "This is our chance."

Huxley looked up. Carthage stood there, coat folded over one arm, flushed and grinning.

Huxley picked up the paper as Carthage sat down at the table with him, pulling the chair close and leaning across.

"What is this?"

Carthage tapped the paper in Huxley's hand. "An audition. Open call across the Celestial Isles. Do you know how old the princess will be this year?"

"Something like ten?"

"Thirteen. Big thing for the monarchs, turning thirteen. She'll choose her royal moniker this year. There's a ball—"

Huxley dropped his gaze, scanning the ad. "Palace Administration is looking for a performing act to present to the princess on her birthday?"

Carthage's south-central burr trilled harder when he was excited. "A contest. Four rounds of auditions performed on four isles: Astoria, Halcyon, Helios, and a final performance on Celestia to decide a winner." He got a faraway look. "Think of it, Huxley — a chance to perform in the Capitol palace. We might even meet the Future Queen of the Celestial Isles."

Huxley did not care about palaces or princesses. He had been raised on a palatial estate himself, heir to an orange grove, but had forfeited those luxuries by leaving Fallsbright to make his own fortune.

We are fine too.

He knew what it meant: *We thought you would have given up by now. Until you're ready to come home and accept your legacy, there's nothing else to say.*

But the orchard was not a legacy Huxley thought he could ever feel proud of. It was something his father had created, and it was labored by the many electricals that toiled for its harvest.

Huxley didn't want to inherit something. He wanted

to sweat and bleed — he even wanted to fail once or twice. He wanted to *make* something.

A fortune, specifically.

That wasn't too much to ask, was it? He wanted to work hard, but he didn't want to work hard for *nothing*.

Astoria, Halcyon, Helios, and the Capitol Isle, Celestia. These weren't the boondocks the Electrical Menagerie had been touring the past six months. These were major stops on the commercial rail lines, bustling metropolises full of wealthy patrons flush with cash and spoiled for entertainment. Just the opportunity to perform in these cities was too good to pass up, and Huxley's spirits rose at once.

He could do it. In a city like Astoria, or New Halcyon, with the good press and prestige the contest would bring, he could fill the house. Standing room only! The company would be saved, and it wouldn't even matter if they won. They'd get the show in the papers, they'd get the ledgers balanced, and they'd come back swinging for a second tour. Maybe, finally, they could actually make a *profit*. The blood faintly pounded in his head just thinking about it.

"All we have to do is come up with the entry fee," said Carthage, bringing Huxley back down to the ground.

"How?" Huxley asked. "The company is bankrupt."

In fact, Huxley was also *personally* bankrupt. His first investment had been a racing kestrel which, on her maiden flight, had promptly gotten lost. Then there had been the stocks he purchased in a company developing long-distance radio technology — just before said company collapsed.

This disastrous tour with the Electrical Menagerie was just his latest financial failure, except that he'd also quit a lucrative job with the casino on Astoria in order to go on tour. A tour which had gradually eaten his savings until he had almost nothing left to live on.

"We'll just have to take out a loan," answered Carthage, as if it were that easy.

"Yes, well... it doesn't exactly work like that," said Huxley. Sylvester Carthage was a mystery. Huxley knew very little about the man, except the kind of stupid things you learned while cohabiting a small train together — what kind of hours the other fellow kept, and how he took his tea.

Carthage was brazen under a spotlight, but shy, almost reclusive, toward Huxley, and Huxley sometimes felt like he was trying to collaborate with a small child. Carthage didn't seem to understand how money worked, and was often compelled by reckless whims. It seemed that somebody with flecks of white at his jaw should understand that the bank wouldn't just *give* you money.

"You have to have good credit in order to take out a loan like this. Or at least collateral. Which, we—"

"We can stake the train," said Carthage. He'd obviously thought of it earlier, from the way he said it so calmly.

But Huxley stopped. The train? Was he serious?

That fifty percent of the train was just about the only thing Arbrook Huxley had left to his name. The ad promised payouts for all three acts that advanced to the final audition on Celestia, but the other auditions were uncompensated. Unless they made it to the final round, the only money they'd see was from selling tickets to the auditions, and he didn't think it would be enough.

If he wanted to keep his train, they didn't just have to sell tickets. They would have to advance all the way through the auditions on Astoria, Halcyon, and Helios. In an open call? Competing against the greatest acts in the realm? The odds were impossible.

He could quit. Get out now, before the whole thing wrecked. Sever their contract, sell his half of the train, and go home. Hug his mother. Have a real breakfast and breathe clean Fallsbright air again.

He looked up at Carthage, who stared somewhat intimidatingly at him, awaiting an answer.

This reminded Huxley of the day they met and shared coffee at a sidewalk cafe on Astoria. He still wasn't sure there wasn't something wrong with Sylvester Carthage. Carthage was naive and very strange, full of unrealistic ideas and old-fashioned ideals.

But if there was one thing he was good at, it was making the *im*possible seem *possible*. That day, standing at an intersection watching Carthage pluck playing cards out of thin air, Huxley felt excited about something in a way he'd never been excited about kestrels or radio parts.

Maybe that was the feeling of finding something to do with yourself that you could actually believe in.

Fell the odds! He *did* believe. They had as good a show as any. Maybe even better. And in those cities, they'd finally have the chance to prove it.

The spotlight was calling. It would have been downright shameful to run the other way.

He stood up and thrust out a hand. "Let's go enter a contest," he said.

Carthage returned the handshake and grinned. "Let's go *win*."

4

A FADING STAR

The caboose car of the train was Carthage's workshop. There was a writing desk and workbench, lit by electric lamps for late-night repairs, and a wall of compartments where he stored parts and materials — copper wiring, gears and cogs, little cans of polish and paint, small bulbs for electrical eyes, sprockets and pulleys, spokes for wheels and an assortment of tires. And, stored at the back in a lead-lined barrel, strapped down so that it wouldn't rock or shake, was the canister of stardust they used for the pyrotechnics.

The train gave a light jolt, rattling the contents of the compartments, and Carthage reached up, putting a hand on an overhead bin to steady himself.

On the floor, his mechanical bear lay lifeless on its side, electrical innards unraveled where he was working to fix a malfunction. He stepped over it and opened a drawer, rifling.

"Say, Dominic?"

There was a quiet squeak of an old wheel, and the

head of a copper electrical appeared, looking around the doorway. "Yes, Master Carthage?"

"Have you seen my loupes?"

"Of course I have," said Dominic. "They're on your head."

"*Ah*." Dominic was right. Carthage was wearing them. He put on the magnifying glasses and knelt to peer inside the cavernous metal belly. "Do you need a new wheel?"

"Why would I need a new wheel?"

"You're squeaking like a mouse." Carthage sat up again. "Fetch me some light, will you?"

Dominic rolled across the car and picked a torch up off the workbench.

"Are you excited, Dominic?"

The little bulbs that indicated Dominic's eyes momentarily winked as he considered. "Should I be?"

Carthage stuck his arm into the belly of the beast, feeling around for the right bundle of wires. "You should."

"Well, then of course I am. What am I excited about?"

Carthage laughed. "Our first audition."

He pulled a fuse from the bear and held it up to the light — blackened and blown. He started to turn around for a new one, but Dominic held one out before he could, arm creaking.

Dominic was more than fifteen years old — ancient, in electrical terms. Carthage liked to paint his performing electricals, which were mostly all tin, in bright colors, but Dominic was made out of copper, and he had decided it was too pretty to paint. Dominic had tarnished these last few years, fading from shiny and pink to a muted red-brown, and Carthage found some strange comfort in the idea they were aging together.

In those earliest days, when Carthage struck out to pursue himself as a street magician, he had nothing — few belongings, no money, and no one in the city he could rely on. It wasn't safe to busk alone, and he thought he was starting to talk to himself too much, so he fashioned Dominic from a household kit that was on sale in a shop window. He didn't like the way these models were assembled, so he pulled out all the parts and reconfigured them in his own way, tinkering and buying new parts as he earned money.

It was many months before he even switched Dominic on, but by the end, Dominic was nothing like the kit he came from. Round the back of his head was a stamp that said *Sachs-Farley*, but his components — and his programming — were 100% Carthage.

He'd been an early accessory to Carthage's act, performing juggling and jokes, but he was too outdated for that now, and stayed aboard the train as a butler instead. His companionship was the oldest and most trusted thing Carthage had.

Carthage had just finished replacing the bear's blown fuse when the train juddered again.

"*Stars*," he heard Huxley say to himself from the doorway, and looked up. Huxley was steadying himself with a hand on the desk, and Carthage saw him risk a glance at the pyrotechnics strapped to the wall. "What's with the turbulence?"

"We aren't on the passenger rail line," answered

Carthage, getting to his feet. "This is an old freight line — the rails are a wee glitchy."

"Well, that sounds safe."

"Afraid of crashing?"

"It's not very high on my to-do list."

"Anyway, it's faster," answered Carthage, plucking a rag off the writing desk to wipe the grease off his hands.

"Crashing? I'd say so."

Carthage had to laugh. "The freight line."

That answer satisfied Huxley. "Engineer says we're beginning our descent. Should be pulling into Astoria Central within half an hour."

"Oh, then we ought to be able to see it from here." He went to the window, Huxley following him, and they leaned to look.

Swirling gray fogs gave way to bright blue as the train exited the clouds and began a descent toward the isle, which floated below and beyond, airborne against a stark blue sky. The train, throwing an occasional spark as she raced along the invisible skyrails, banked for final approach, and the isle vanished from their line of sight.

"Astoria," Carthage said. It seemed funny that their new venture was beginning in the same place they all met for the first time. "Here we are again."

ASTORIA CENTRAL WAS totally unlike the depot on Carpathia. It was one of the busiest rail stations in the Central Isles, bustling and expansive, with high silver arches and a domed glass ceiling that let in natural light, and the people on the platforms wore bold colors and good fabrics like satins and velvets.

They were also far less impressed by the blue train when she finally chugged into Platform 16. Carthage watched through the window of the dining car as people walking alongside the platform glanced at the train, took it in back to front, and then kept walking.

An unpleasant feeling pressed down on his shoulders, and he moved away from the window.

Huxley was also looking out the window. He'd been living and working on Astoria when they met, and Carthage wondered what the young man thought about returning.

"Glad to be home?" he decided to ask.

"Home?" Huxley's puzzled look told Carthage all he needed to know.

At the depot, they finished the paperwork necessary to audition and handed over their fee. The bank had granted them their loan, albeit at what Huxley complained was a highway robbery rate of interest. With the paperwork sorted, they unloaded what cargo they needed and left the train at the depot, hauling the gear by convoy down to the camp where auditions were being held.

The carnival camp was outside the industrial district of the city, right on edge of the Astorian sea. The air tasted like salt, and although the land was patched with soft dirt and grass, small seashells occasionally crunched underfoot as they were unearthed from the dirt.

At the center of the camp was a large big top, where the auditions would be held, and around it the performing troupes and traveling celebrities had pitched their own tents to live and rehearse in.

Carthage thought the exorbitant entry fee was probably to keep vagrant performers and caravan roadshows out of the competition, which troubled him for two reasons. The principle bothered him, firstly. But he was also worried to realize he'd be matched against a crop of competitors with far better resources.

They staked out their territory — literally — and while the electrical crew raised the tent and moved production equipment, Carthage and Huxley went to work putting up posters advertising their show. The auditions would be ticketed, the profits from which would support them as they competed.

Their closest neighbor was a periwinkle tent ribbed in silver, and signs displayed the shadowy portrait of a feminine figure wreathed in twirls of gray smoke that resembled wings. The titles said *Andromeda Skyhawke — Mistress of Illusion. Prepare to be astonished!*

"Mr. Sylvester Carthage?"

Carthage turned from where he watched Huxley hanging a banner to face a protectorate standing behind him.

The protectorate was tall and thin, with ginger hair parted to one side and a combed mustache. The afternoon sunlight gleamed off the gold bars pinned to the epaulets and breast of his navy blue uniform.

"Aye?" asked Carthage.

"Lord Protectorate Miles Vicewar." He didn't offer

a handshake. "I would like to speak with you and your associate — privately."

★

WITH NO FURTHER explanation, Vicewar escorted them to his own private tent, which was adjacent to the big top in the middle of camp. Inside was a small security office, spartan except for the massive mahogany desk which Vicewar had somehow transported to this campsite. He sat down one on side of it and indicated Carthage and Huxley should do the same.

Huxley looked at Carthage. Carthage sensed a question in that look. *What did you do?*

Nowt, he denied by shaking his head. Then gave a pointed stare back: *What did* you *do?*

Huxley shrugged, which was not reassuring.

"I am part of the Palace Protectorate," began Vicewar. "It's my duty to protect our Future Celestial Queen. As such, I am here to scrutinize every performer and producer attending this..." he waved his pen in the air, distastefully, like he didn't really like the whole business. "This *sideshow.*"

"Is the princess in danger?" Carthage asked.

"The princess is always in danger," Vicewar replied. "That's the nature of being a princess. But *you* will show proper deference by caring to refer to her as *Our Celestial Lady* — not 'the princess', as if you were familiar with her."

Carthage furrowed his brow, trying to sound sincere. "My humblest apologies, Protectorate."

"I am the *Lord* Protectorate," Vicewar corrected.

Huxley, who had his arms crossed, clapped a hand

over his mouth. Carthage realized Huxley was laughing, and kicked him in the shin. The last thing they needed was to be ejected from the competition for offending a protectorate. Er... a *lord* protectorate.

Vicewar looked down at his paperwork — carbons of their personal passbooks.

"Now," he said, "you are S.F. Carthage, performer and proprietor?"

"Yes, Lord Protectorate."

"Except that Carthage is not your real name."

Carthage ran his tongue over his teeth. He hadn't thought there was any reason for this to arise as an issue. "I was born Cannongate," he said. "But Carthage *is* my 'real' name. I took it legally."

Huxley raised his brows. This was news to him.

Vicewar looked to him. "And you are A.Q. Huxley, producer and manager?"

"That's correct," said Huxley. "Except that I am the *Executive* Producer."

Carthage kicked him harder this time.

"I see that you're from Fallsbright."

"It's true."

"Are you a Terraformist?"

Huxley straightened in his seat. "Stars no. I'm a Monarchist, of course — like you."

"The Terraformists wouldn't hesitate to abduct the Future Queen," said Vicewar. "Or even to kill her. I will be keeping a close eye on everyone here. I expect that any upstanding citizens will do the right thing in reporting any... *shenanigans*, should they occur."

With that, he let them go.

They walked back through the carnival in silence as competing strains of calliope music played from opposite directions. When they reached their tent, Huxley turned to Carthage, somewhat hotly.

"I'm not turning anybody in just for being a Terraformist, if that's what he expects. It's not illegal." Then, he seemed worried that he might have said too much. "I mean, *I'm* a Monarchist, of course, like I said..."

Carthage didn't even want to touch the topic. This carnival, filled with colors and sounds and the combustible element of opportunity, seemed too dreamlike to be ruined by politics. The only thing he wanted to worry about was his audition. He certainly didn't want to know any of Huxley's private opinions. Unsure of what else to say, he remained silent.

"Anyway," said Huxley, a hint of accusation in his voice, "Why did *you* change your name?"

Carthage looked off. That was a topic he didn't particularly want to touch, either. But he didn't think Huxley would accept a brush-off. "I needed distance from my family," he answered.

Huxley softened, so maybe he understood that.

"We ought to get back to work," Carthage said, turning away. "We've an audition to rehearse."

THE FIRST AUDITIONS began that evening. Carthage wanted to keep rehearsing until the next day, when it would be their turn, but after a full afternoon of rehearsal,

Huxley declared that they should have some dinner and catch a few of the auditions.

"First," he said, "because your voice is scratchy and I don't want it to go. Second, we should size up the competition."

Carthage's voice wasn't scratchy, and he suspected Huxley was really just tired of rehearsing and wanted to take in some entertainment. But Carthage shared Huxley's curiosity about the other entertainers, and couldn't protest too earnestly. They ate a cold picnic for dinner and put on their coats to go out.

It was dark, and a cool air enlivened Carthage as they walked through the fairground. He found himself feeling glad that Huxley insisted on calling work for the evening. Breathing fresh air and stretching his legs was something he didn't know he needed.

The smells of popcorn and spun sugar danced on the breeze, mingled occasionally with a salty, scaly whiff of the ocean.

"What shall we see?" Carthage asked Huxley, who thumbed through a schedule.

"Lior Bonaventure," said Huxley, and seemed excited. They ducked down an alley between two red tents, emerging onto a wide pathway flocked with people. The crowd migrated, chattering, toward the big top in the center of the fairground. Somewhere, a barker was hawking something. Carthage and Huxley followed the people.

"What has he done?"

"Lior Bonaventure?" Huxley looked surprised. "Only

one of the finest horse trainers in the Isles! Three-time dressage champion. We'll get to see his world-famous flying stallions."

"Do you ride dressage?"

Huxley laughed. "Me? No. I always rode jumpers. What about you?"

"Me?"

"Didn't you say something about growing up in the country? Didn't you have horses?"

The family had horses. And his sisters had a pony, which they shared. But he'd never been allowed to ride. Once, the old man who groomed the animals lifted Sylvester onto the back of the family hack, a sturdy old cob with a lamb's disposition. There'd been little danger, but Sylvester's father found out, and the groom was nearly let go.

Spending the middle years of his life in the city, there'd been little opportunity to learn horsemanship. As an adult, he'd only properly ridden a horse once or twice. And "properly" was probably being generous.

But he'd read plenty of books about them. Encyclopedias of the varieties, and chivalry stories about knights and their horses dying together in battle, and penny serials with heroes that chased flying mustangs across the sky.

"I love horses," he answered, which omitted the breadth of the truth, but was also not a lie.

Lior Bonaventure proved to be a broadly built and somewhat heavy middle-aged man, with dark skin, a strong voice, and the startling alacrity of a ballerina. He had a way of commanding the room without seeming like too much of a performer, and a confidence that suggested many years in the spotlight.

His stallions, brindled mustangs from the regions of Fallsbright, were much the same — large and graceful, with an understated way of being breathtaking. Their dark coats, ribbed with gold, were polished to gleaming, and they wore halters inlaid with pearls.

Bonaventure demonstrated the classical dressage airs from the ground, directing the horses to leap and prance with nowt but a long whip, which he waved in the air like an orchestra conductor. And then, bareback, he sat astride the darkest stallion and galloped it around the ring. Turning into the center, the horse leapt into the air — the capriole, Carthage recalled, one of the most dramatic and difficult airs for man and beast. The horse rose in the air, higher than seemed possible — and then hung there, defying gravity as if someone had painted it that way in portrait. The audience gasped.

Carthage's breath caught, too.

After ten or fifteen seconds, the horse landed neatly, and then reared, striking with its forelegs to thundering applause.

Carthage and Huxley, both seeming to forget momentarily that they were competing against Bonaventure, gave him a standing ovation. He took a bow, as did his stallions.

The next thing they saw was a highly accomplished theatrical troupe, The Abernathy Players, which performed a one-act play from the acclaimed playwright

Silas Abernathy. It was a slow, ponderous storyline about a man in love with his rival's sister, and it ended with the man being stabbed in the back and dying as he collapsed upon his writing desk and penned a sonnet for the woman he loved.

Carthage thought it was far too depressing and grisly, especially since they were auditioning to perform for the twelve-year-old princess. But Silas Abernathy was in attendance, and the audience raged with applause while he stood up on the front row and took a bow.

Huxley, who had gone to sleep sometime around the third soliloquy, sat up when he heard the applause.

"What did I miss?"

"Seven more soliloquies and a stabbing," Carthage answered.

The final audition they attended — the final audition of the night, in fact — was that of Andromeda Skyhawke, Mistress of Illusion.

As the show began, the lights dimmed, and an electrical stagehand played a mystical strain on the panpipes. A single spotlight faded up on a hawk trapped within a small cage.

A hush fell over the audience as the moment stretched too long, and the hawk screamed and flapped its wings, brushing the bars of the cage. In a flash of white, the cage burst open, shattering into a plume of smoke, and a woman appeared in place of the hawk.

She was tall, with very fair hair that glowed almost white under the lights, wreathed in a sleek dress of feathers and wearing a mask with a long beak. She lifted her arm, flourishing, and revealed a train of long pinions that resembled a raised wing. The pale smoke swirled around her, and the audience erupted with applause.

She went on to perform an interesting restoration act, in which she burned a framed portrait of a sailing ship, then returned it to its original state by painting on it with a brush and a bottle of Astorian seawater. She was a masterful performer, playful and coy, and she worked without any patter — speaking only in her gestures and the wry expressions she made to the audience. Although it was quite clear to Carthage how it was done, he found that she sold the effect so earnestly he didn't really care.

He sat back. "She's good."

Huxley sat forward. "She's *incredible*."

Huxley was right. Carthage began to watch the audience, instead, and the smile she evoked in him faded. She had her patrons sitting forward, eyes wide and mouths agape.

And she had filled every seat in the house.

His audition was tomorrow. He had to follow *this*? A glance at the palace judges proctoring the auditions revealed that they were smiling and applauding, too.

For the first time, he wondered if he might not win.

That was non-negotiable. His will resolved, and he stood to go as soon as Miss Skyhawke took her bows. Huxley had been right in what he said: it was important to size up the competition. Now that Carthage had seen the competition — the powerful Bonaventure, the popular Abernathy, and the talented Miss Skyhawke only being a sample of what they faced — it was clear the time to be wide-eyed was over.

Outside, as the crowd dispersed, he put on his hat. But Huxley lingered, fidgeting with his hat instead of putting it on.

"Sommat the matter?" Carthage asked.

"Nothing. I was just thinking — perhaps I'll stick around and introduce myself. I'd like to acquaint myself with some of the other acts."

Fascinating development, since Huxley expressed no interest in acquainting with Lior Bonaventure or Silas Abernathy.

"There were some Skyhawkes," said Carthage, "I think twenty years ago, that owned the patents on an aqueous method of mining copper. Last I heard of the family, they bought up foreign mines and were living abroad. If this woman is some relation, then she's heir to more money than you or I will ever see — and far above our station."

Huxley laughed. "Speak for yourself, Carthage."

Carthage stepped closer to lower his voice. "We have no time for distractions. Particularly not with the competition. I mean it when I say you and I are out of our league here. The caliber of these competitors has me concerned. We look downright provincial in comparison."

"Well," said Huxley, and put on his hat. "There are worse things to be."

"For peace of mind," Carthage answered, "I think we should run through the audition one more time."

Huxley sighed, but followed him.

THEY HAD ALMOST reached their tent when Carthage spied someone standing nearby, under a lamp. A woman. She turned, making eye contact, and he shuffled to a halt, then turned quickly to Huxley.

"Go on," he said. "I'll be along in a minute."

Huxley seemed puzzled, but avoided further protest and accepted being sent away.

Carthage took off his hat as he approached her. "Elys?"

"Sylvester," she replied. His sister had her black hair pulled back behind her head, and she wore a long-sleeved dress in a blue so dark it looked almost like mourning clothes. The only adornment she wore was the silver locket on a chain, which he knew she never took off.

He'd sent her a letter to share his excitement about this audition, and regretted that now. He had the feeling that he was about to be chastised, as if she were a nun and he had just been running through the church.

"What are you doing here?" he asked. She lived on Atlas, where they were born, which was hours away.

With a straight back, Elys closed the distance. "I'm here to stop you," she said.

"Stop me?" He tried to feign surprise. Second-oldest Elys had been a perfect child to her parents, but a thorn to her siblings. There was nothing they did without Elys telling on them. With both parents now absent, it seemed that she had promoted herself from just tattling on him to outright scolding him. "Stop me from what?"

"This isn't the kind of attention you want," she said. "The tabloids are already crawling over this contest. You're walking blindly into a wolf's den of scandal."

"I'm not afraid," he answered.

"This isn't about *you*," she said. "Our sisters are trying to lead quiet and respectable lives."

"I already took a different name. Do you want me to hide the rest of my life?"

"There's a far cry between *hiding* and making a spectacle of yourself. It's only a matter of time before someone learns who you really are. Thrusting yourself into the limelight will only expose our family to more shame. "

He wouldn't stand here and be lectured by anyone, especially his wee sister. He turned to go. "This is something I have to do."

"Haven't you done enough?" she muttered.

He took a sharp breath that felt like a knife between his ribs. Tightened the fist holding his hat, crushing the brim, and turned back to her. "Are you accusing me of something?"

They were both still for a moment. A held breath.

It seemed she was unwilling to say it to his face.

"Try to be reasonable, Sylvester," she said finally.

"Don't speak to me like a *child*, Elys!"

Ignited, some sudden color came into her pale skin, a sharp spark in her dark eyes. "I'll speak to you exactly as you *deserve* to be spoken to. You have no concept of your own limitations. I wish you would come back to Atlas."

"Well," he said. "Then we come to it. It isn't our family history you're ashamed of. It's *me*."

"That is not at all what I said."

But it was what she meant. They hadn't argued about

this in years. For her to bring it up now was a kick to the knees. He knew what *come back to Atlas* meant. When he moved off the isle, his family fought vigorously to make him stay. They said they were afraid of him living alone in a flat in the city, and tried to convince him to commit himself to a home for convalescents.

"I am not fine china." He leaned close to her, severe. "I'll not be handled by you the way I was handled by mother and father—"

"Sly—"

"—I am not something fragile, only to be brought down on *special occasions!*"

She blinked, and her mouth snapped shut, as if that stung.

Did it? Good.

He put his hat back on, signaling that he was done.

Her mouth remained firmly closed. Perhaps she was done, as well.

"I appreciate your visit," he said. "Where can I take you?"

"I have an escort," she answered. "But thank you."

"Then I'm afraid this is good evening." He turned away. "I have an audition tomorrow."

She waited until he was a few paces away before she spoke again.

"Do you ever think about that day, Sly Fox?" There was a tremor in her voice, a knife's edge of vulnerability. The use of that pet name, which she had not used in years, jarred him. He knew which day she meant, and the answer was *yes*. But he pretended he didn't hear her.

"Because I think about it all the time," was the last thing he heard her say. Quietly. To herself.

So do I.

But he kept walking.

★

SYLVESTER FOX CARTHAGE did not get stage fright. Onstage, his direction was clear — it was the rest of life that daunted him, feeling far too easy to miss an important cue.

But the day of the audition descended him into almost sheer panic, and the more they rehearsed, the *worse* he felt about the show. In the final hour, when he was supposed to be warming up, he found himself pacing backstage, and the high strains of otherwise cheerful music playing in the front of house gnawed for some reason at his nerves.

Elys's sudden appearance on Astoria had rattled him far more than he cared to admit. He hadn't slept much, finding himself preoccupied by memories he didn't care to think on, and this wasn't the frame of mind he needed to perform at all.

One key to illusion was that people had to *agree* to believing in it. The other key was that *he* also had to believe it. He didn't think any trick became truly worthwhile until he'd done it so many times he stopped thinking consciously about the technique — like a musician who no longer needed to read the music — and started believing in the effect himself.

Fiction, and theater, and magic, he thought, all had

that in common. It was a kind of a collaboration, in which performer and patron had to playact together.

Since he'd seen Elys, he felt entirely aware of his own technique. Painfully aware, in fact, of *himself*. Completely false.

He had to confess the feeling had a name. His sister had given him stage fright.

Unable to bear the roiling pressure building inside him backstage, he went outside for a breath of clear sea air.

He'd been ignorant to think his sister would share his excitement about the contest. When had Elys been excited about anything but ruining someone else's joy?

She was good at it, too. The carnival, colors washed away by darkness, seemed dressed as lifelessly as his sister. He had to wonder if she was right. Was he only making a *spectacle* of himself?

They were outclassed. Perhaps Huxley didn't realize it, but Carthage did. They didn't belong here.

That was a familiar feeling.

There was murmuring from a few people nearby, and motion in the sky drew Carthage's eye.

A star was moving.

Carthage had been devoutly religious his whole life. As a boy, one of the books he devoured was the Holy Canon, and he was deeply compelled by the stories of creation. The way God had formed the terrestrial plane, pulling the aether sea out like a rug beneath the floating isles, hanging the Stars above. Set in place to serve humanity, each star had a name and a purpose to give light, heat, and power to life below.

There were many modern people that now worshiped the Stars, not just the Hanger of them. They set out shrines during the holidays, and attempted to divine the future by the constellations that appeared when they did.

Carthage knew better. Unlike God above, who stayed fixed and unchanging in Heaven, the Stars were capricious. They moved restlessly in the sky, they courted and wrestled, they retreated when men called upon them.

Sometimes, they even fell.

There was another man stopped on the path near Carthage. Staring up.

"Which is that?" Carthage asked the stranger.

"Veris. It collided with Vyskander last month. The almanacs say it's dying."

There had to be nothing worse than a dying star. Its light pulsed, gaping for breath, as it crawled sluggishly across the sky. Carthage could hardly stomach it. It seemed cruel that such beautiful things should stagger and die.

Others were looking up now too. Pointing and murmuring.

No stars had died in close to a hundred years. If Veris fell, it might bring starshowers, which flushed the realm with stardust and brought eras of prosperity. Perhaps it might even cool off and become an isle — the histories said Fallsbright was a star, once. But chunks of it might also hurtle into a city, or shed flaming bits onto crops, and bring a depression with it instead.

Veris slowed, then stopped. The onlookers let out a subtle breath.

As Carthage stared into the sky, courage rose up in his chest.

So the almanacs said Veris was dying? Well, even the almanacs could be wrong.

As was Elys. She'd *always* been wrong.

He did not belong locked away. He didn't need sighs, or sympathy, or to be eulogized like some terminal thing.

Hold on, he told the flickering star. *You may yet prove them wrong.*

"There you are!" said Huxley as he came up behind. "Come inside! We're five till curtain." Huxley's voice had a sharp timbre of panic. Panic Carthage no longer felt.

He put on his hat and felt his confidence return. Sylvester Carthage did not get stage fright. Life was daunting, but onstage, his direction was clear.

Onstage, he was a star.

THE CONTEST JUDGES were sitting at a table on the front row, right where Carthage could see them.

They looked tired. They'd seen dozens of acts across the past two days. But Huxley had been hustling to sell tickets since the Menagerie arrived on Astoria, and the good news was that the venue was almost full. They'd even taken the financial risk of giving away a handful of comp tickets to the local children's choir, whom Carthage saw Huxley had strategically seated a few rows behind the judges. Good. It was difficult to have a good show in a half-empty venue. An audience was always more self-conscious when it was small.

Tonight, he opened with his escape-from-the-looking-glass effect, which got them paying attention. Then he did another routine they'd done many times on the tour.

It began with him pulling a dusty sheet off of an electrical skeleton, made awkwardly of welded-together parts of other things, like watering cans and old pipes. He liked this bit because he could use some audience participation. Taking off his hat, he gave it to one of the judges to reach inside. The judge made a show of feeling around inside the hat, perhaps with a bit too much determination. Carthage thought she was looking for some kind of compartment or false bottom.

"Don't get lost," he prompted when the examination went on just a bit too long, and the audience laughed at the judge's expense.

He took the hat back, shook it out, and blew into it like he was blowing out a candle. Then he offered it to her again. The judge reached inside, and Carthage relished that sudden bolt of surprise across her features when she found something she wasn't expecting. She pulled the gear from the hat and held it overhead to an answering cry from the audience.

He took the gear, fixing it to a rod on the electrical skeleton. Then began to rifle through the hat again, producing a series of useless items and discarding them over his shoulder. A horn. A wooden spoon. An electrical bird, which elicited shouts of surprise when he tossed it toward the rafters and it flew away. And then an electrical snake.

He jolted as it hissed at him, and somewhere a child shrieked with laughter as he dropped the snake back into the hat. Nothing fell out when he turned it over and shook it out, so — carefully — he put his hand back inside.

This time, he found what he was looking for. Pulling the spanner from the hat, he held it triumphantly over his head.

Putting his hat back on, he began to tighten the nuts and bolts on the skeletal electrical. Then, spinning its lifeless, half-formed figure all the way around for the audience to see, he tossed the sheet back over its head.

Leaned close. Breathed on it.

Leaving it covered, he took a few steps away and rubbed his hands together. Warming up. "Shall we wake him?" he asked the audience. There were shouts of agreement, especially from the children. He pointed at them directly. "I need your help!"

He counted down with his fingers in the air, and the electrical band scored him.

Three.

Two.

One.

On one, he shouted with the audience: *"Wake up!"*

He raised a hand, beckoning. Under the sheet, the electrical arm raised with a jerk.

The crowd gasped.

He raised his other hand, and the electrical mirrored him.

Crossing the distance together to meet in the middle, Carthage took the sheet in hand and yanked. Underneath, the lifeless skeleton had transformed into a living electrical. Jasper, round tin body painted in a gleaming and cheerful yellow, rubbed his electric eyes as he was revealed, then waved to the audience.

The audience cheered back.

Jasper's round body and one wheel gave him a silly appearance. He did juggling, and made an excellent comedic foil. Having now come alive, he produced a set of balls and began to demonstrate his design. Carthage liked to make Jasper's juggling balls disappear, much to the confusion and dismay of the electrical, only then to make them reappear, but accidentally in triplicate, as if his own magic had gone awry. The audition ended with them juggling together, man and machine, passing balls back and forth and trying desperately to keep all of them in the air.

Carthage could hear the children roaring with laughter, but when he looked, he saw the judges were laughing, too.

Sitting forward.

Watching.

When he and Jasper took their bows, Carthage laid a hand over his heart. Trying to hold it back from racing right out of his chest. The audience was alight, and every doubt he ever had vanished — at least for the moment.

★

THE RESULTS WERE announced two hours later, just outside the big top. An eager crowd of performers assembled in advance, and an electric current of conversation crackled through the crowd.

Carthage joined Huxley, who had claimed a spot close to the podium where the judges would render a decision. He drank from a silver flask, which he held out to Carthage.

Carthage gave him a disapproving look. While at work?

"It's *coffee*," said Huxley. "Stars, you're worse than the nuns at boarding academy."

Relenting, Carthage took the flask. He drank a swig and nearly choked.

"What's wrong?"

"It's *cold.*"

"Well, it's been in my coat since this morning."

Carthage wanted to spit the lingering traces out of his mouth, but that would have been improper. He swallowed his own grimace.

"Don't offer me anything that's been in your coat since morning ever again."

"Good evening!" called a new voice. Carthage and Huxley both turned to see Silas Abernathy striding toward them.

The young playwright's hands were pushed deep into the pockets of his tweed trousers. He wore a paisley vest and matching bow tie at his collar. A cool smile turned up the corner of his mustache. "Must say, you gents put on quite a show. So... quaint and old-fashioned."

Huxley took another swig of cold coffee.

"And you're Mr. Abernathy," said Carthage, opting to

be gracious. "I must say, I've never met a writer before. How fun it must be to tell stories for a living."

"Well, I wouldn't call it *fun*. It takes a great deal of work to produce a play."

Carthage slipped his hands into his pockets, mirroring Abernathy's stance. "Is that a fact?"

"Of course. There is the staging, and the technical matters, collaborating with the clearinghouse, and of course then we have weeks and weeks of rehearsals."

"*Rehearsals*," said Huxley, breaking his silence. He thumped the flask against his forehead. "Why didn't *we* think of that?"

The young men regarded one another for a moment. Abernathy's cool smile edged up into a downright smirk.

"I admire the spunk you have," he said to Carthage directly. "The greatest performers in the Celestial Isles are all vying for the outcome. To turn up here with your... roadshow shows real mettle."

Carthage said nothing. In his pockets, he closed his fingers into fists.

"Don't you have somewhere more important to be, Abernathy?" asked Huxley. His tone was careless, almost bored. But Carthage wondered if Abernathy detected the underlying threat. He didn't think Abernathy or his paisley coattails would fare well in a fight with Huxley, even if he was taller.

"I'm here to *warn* you," said Abernathy. "There are things going on behind the scenes that two hapless fellows like you don't begin to want a part of."

Carthage furrowed his brow. "What does that mean?"

Before Abernathy could reply, someone blew a shrill whistle. The crowd shifted as a man climbed onto the podium. It was the principal judge, a small, bespectacled man who looked perpetually like he'd just been sucking on a lemon.

"The results of the open auditions," the judge began, "are as follows..."

Carthage turned back to Abernathy. But Abernathy was gone, and the crowd pressed into his place.

The judge adjusted his spectacles. "Firstly, The Abernathy Players..."

Beside Carthage, Huxley sighed. Carthage restrained his sigh, but he felt the same. Now even the good news of advancing would be tempered by the knowledge they would be traveling in a caravan with the oh-so-charming Silas Abernathy. Abernathy ascended the podium to claim his winning certificate.

"I'd like to thank my troupe for—" But he was ushered offstage before he could finish his acceptance speech.

"Alastair Hemlock, the Silent Man..."

In stark opposition to Abernathy, the mime just took his certificate and bowed.

"Lior Bonaventure and his horses..."

Bonaventure took the certificate without even a second glance at the crowd.

Beside Carthage, Huxley shifted his weight. There were only two places left.

"Miss Skyhawke, Mistress of Illusion..."

The lady, hitching her skirts, sprang upon the podium

with a surprising athleticism, smiling as she received her certificate.

"Lastly..." There was a nerve-wracking pause as the judge adjusted his spectacles. Huxley muttered something Carthage thought was either an oath or a prayer. Carthage, despite his overall confidence, found himself staring at the ground.

"The fifth and final spot goes to... The Electrical Menagerie."

Carthage looked up.

The crowd murmured, and people began turning toward them.

Neither of them reacted at first. A surge of adrenaline hit Carthage, paralyzing him. He wanted to scream, or tear off at a dead run and make laps around the campsite, but those weren't things he thought he should he do. He froze instead.

Huxley clapped him on the back. No, pushed him forward.

Together, they ascended the podium. Despite the many eyes on them, Carthage was afraid to even smile. Huxley took the certificate, and then seized Carthage in a handshake and pulled him closer. It was only after a flashbulb went off, halfway blinding him, that Carthage realized Huxley was posing them.

Huxley pointed to the reporters that crowded the stage. "The Electrical Menagerie will reveal even more never-before-seen wonders at its debut performance on Halcyon — *and* on Helios and Celestia after that. I'm A.Q. Huxley, and you can quote me!"

They'd done it.

The Electrical Menagerie, so close to bankruptcy just days before, was headed to Halcyon. That joy boiling inside Carthage combusted. With a holler, he flipped his hat into the air, and as he caught it on his head, flashbulbs went off all around him like lightning strikes.

RUNAWAY THINGS

It was Huxley's first time having his picture taken in the newspaper, and he wanted someone to celebrate with. Carthage seemed excited, too, but disappeared as soon as they got back to their campsite.

Huxley rediscovered him a few minutes later, fussing with one of the stagehand electricals. He walked into the tent just in time to hear Carthage reset the electrical with the master password:

"*Vermilion*."

The electrical's eyes winked out momentarily, then came back on, pulsing this time.

"I am your operator," said Carthage. "Requesting administrative access."

"Granted, operator." The electrical's eyes steadied.

"Report all errors beginning yesterday."

"One error. Unexpected shutdown at 14:23."

Carthage clicked his tongue. "I thought so," he said. "Deactivate."

The electrical powered down.

"What are you doing?" Huxley asked.

"This one is having some problem with the power supply," said Carthage, and reached for his toolbox. The working electricals, which they placed under heavy demand, frequently broke down.

"You know," said Huxley, "That's the trouble with electricals. If we had a live crew, we wouldn't have to fix them all the time."

"Aye, but then we'd have all those personalities."

"And?"

"And, we'd have to *pay* them."

Point taken.

Huxley checked his watch. It wasn't too late to catch a train into downtown. Astoria had fifteen musical theaters, restaurants, gaming parlors, museums, and even the very first twenty-four-hour aqua-gymnasium.

"The night trains are still running," he said to Carthage, hoping his companion might pounce on the idea.

Carthage, rolling up his sleeves, looked back at him, perplexed.

"I'm hungry," said Huxley when that didn't work. "Do you want something to eat?"

"There are leftovers in the hamper," said Carthage, turning his back to dig through his toolbox.

Huxley left the tent and stood outside where the path forked, holding his hat.

The campsite was a bustle of activity as onlookers dispersed and losing contenders began to pull up stake. The way the air stuck to Huxley suggested it might storm. Maybe others had the same thought. There were gruff shouts shared between workers as campsites struck and tents collapsed.

Although it was alive, it felt empty. It was Huxley's first time having his picture taken in the newspaper, and it seemed he should tell someone. But there was no one around to tell. Briefly, he thought about finding the nearest telegraph office and wiring Fallsbright. Maybe his friends from academy would like to hear what happened.

Then again, his friends from academy, who were now all doctors and lawyers, had stopped replying to his letters some time ago.

A strain of opera playing on a phonograph turned his head. Light spilled along the dark pathway from the half-open periwinkle tent that belonged to Miss Andromeda Skyhawke.

Huxley put his hat back on. It was good sportsmanship, not to mention common decency, for a man to congratulate a winning lady. Especially a pretty lady. Doubly-especially a pretty lady who would be traveling with them for the foreseeable future.

ON THE THRESHOLD of the half-open doorway, Huxley cleared his throat and paused there, waiting for an invitation inside. The lady was at her dressing table, re-pinning her hair. She glanced up and saw him behind her in the looking glass. She still wore the mysterious, hooked mask.

For a moment, her eyes narrowed and her mouth pressed together in what seemed to be the spark of a suppressed grin.

"A.Q. Huxley," she said, and continued to pin her hair without turning around.

That was his invitation. He stepped inside, sweeping his hat off. Navigating around a costume rack, which brushed against his arm with feathers and silver sequins, he took a meaningful look around at what she had backstage. The hawk she had used in her performance was tethered by the foot to a perch nearby. There was a magic box which she'd used to make herself disappear, and some other interesting shapes concealed under dark purple cloths. One trunk of props stood with its lid open, and he stood beside it, to see if he could steal a glance inside. "You know my name," he said, pleasantly surprised.

She laughed. "Followed, if I'm not mistaken, by the surname *'And You Can Quote Me'*."

"Well, since you seem to know who I am, may I have the pleasure?"

She turned away from the mirror and rose from the dressing table, matching his height. Perhaps she was wearing heels under the many skirts that bustled about her ankles.

On second glance, she didn't match his height. She looked down just slightly.

Yes, let's go with that. Probably wearing heels.

"Andromeda Skyhawke," she said, "Mistress of Illusion."

Huxley expected her to offer a hand to kiss the way women of the gentry usually did, but she didn't. He forfeited that gesture and bowed lightly at the waist

MOLLIE E. REEDER

instead. "Arbrook Huxley," he said. "I was wondering if we might get better acquainted over a meal?"

She raised a brow. "Acquainted?"

"Professionally, of course. It appears we're traveling companions."

"It appears we're also competitors," she said. "And — if I didn't know better — I'd think you were trying to take advantage of a rival." Moving past him, she shut the trunk of props, concealing her trade secrets with a click.

He followed her between two silver drapes, into her rehearsal space. "Well, if you aren't comfortable talking business—" he swerved to dodge two electrical stagehands carrying a piece of truss. "—then we'll just have to keep dinner strictly personal."

She turned. "I doubt anything is ever *strictly* personal with you, Mr. Huxley." Then, something softened her gaze. She reached up and took away the mask. With her eyes no longer hooded, she looked much younger, perhaps his age. Unmasked, the glamour and the poise were gone. The Mistress of Illusion was an illusion herself — merely a character this young woman played. But Andromeda was twice as beautiful just as herself.

"Perhaps that's something we have in common," she said. "I don't do the personal very well — I'm afraid that you will find me ultimately single-minded."

He ran his thumb along the satin band inside his hat, prepared to say aspiration was something he admired in anyone.

The scream of a horse never gave him the chance.

"*Stars*," breathed Andromeda, head jerking toward the

• 64

open doorway. He'd never heard a woman of the upper class swear before, but he echoed the sentiment.

Another sharp whinny pierced the night.

It was the sound of a horse in terror.

As Huxley burst outside into the cool darkness, it took his eyes a moment to adjust. There were dim shapes of people running, and a woman screamed. Although he was not fully certain yet what was happening, instinct carried him at a run toward the sound. He realized then that Andromeda was at his elbow, keeping pace.

"The horses!" someone cried. Cloud-spotted lesser light revealed the oncoming flash of pearls set in halters as Lior Bonaventure's stallions galloped wild through the camp — Huxley and Andromeda directly in their path. As he grabbed her, they stumbled back together and went to the ground.

He pressed her to the dirt and shielded her head with his body, risking a glance upward to glimpse a dark shape eclipse the Lesser Lights as it leapt and sailed over them — into the sky.

Another stallion skidded short of them and reared up, towering, forelegs slicing the air. A rope, lashed over its nose and neck, dangled and dragged behind it, tangled up on a...

On a *man*. The horse was dragging someone by the leg as it ran wild.

Huxley jumped to his feet, and the horse reared up again, screaming in fear. He saw now that there was a saddle on the stallion's back, slipping askew where the girth had loosened, stirrup iron banging the animal's side.

Huxley lurched, seizing the rope that dangled, too tightly, around the horse's face, and was nearly yanked off his feet as the horse leapt. The rope burned through his hand as he tightened his grasp, half trying to stop the horse and half just trying to hang on.

The horse's legs clattered through empty air, and Huxley seized for a handhold on the saddle as they both went airborne. Now *he* was being dragged — right into the sky.

"Whoa!" he yelled as he pulled, hard, on the rope. Getting the hand that held the rope wedged into the tightly braided mane, he pulled himself over the horse's back and straddled its lopsided saddle. "*Whoa!*"

The horse descended, pulling up short. Huxley leaned forward and worked the rope off its face and over its neck, then jumped off as it trotted away.

Andromeda was crouched over the man in the dirt. The man lay face-down, and the long track his body left along the path was wet. Huxley took the man by the arm and turned him over.

Andromeda gasped. "*Silas Abernathy?*"

Abernathy reeked of blood and booze. A gash on his head colored his face and shirtfront red. He didn't move.

Huxley took the playwright by the wrist, Abernathy's hand flopping in his grasp, and pulled at Abernathy's necktie with his other hand. Pulling the tie loose, he leaned close to Abernathy's mouth. The playwright was cold.

"He isn't breathing," said Huxley, and felt lower on the wrist for a pulse, not quite believing it.

"Do you mean...?"

Huxley looked up to see an unmasked horror written on Andromeda's face. She didn't finish the sentence. A crowd was beginning to gather, pressing in around them. He looked down at Abernathy again and realized it was true.

Silas Abernathy was dead.

HUXLEY STOOD BESIDE Carthage as the principal judge addressed the contenders. Everyone appeared to be present — except for Lior Bonaventure, who was said to still be rounding up his horses. It was very late at night, or perhaps very early in the morning. Huxley wasn't sure anymore.

"The Abernathy Players have decided to continue on to Halcyon despite this unfortunate accident," the judge said. A glance at the theater troupe revealed that they huddled together in a strand, faces bright with shock. "The timetable of auditions remains unchanged. We will see you all on Halcyon in three days."

Without any words of sympathy, the judge descended his podium and walked away.

Andromeda was standing near to Huxley. She seemed shaken, and sighed with relief as a burly man approached and placed his brown wool coat over her shoulders. Huxley realized with a start that she was standing there in nothing but a dress, and felt confused about why or how he'd lapsed in failing to offer her his own coat.

"Sergei," she said, turning to the man. "There you are!"

Sergei was large, with unkempt black hair and mutton chops. Huxley recognized him to be the lady's manager. "You are alright?" he asked her in a heavy Alsatian brogue.

"Yes, I'm fine." Dirt scuffed her skirts, and the pins in her hair had come loose, so that wisps of it framed her face.

"Let's go. No place for a lady."

Pulling his coat tighter over her shoulders, she said nothing to Huxley as she followed her manager away from the scene.

Lord Protectorate Vicewar was nearby, holding a notebook and a fountain pen.

"Lord Protectorate," called Carthage, sounding troubled. "Can you tell us what happened?"

Vicewar shut his notebook and slipped the pen into the breast pocket of his uniform, so that only the gold clip showed. "Well," he said. "After examination of the body, and cross-examination of the witnesses, including Mr. Huxley and the lady — it appears to be open-and-shut. The rapscallion got roaring drunk and decided to go for a joyride. Kicked to death, judging by the gash on his head. The horses worked into a frenzy and broke out. An unfortunate accident brought on by too much revelry."

"Then it was an accident," said Carthage. "Like the judge said?"

"I see no sign of foul play," Vicewar answered, then scrutinized them. "Is there any reason it might not be an accident?"

"Abernathy made a curious remark to us earlier tonight," said Carthage.

"What kind of remark?"

"Just that there was some kind of behind-the-scenes drama."

Vicewar rolled his eyes, tucking away his notebook. "As there always is whenever actors and artists get involved."

Huxley thought about the strange exchange they had with Abernathy before the results were rendered. Perhaps the playwright's cryptic threat — or warning, as Abernathy called it — had been a joke to unnerve them.

But he kept remembering Abernathy's body lying turned-over in the soft dirt, and something about it didn't feel right. In his memory, he crouched over the body again: Abernathy was pale, cold, and reeked of liquor.

"Huxley?"

Huxley, returning to the present, refocused to realize Vicewar had walked away. Carthage was staring at Huxley's front. Looking down, Huxley realized there was blood sticking like rust to his coat. He touched it and wondered if it would come out.

"Huxley?"

"Huh?"

"Perhaps you should retire for the evening," said Carthage.

"Abernathy smelled overwhelmingly like booze," said Huxley.

"Vicewar suggested he was celebrating."

"Exactly," said Huxley. "He was arrogant, pretentious,

rich, and he was *celebrating*. But I know cheap liquor when I smell it. Abernathy reeked of *swill*."

There was a moment of silence as they both pondered this.

Carthage had worried lines around his eyes. "You and I ought to keep our heads down, Huxley. This isn't the sort of thing we came here to be mixed up in."

"You think Abernathy was murdered?"

"No," said Carthage, not very convincingly. "I'm sure it was an accident, as the Protectorate said... still, we aren't among friends here. Perhaps we should beware of accidents ourselves."

HALCYON

Traveling with the judges was a critic who wrote columns for the *Celestial Gazette* and was syndicated in sixteen others. Her first review ran in the papers the day after the results were announced, just after the performers vacated the seaside camp and departed for the next stop on Halcyon.

In it, she praised the "fresh talent" of Miss Skyhawke, criticized the "overwrought routines" of Alastair Hemlock the Silent Man, and dedicated an entire paragraph to eulogizing the late, great Silas Abernathy.

She did not mention Carthage's show at all.

Across the next day or two, as they traveled to Halcyon, he found himself repeatedly opening the paper and looking at it again, as if waiting for a correction to blink into place at the bottom of the column. But he knew that the oversight was no oversight at all. Alastair Hemlock had been, at least, *bad* enough to warrant the critic's time.

The Electrical Menagerie had simply been a waste of it.

Lowering the holopaper to lay it beside his teacup revealed Dominic staring at him, kettle in hand. The train was half a day from Halcyon, and the skies outside the dining car were silky blue and dotted with clouds.

"Would you like something else to read?" the electrical asked.

"No," said Carthage. "This is fine."

"Well, I think your memory is failing," said Dominic, refilling Carthage's teacup. "You've read that one already."

"My memory isn't failing." Carthage rolled his eyes. "Sometimes people like to read the same things over and over again. There's nothing wrong with that."

Huxley sat down across from Carthage with a casual thump, rattling the china. Carthage reached to steady his teacup. Huxley picked the paper off the table, disappearing behind it momentarily as he opened it. Dominic set a second cup on the table and poured Huxley some tea.

"Stars! Don't we have anything *else* to read?" Huxley slapped the paper back down on the table, rattling Carthage's teacup again. This time, Carthage grabbed the cup off its saucer, lifting it away from the table before it could slosh. "When are the steelworkers going to riot again so we can finally get something *interesting* on the front page?"

Carthage didn't answer. That outburst was as close as they'd come to actually discussing their glaring omission from the critic's review. Although it was clear that neither of them took it favorably, neither of them seemed willing to admit that.

Huxley silenced himself with a mouthful of tea, but then coughed. "What *is* this?"

"Chamomile tea," said Dominic. "You were using hostile language. I thought some chamomile might soothe you."

"Well, it doesn't soothe me. It makes me angry. Go get me some coffee."

Carthage took a drink. He didn't mind chamomile tea, although it wasn't exactly soothing him, either. His notebook was open in front of him, but the page was blank. He tapped a restless pattern between the lines, looking out the window.

The next audition had to be better than the first. It had to be *so* good that the critics couldn't ignore it. The trouble was that these were society journalists. It had been easy to impress tenant farmers and wee children. But the people of the Central Isles weren't easily fooled.

Outside the window, clouds formed what looked like a long range of mountain peaks. Looking closer, Carthage saw a castle, banners splayed from spires. A dragon curled around a moat, white smoke puffing from its snout. A lady danced with a jester. A man on a horse galloped across the sky with a lance. A lion rose up on its haunches to meet him. Here was a swan, wings raised in flight, and there was a crown — to make a king out of the fool.

"Huxley," said Carthage, humbled by the beauty of the expanse, "Look at the sky."

Huxley looked. "I don't see anything," he said.

Of course not. Carthage turned back to the blank pages

of his notebook. If only he could translate, somehow, that thing that rose up in his chest when he looked out the window. But it was beyond words, and it was bigger than pictures. What were the blueprints to the door into his own mind?

"What are you working on?" Huxley asked.

"Sommat incredible," Carthage answered. Something mystifying, spectacular, and too good for *anyone* to ignore.

"What is it?"

Carthage shut his notebook. He needed more time to think. "I'm not sure yet."

THE SECOND AUDITION was to be held in what had once been the amphitheater at the ruins on the cliffs overlooking New Halcyon. The closest rail depot was down in the valley, so contest administration laid a new landrail junction so that the performers could pull trains right into the field and make camp around the amphitheater.

As Huxley oversaw the electricals' assembly of their campsite, Carthage left the train to stretch his legs. Tucking his pen behind his ear, and his notebook under his arm, he walked slowly through the camp.

The field surrounding the ruins was flat and pleasantly cushioned with green grass, but the air felt choked by the many industrial smokestacks that spit smog from New Halcyon in the valley below. He was glad to have a few days to adjust to the thin air before he had to perform.

It was late afternoon, and sunlight was chased by the

high-altitude breezes, alternating between warm and cool. His was one of the last companies to arrive, and all of the other performers were underway with preparations. In the shadow of the amphitheater, locals raised booths and strung scarlet-and-gold bunting, lining the pathways with vendor tables and carnival games. Wind buffeted the hillside, jangling bells strung overhead.

Lior Bonaventure's horses were together in a corral, and Carthage paused to open his notebook and sketch one that raised its proud neck and looked over the rails at him.

Lior Bonaventure walked up with another horse, and the bells made it snort and kick its heels.

"I'm glad to see you got all your horses back, Mr. Bonaventure," Carthage said.

"No thanks to that *hack* Abernathy," said Bonaventure.

Carthage furrowed his brow. No love lost for Abernathy, but the man *was* dead. It seemed wrong to speak ill of him now.

The stallion bumped Bonaventure playfully, knocking his hat askew. A harsh stripe was burned across the horse's nose, where the fur and skin had been torn away by a rope. Bonaventure stroked its face, gently, mindful of the healing scars. "I hear your boy is some kind of rough rider."

It took Carthage a moment to realize Bonaventure meant Huxley. "He's very spirited," said Carthage. "He lacks nothing in boldness."

"Well, he kept poor Zephyr here from galloping right

up to the Stars. I owe your outfit a debt. If the two of you ever need anything, you have a friend in Bonaventure."

Carthage smiled and took his hat off in a gesture of gratitude. "I wish you the best, Mr. Bonaventure."

"I never needed wishes," answered Bonaventure, leading the horse away with a friendly grin. "You keep those for yourself."

Following the widest path, which was what was left of an ancient road, Carthage headed to the amphitheater, the only standing part of the ruins. The rest had been sacked during the fall of the Second Empire some eleven hundred years ago, but the amphitheater remained resolute. Its red sandstone walls towered against the late afternoon sky, and even the eagles carved over its archway were still recognizable, although time had worn away the finer features.

Walking into the ring, Carthage looked up. Contest administration had raised a tent top over the open roof of the amphitheater, and electricals scurried to assemble the steel truss that would hold lighting and flies overhead. Carthage wished the roof of the amphitheater had been left open. How fantastic would it be to perform under the canopy of stars?

The amphitheater had the hollow, sacred feeling of an empty church. He sat down on the front row, took out his notebook, and began to draw a top-down diagram, thinking about the staging of his next performance.

After a few minutes, he glanced up to see Miss Skyhawke walking with her manager Sergei on the other side of the ring. It appeared they were doing the same thing he was. When she noticed him, the corner of her mouth turned up in a wry smile, and she gave him a polite wave.

He tipped his head down in deference, and she turned back to talking with Sergei. Carthage watched them for a moment longer. What sort of tricks did the Mistress of Illusion have up her sleeves this time? She looked at home here on this ancient stage, like one of the muses carved into the sandstone walls. Hands on her hips, she surveyed the ring and gestured to Sergei where she thought her props should go.

It didn't escape Carthage that Huxley and Miss Skyhawke happened to be in the same place at the same time when the horses got loose. He'd already warned Huxley once, but he worried even more now. The lady was cunning, charming... and, was she more talented than him?

He didn't feel that anything came naturally to him. He'd spent a lifetime learning what he knew, and every bit of it came at a painful price.

The young woman, on the other hand, seemed as if she were simply born to occupy a stage. He sensed in her a desperation to win, and didn't doubt for a second she would — if they let her.

To have any chance, he needed Huxley thinking straight and playing close to vest, not cavorting with the competition. Whatever familiarity had already transpired between them that night was now history. But Carthage resolved to intervene if it evolved.

They would have to work harder, and smarter, to win. And they would need a *really* good show.

Something circled his head. He looked up to find that it was a butterfly. An Alsatian echowing, to be precise, and a female by the long swallowtail it had. As a boy, his favorite encyclopedia had been the *Natural History of Insects*. He'd spent hours memorizing the varieties.

Its blue-green wings shimmered as it fluttered toward him. It bumped into him and stuck there, probably tired. Crawling up his front, its tender feet felt the wool of his coat and the lapel of his red vest.

Then, as he watched, it performed its magic trick for him. With a slight shudder, as if throwing off some old outfit, the blue-green wings transformed to a radiant magenta.

Of course — *transformation!*

The ideas that had been percolating in his mind all morning now whistled like a kettle ready for tea. Closing his notebook with a clap, he rose to his feet. The butterfly, startled by his sudden movement, lurched away.

He headed back outside, momentarily blinded by the sunlight, only to collide with the wiry frame of a taller man. His eyes adjusted to reveal Alastair Hemlock, the Silent Man, who went quickly to his knees and scrambled to collect the things he'd dropped.

"Terribly sorry," said Carthage, kneeling to help, "I didn't see you there."

Hemlock had dropped a shoulder bag of personal effects — a tin of makeup, a comb, a green apple, a watch. He hurried to shove everything back in his bag with long and bony fingers. Then, looking up, he nodded what might have been a thank-you. He was tall and sallow, a sickly complexion rendered downright corpse-like by the traces of white greasepaint that clung to his face.

"Good show," he said, startling Carthage by speaking. It was a low, gritty voice that didn't match his thin frame. "Break a leg." Holding the bag tighter this time, Hemlock hurried off.

Carthage picked up his fallen notebook and flicked the grit off its cover.

Never trust a mime, jarred through his brain as he glanced at Hemlock's retreating form. It was a strange old street performer's adage, oft-repeated to him when he was learning the trade on the sidewalks of Astoria. But as he returned to the train, he forgot about the encounter entirely.

It was time to work.

★

THERE WERE JUST a few short days before the next audition, and much to do, so Carthage worked through the night. First, he designed a prototype butterfly. Then, having Dominic take the prototype and translate it to schematics, transmitted the specifications to the stagehand electricals for them to reproduce.

Carthage hoped they would fabricate the butterflies well enough to pass his inspection. He typically built all of his props himself, but there was no time. Because of the shared performance space, everyone had allotted times to rehearse. Their first full day in the amphitheater began bright and early the following morning.

To begin, he and Huxley blocked the amphitheater. Huxley, with a roll of string, placed marks down where Carthage and the performing electricals would enter, cross, and exit. Then they planned the lighting cues, which would be programmed to the lighting electrical, and Huxley selected sheet music for the band.

Midday, they started their first run-through, but it was mired by problems immediately. Jasper, who was supposed to go on with Carthage to open the show, had a badly malfunctioning arm servo which started sparking, and which also sparked an argument.

"There's no *time*," declared Huxley, and crossed Jasper off his script with red ink. "We'll fix him on our way to Helios. He'll just have to sit this one out."

But scratching Jasper meant rewriting — and re-blocking — the opening act. They put their heads together and agreed to open instead with Marietta, the operetta electrical, who required very little blocking, and the run-through resumed from the top.

"Everyone will love me," said Marietta, who was painted magenta and had a round head and body. "I am the best electrical in the Menagerie."

"Can you silence her?" Huxley complained, the third time she told them that.

"You are untalented," the electrical told him. "And jealous of me."

For several entrances and exits, Carthage had to run up and down the steps that ran down the center aisles of the amphitheater. Huxley took out his watch and they practiced these transitions, timing them, but they were too slow.

Huxley scratched the back of his head, looking at his book. "We'll have to cut something," he said. "We're two minutes over our time. One of these musical cues needs the ax, and maybe we can lose one of the blackouts."

Carthage paused to catch his breath just inside the ring. "We're sloppy," he said, loud enough for the performing electricals to hear. "We need more practice. Let's do it again."

They did. Again and again and again. An hour later, Huxley reported that they'd shaved thirty seconds off the transitions. Then they moved on to the finale, a rough staging since none of the props were finished.

"Carthage," said Huxley when they finished walking through it, "if you pull this off, I'll buy you a steak."

Carthage didn't feel very motivated by a steak dinner, but the anticipation of the act was enough.

"I'll give them sommat to talk about this time," he promised.

What followed were notes from Huxley, and then a few adjustments to blocking based on those. The band played two arrangements for Carthage to pick between, and then there was some disagreement over costumes, but by then, Carthage's head was starting to feel blurred. They'd skipped breakfast and worked through lunch.

Huxley looked at his watch. "How about we stop for dinner?"

Cold pinpricks needled at Carthage's knees. That

happened sometimes, and it warned he'd overtaxed his legs. He was risking pain tomorrow if he continued.

But the audition was still running almost a minute and a half over. He would only have the amphitheater once more before it was time to perform, and that was only a half-day rehearsal.

"Let's work on the transitions a wee longer," he said.

Huxley sagged. But he reset his watch, and they went back to work.

★

LEANING FORWARD TO pull the tab on the shade, Carthage let morning light spill onto his workbench.

The mechanical frame of a butterfly sat in front of him, and he put on his loupes to affix its holopaper wings. The loupes made prisms at the edges as light caught the lenses, sparkling in his peripheral vision. Frowning as the electrical butterfly jerked unnaturally, he used a pair of tweezers to adjust the tension rod between the wings.

Huxley knocked as he entered.

Carthage reached to switch lenses so that he could look even closer at the nearly microscopic components of the butterfly.

"Carthage?"

Carthage turned, but Huxley looked grotesque and distorted behind the lenses. He took them off. "Aye?"

"I asked what color you were wearing..." Huxley stifled a yawn behind the back of his hand. "For the pictures today."

Pictures? Carthage furrowed his brow.

Huxley waited for a moment, then tried to clarify. "You know, the photographs?"

"Photographs?"

"Didn't I...? Well, maybe I forgot." Huxley scrubbed his face. He hadn't shaved, and his hair still looked sleep-tossed. "We're taking photographs today. I'm wearing black, so... pick something that doesn't clash. But don't pick something that matches, either. I don't want to look like I tried to match you."

Carthage put his loupes back on. "Tell Dominic to pick a coat for me," he said.

"When was the last time you ate something?" Huxley asked, looking around the workshop. "Or... slept?"

The electrical butterfly flexed its wings, as if at rest on a flower, and Carthage sat back, excited. It was electrifying to bring something to life. "Look at this," he said, turning to flip open his notebook. "I—" He was startled to find the page empty.

They *all* were.

"This isn't mine," he said, and pulled the loupes off. They clattered as he set them down. "This must be Alastair Hemlock's."

"Hemlock?"

"We bumped into each other the day before yesterday... we must have switched books." Carthage frowned as he thumbed through the blank pages. Something about it didn't seem right. "Funny that it would be empty. The binding looks so worn."

"Ah," said Huxley, and crossed over to join him. "Don't you know this trick?"

"Trick?"

Huxley took the book from him. "We did this all the time at boarding academy. To hide our star sagas from the nuns. It just needs a good—" he whacked the book, hard, against the edge of the workbench, then reopened it. Words flicked up, letters jittering for a moment, then arranging into straight lines.

Carthage took the book back, fascinated. He knew plenty of things, but there was a startling sense of loss to realize there were certain things he'd never learned because there were some things children only learned from friends.

Of course, he'd also never learned to lie to nuns. So maybe there was an upside to his estrangement from boyhood culture.

He focused on the letters. The print was black and uniform height, written in capital lettering. The printing style favored in the Northeastern Isles, and Fallsbright.

MAN MUST TAKE HOLD OF HIS OWN DESTINY BY
RESHAPING THE STARS TO HIS PURPOSE.

Carthage frowned and flipped to another page.

1. EACH MAN IS A TYPE OF ROYALTY HIMSELF.
2. TRADITION IS A LASHING.
3. INFAMY OVER OBSCURITY.
4. THE STARS ARE ALSO MORTAL.

Carthage felt a jab as he knew what this was. He closed

it and looked at his companion, but from the look on Huxley's face, he knew, too.

"I'll return this to Hemlock," said Huxley. "And get your book back. Will we keep this between ourselves?"

Huxley's tone held a bigger question.

"Why do you think Hemlock was hiding this?" Carthage asked, leading.

"I'm sure he thought he might be ejected from the competition if Protectorate Vicewar knew he was reading the Terraformist Manifesto. And I'm sure he was right."

"People with clear consciences don't keep secrets," declared Carthage. But a subtle twinge followed. Didn't he have secrets, too?

Huxley seemed flustered, an effect magnified by his tousled hair and shadow of a beard. "Well, sometimes, people just want to do something secretly. And it doesn't mean they did anything wrong. I mean, sometimes, you just want to read your star sagas without anyone knocking you on the knuckles for it. Or, maybe, you want to read the Terraformist Manifesto because you're curious and it isn't illegal. So anyway. I'll return this to him." He plucked the book up. "And I'll wear my black coat. Don't match me."

Carthage, frowning, turned back to his work as Huxley left. He didn't like the idea of reporting Hemlock to the Protectorate — not for reading a book, even one filled with poor philosophies. But the words jarred him again:

Never trust a mime.

Just what other secrets was the so-called Silent Man hiding?

"Huxley," he called, sitting up. Huxley reappeared in the doorway a moment later. Carthage frowned at him, worried, and indicated the book. "Tread carefully," he said. "Already one of us has turned up dead."

The defensive look slipped out of Huxley's eyes, and he clenched his jaw at the mention of Abernathy. Nodding, seeming to consent to Carthage's wisdom for once, he turned away with a sober expression.

Carthage turned back to work, inhaled, and tried to turn his mind to more pleasant thoughts.

It will all be worth it, he told himself. Celestia was calling, and so was the stage.

But it was hard to ignore the way those cold pricks he'd started feeling last night had spread from his knees down his shins.

MACHINATIONS

Halcyon was a green isle, spotted with red sandstone. The yellow Principal Star stood in a blue sky.

Huxley wore black.

It was his battle color, like a gunslinger or a gladiator. The black waistcoat with gold thread, the black coat with velvet filigree. The gold watch fob, a black tie.

Ainsley Belvedere welcomed him for tea just after noon. She'd been an actress before she was a critic. He'd seen her in the movies. Now she wrote for the *Celestial Gazette*, and she was syndicated in sixteen local papers.

She also wore black.

Black hooped skirts, black pearls at her throat. A black net in her pale hair.

She had a press room across from Protectorate Vicewar's security tent, and her own private salon adjacent to that. The salon was fully furnished with a writing desk and glass lamps, tea tables and couches. Huxley sat on a sofa with clawed feet and upholstery pinstriped in rose gold. The journalist sat across from him and sipped tea out of bone china painted with constellations.

"How is your tea?" she asked him.

Weak. It tasted like lukewarm milk. But that was the fashion in the Central Isles.

"Stellar," he said, and set it down in its saucer so he wouldn't have to drink it anymore. "I'd like to hear the odds."

"The honest odds?"

He clasped his hands between his knees. "Yes."

She set her teacup down across from his, dabbed her mouth on a lace napkin. "The contest goes to Lior Bonaventure."

Huxley sucked a breath and tried to conceal his disappointment. "And my show?"

"You'll be voted out at Helios."

Well, that was a lined pocket in a rag coat. "Then you think we have a chance of winning here, in Halcyon."

Her eyes were cool as the dark pearls that clung to her throat. "Only due to the tremendous setback the Abernathy Players have endured," the critic answered. "It was unlucky to lose the playwright, but rehearsals here in Halcyon have continued the trend."

Huxley had heard that, too. The Players' alloted rehearsal in the amphitheater had been cut short by an electrical blackout, and two trunks of costumes had almost been lost when someone left a lamp burning unattended. Rumors were beginning to swirl of sabotage.

He wanted to know more. The critic had been allowed to watch some of the rehearsals. She had an inside line no one else had. He also wanted to test the bridge, and sometimes the only way to do that was put your weight on it.

"Is it true the play has already been rewritten twice?"

A sly smile flashed across her face. "I don't suppose I should tell you that, Mr. Huxley."

"You had a low opinion of Alastair Hemlock in your last commentary," Huxley said. "But you think that I'll go home first?"

"The mime is a professional," she answered. "He may be bad, but at least he's good at it."

Huxley could stomach being called names, and he wished she would. If she called him names, at least he would have some clipping to enclose in an envelope and send home. Something to prove that he'd *done* something, even something hated.

He wasn't on some reckless fling, even if that was what everyone at home whispered. He wasn't carousing or looking for a way to escape responsibility.

Not anymore.

He was *working*, harder than he'd ever worked in his life. His arms were heavy. His eyes felt like sandpaper when he blinked. The previous day's fifteen-hour rehearsal clung to him even after a night's sleep.

He had a real job. A real business. And not just a real show. A *good* one. If only his family could — if only they *would* — come to see for themselves. Then they would understand.

But how was he ever going to get them to come see his show if nobody wrote about it?

"Miss Skyhawke has raw talent," the critic went on with her prediction. "Perhaps the most daring act I've seen in years. But she's cut from just the same cloth as you. This competition means far too much to her. She *can't* fail. Which is why she will." She took a sip of tea. Observed him. "Your whipped look exactly proves my point. You're young and have no guile. Completely wrapped up in your feelings. This is show business, Mr. Huxley. You can't afford to take any of it personal."

No guile? Now *she* was the one walking a rotted bridge.

"Tell me," Huxley said. "How much do you cost?"

"I beg your pardon."

He'd worn his black coat today, and it wasn't to sip weak tea and exchange backhanded remarks. It was his battle color.

"I read what you wrote about Abernathy," he said. "I want you to do that for me."

Her look was cutting. "Eulogize you?"

"I met Abernathy. He was none of those things you said. So how much do you cost?"

"Mr. Huxley..." She set her teacup down with a quiet clank. "I am a licensed member of the Press Corps, and I have an integrity to uphold."

"Integrity?" He laughed. "You're an entertainment critic."

"You'll catch more flies with *honey*, sir."

"Oh, ma'am — what I'm trying to catch has a taste for *vinegar*."

She opened her mouth, then faintly smiled and closed it.

It was very satisfying to have the last word. He felt more awake than he had all morning. He reached deep into his black coat and withdrew his black checkbook. Opened his fountain pen and signed his name in black ink.

She watched him slip the check under his saucer, and did not object.

"Thank you for tea." He stood up and put on his hat. "I look forward to your review."

"I look forward to your show," she answered. "I hear it's going to be quite good."

He walked out with his head high, and only paused to swallow a stinging heart once he was outside.

Huxley still had Alastair Hemlock's holo-hacked manifesto. He'd tried returning it first thing that morning, before pictures. Carthage was anxious about his missing notebook. But Hemlock hadn't answered when Huxley came calling.

Now Huxley cut through camp, determined to try again. Hemlock was traveling by airship, not by train, and he traveled alone, not even with a publicist or manager. Huxley rounded a corner and saw Hemlock's small tent, but Hemlock was leaving.

Huxley opened his mouth to call out, but something closed it again. Hemlock had a fast, nervous gait. He darted down an alley between the two royal blue tents where Palace Administration worked, headed toward the amphitheater.

Huxley, instead of calling out, followed him.

Passing through the small carnival the locals were hosting, Hemlock went left at a red maypole and circled to enter the amphitheater through a side entrance. He disappeared under the shadowed archway.

Huxley, walking quietly through the grass, ducked into the darkened amphitheater behind him. He found himself standing in the unlit concourse that ringed the arena itself. But where was Hemlock?

In the amphitheater, Miss Skyhawke was rehearsing. Her voice, and her manager's, blended as the dialogue bounced off the stone. The words were indistinct. A few notes played on a violin.

Huxley passed between the pillars. The stone columns that supported the architecture, carved with faded reliefs, felt like a forest of trees. There were many places to hide.

Footsteps tapped nearby. It was hard to tell if they were coming or going. Huxley's left arm tensed, and he held the fingers of his hand open.

Hemlock gasped as he rounded a pillar and came face-to-face with Huxley. His too-white face shone like a ghost in the darkness. He reeled back, and his eyes searched Huxley.

"Were you *following* me?" he rasped. It was the phlegm-weighted, gristled voice of someone who smoked a lot. No wonder he was the "Silent Man".

Huxley reached into his coat and withdrew the black book. "You accidentally exchanged books with my colleague. I came to switch them back."

Hemlock's brows went up. He opened the bag he carried and took out Carthage's journal, gladly trading.

"Interesting reading material," said Huxley.

"Oh?" Hemlock paused, holding his book.

Huxley gave a stupid laugh. "Yeah. All those blank pages?"

"Yes... of course." Hemlock hid the manifesto away in his bag, but still seemed nervous. The greasepaint around his hairline was beginning to run. There was a pause, and he went on to answer a question Huxley never asked. "I was just... I was just coming to borrow some spirit gum. I was going to ask the lady's manager, but they look busy. I'll have to come back later. Thanks again."

With that, he brushed past Huxley and left.

In Hemlock's wake, Huxley felt chilled. He didn't realize how hard his heart had been pounding until it softened.

Emerging from the shadows, he exited into the amphitheater down one of the center aisles. Andromeda Skyhawke had just turned away from her manager and was taking a drink of water. Sergei, the manager, stood nearby talking to the principal judge.

"Mr. Huxley!" Andromeda spotted him and straightened. "To what do I owe the pleasure?"

He crossed between stone and sawdust, entering the ring with her. She approached him, but looked over her shoulder at Sergei, who was watching them. The gaze felt to Huxley the way overbearing fathers sometimes looked at him. Perhaps Andromeda felt the same, because she stopped a more-than-proper distance apart.

Huxley took off his hat and bowed lightly. Glancing to make sure no one was going to overhear them, he spoke in a low voice. "The mime was skulking around here," he said. "I thought you might like to know."

"Skulking? What do you suppose he wanted?"

"He claimed that he wanted spirit gum. But he fled once he realized I had followed him."

Something played at the corner of her mouth. "Look at you, rousting ruffians. It's barely lunch."

Huxley took a few steps closer so he could lower his voice again. He opened his mouth, but overhead there was a sharp pop.

Andromeda's eyes darted upward, and her coy grin melted into terror. "Huxley!"

A shower of white spots stung him on the back of the neck and the hand, but Andromeda knocked him out of the way and to the ground before he could really think through it. Plummeting from the truss overhead, a heavy light crashed to the ground, shattering glass where he'd just been standing.

Stunned, he looked up to find himself entangled — again — with Andromeda Skyhawke.

"We have *got* to stop meeting like this," she said. Her hand steadied on his left arm, and her expression flickered when she felt something up his sleeve. A question crossed her face, but she didn't voice it.

"Well, consider us ev—" Sergei hauled Huxley to his feet, away from Andromeda, before he could finish the sentence.

The principal judge knelt to examine the fallen light, frowning at the warped clamp. "Someone might have been killed."

"An accident, I'm sure," Andromeda answered as Sergei gave her his hand, but looked up at the steel truss that dangled in the darkness overhead and had a troubled expression.

"Awful lot of those going around," muttered Huxley, swatting sawdust off his coat.

Sergei pushed Huxley's hat back at him. "You," he said, "are bad luck! Stay away from my rehearsal!"

Andromeda waved at Huxley, apologetic. He tipped his hat in thanks and left, giving her privacy to rehearse again.

An awful lot of accidents. And one of them already ended in a man's death.

He exhaled as he discovered a shard of glass in his hair. This competition was cutthroat enough, and now it seemed they had an *actual* cutthroat to worry about. The judge was right. Huxley had brushed too close to being a second fatality. But he'd only been there by chance. If the falling light was anything but an unfortunate accident, there was only one person it could have been intended for, and that was Andromeda Skyhawke.

He only hoped she heeded the warning.

8

TRANSFORMATA

The 'Abernathy Players' second audition turned out to be a dramatization of Silas Abernathy's life. Carthage thought the script was full of embellishment, not the least of which being the depiction of Silas Abernathy as a swashbuckling hero.

The reenactment of Abernathy's death felt particularly uncomfortable, since the true and gruesome details were all omitted in favor of a fictionalized ending in which it was implied Abernathy did not die but instead rode a flying stallion into the sky, never to be seen again.

Huxley seemed especially off-put by the play, maybe because he'd seen the man trampled to death and the tragedy was romanticized, or maybe because a character appeared that was obviously supposed to be him, except that she was a woman and cried over Abernathy as he departed.

Carthage noticed that while turnout was high, response from the audience was tepid. Halcyon, which had built its fortune in manufacturing, was less educated and less artistic than Astoria, and the audience didn't really seem interested in dead playwrights. But even the judges clapped somewhat uncomfortably when the play was over, a far cry from the standing ovation the troupe received after their first audition.

Lior Bonaventure took advantage of the high ceiling of the amphitheater to gallop his horses like a flying carousel. Lighting cast the shadows of dancing horses across the ancient walls, and an audience of all ages seemed charmed. Once more, Carthage found himself marveling at Bonaventure's stage presence. He was a formidable challenger.

Miss Skyhawke performed a startling levitation effect that concluded as a transformation effect when, in a clap and a bolt, the levitating illusionist turned herself into a hawk and flew over the audience.

Carthage, even knowing it was a trick, felt his heart drop in shock as it happened.

He slightly resented her for eliciting that in him. Of course it was only an illusion. But he wasn't entirely sure how she did it, and also resented that it would keep him awake for days until he figured it out.

By the applause she received, there was no question that she was the favorite of the evening. He caught himself clapping despite himself. She deserved it.

As for Alastair Hemlock's audition, they missed that one, since he went on just before them. But they did hear the crowd laughing. Now that Carthage had encountered Hemlock in person, the idea of him making anyone laugh was hard to fathom.

Backstage, Carthage looked one last time at his watch. Yesterday, they had just a few extra hours for another run-through in the amphitheater, and this time they came just under the time they were allotted.

"You ready?" Huxley asked.

Almost. Carthage tied his silk cravat. "Are there journalists here?"

"A few local writers from Halcyon. And of course Ms. Belvedere, traveling with us."

"Where is she?"

Huxley hesitated.

Dominic held out his coat, and Carthage bent backwards to step into it. It was a new coat, with butterflies stitched up the tails. "I won't let her intimidate me. Where is she sitting?"

"Section B. The front row."

"Excellent," Carthage said, and shook out the coat. "A front-row seat."

Ms. Ainsley Belvedere, sitting on the front row, wore a net over her face. But it did not hide her bland expression quite well enough. She looked uninterested, as if she'd written her article before ever seeing the show.

Carthage opened lightly with comedy and music, bantering with Marietta the operetta electrical. She sang Fodor's 3rd Movement, *Transformata*, and then Carthage performed an effect that brought a dead bouquet of roses back to color and life.

He was glad Ms. Belvedere was sitting so close. It gave him a chance to observe her, and several times throughout the show he cheated his performance toward her so that she would have the best angles. It confused the electricals performing with him, who then had to adjust their preprogrammed blocking, but they would have to process quickly and adapt.

The lights were beginning to burn him, and he felt lightheaded in the heat. He was sweating under the heavy coat, and sweat ran tracks under his collar and down the small of his back.

Unfortunately, his efforts to woo Ms. Belvedere had little effect. Several times, motion drew his peripheral vision when she lifted a pencil to write something. But her face remained static, as if she were balancing her checkbook.

She *was* balancing her checkbook, for all he knew. She seemed distracted.

Every time she looked down, he got a little hotter. She looked at him like she might look at a specimen, like his wings were pinned to a white board. He'd fed himself busking sidewalks, and he knew there were certain people that would look at you once and pass a coin into your hat without actually watching the show. As if you were a panhandler and not a performer. As if they could pay for the right to otherwise ignore you.

He'd seen some of Ainsley Belvedere's moving pictures. He loved *The End of Contemptua*, he'd seen it in the cinemas three times. Every single time, as the lights went low and the projector clacked aloud in the sacred silence of the theater, he locked his gaze on the holographic picture and never once looked away. He'd barely even blinked. When it was over, he applauded for the players, even though they would never hear it.

Someone in the second row touched her shoulder, and she turned around to answer. The other person leaned close to her ear, and then Ainsley Belvedere laughed. Not with him. Not even *at* him. Then she whispered something back, and it became clear that she was actually having a *conversation* while she sat on the front row of his show.

The band kicked uptempo as what was supposed to be a transition into the finale started. Carthage raised his arm, appearing to flourish. Flashed the back of his hand toward Huxley, who would be somewhere behind him, managing.

Three fingers pointed straight up: *trigger the blast caps.*

It wasn't time for the final pyrotechnic cue. He was jumping it early, and he worried Huxley might think he was confused and stick to the script instead.

Trust me, he willed.

There was a fraction of a pause.

The arena lit up as the stardust ignited. Carthage had signaled for it, but it came so suddenly it startled even him. The blast caps were in a sequence, but the fuses were short. The blasts felt and sounded simultaneous as the amphitheater momentarily blazed like daylight. The audience jolted at the sudden thunderclap.

The stardust was tinted with dyed phosphorus. Crimson and turquoise smoke billowed around Carthage. The air still sparked as flecks of stardust continued to ignite midair. His ears rang and his mouth sizzled. The amphitheater stared.

He took off his hat to beat a bit of red tint off of his sleeve. "Is everyone awake?" he asked.

The audience let out the breath in a ripple of giddy laughter. Carthage put his hat back on and looked at Ainsley Belvedere. Her hand was pressed over her heart, and she faced him.

Now the show could go on.

Marietta began a haunting reprise of *Transformata*.

Carthage produced an electrical butterfly out of his sleeve. It perched on his fingertip, wings flexed, then he cast it into the air. The audience was quiet now, rapt, as it flew away.

He took a coin out of his pocket and transformed it into another butterfly. Pulled another out of his hat. Shook his coat and released two more. They fluttered up and away, beyond the lighting and the truss, vanishing into the dark.

He flourished to his left. A spotlight illuminated butterflies perched on the outstretched arms of the stone reliefs. These swooped low, and he saw several local children leap from their chairs, trying to catch them, as they flew up and away.

He flourished to his right, and the butterflies reappeared from the rafters in a synchronized swirl, circling him. The audience murmured as the butterflies alighted on his head, shoulders, and outstretched arms.

He brought his feet together and pointed one finger straight up.

Blackout.

Above, white stars twinkled in a black sky.

He held the moment, savoring it, watching faces that turned up in wonder. The sky shimmered like a rippling pond as a slight glitch shivered across it.

Then he brought his arm down, the lights came back on, and the sky collapsed into hundreds of butterflies.

The holopaper wings changed color as the butterflies scattered from the ceiling. From black, specked with stars, to radiant blues and greens. The butterflies descended into the audience, swirling around the amphitheater, and there were answering shrieks of delight. The stage lights cast whirling shadows on the sandstone walls as the butterflies filled the room.

Carthage looked at Ainsley Belvedere. She wasn't looking at him. She was watching his butterflies. Head tilted back, mouth turned up in a look of wonder. She lifted a hand, and one of the electrical butterflies landed on it, crawling over her knuckles.

The look of wonder burst into a downright smile.

Carthage pulled a deep breath and felt a smile escape, too. The butterfly flew away, and she looked right at him, catching his gaze. Still smiling, he swept off his hat and bowed to her.

He heard the audience clap, but he was more interested in this one person, who had come to his show with her mind made up and had it completely changed.

★

THE PRINCIPAL JUDGE announced the results of the Halcyon audition outside the Palace Administration tent. The darkness of nighttime brought a cold air to the hillside, and Huxley crossed his arms over himself, but Carthage stood in a waistcoat and bare shirtsleeves and found it pleasantly cool. He was still warm from stage lights and adrenaline, and the outdoor air, even tinged with smog as it always was, tasted fresher than the indoors.

At the podium, the judge shuffled his note cards. "Advancing to Helios," he began. "Lior Bonaventure."

Bonaventure turned and left as soon as he heard his name, apparently unconcerned about who his competitors would be.

"Miss Skyhawke."

Carthage caught several onlookers nodding along with this news. That was an expected outcome.

"The Electrical Menagerie."

Carthage clenched a fist in victory and shot Huxley a grin that he thought probably looked a wee punch-drunk. Crowing, Huxley threw up his arms, so excited it seemed like he might actually tackle Carthage in some kind of hug. Carthage braced himself and was relieved when that didn't come.

Helios! Carthage shut his eyes for a moment, but when he opened them again, he caught two journalists settling a bet on the sidelines. Not so much an expected outcome, then. He steeled himself. The stakes would be higher in Helios, where they'd be forced to prove Halcyon wasn't just beginner's luck. Somehow, he'd have to top what he just did. Could he follow his own act?

Yes, of course. A newfound bolt of energy coursed through him. There was no limit to what he could accomplish. Ideas already crackled at the edges of his mind, and his heart tried to float out of his mouth.

Nothing could bar him. Anything that didn't exist, he could invent. Imagination and innovation had never failed him. Nothing could overcome the power of a dream. His mind and his hands were all he needed, and they were readier than ever. Firing like new spark plugs in a combustion engine.

"Lastly..." The judge took off his reading spectacles and slipped them into a coat pocket. He looked up and recited the final act to advance: "Alastair Hemlock."

THE TRAIN WAS underway in a matter of hours. As it raced away from Halcyon, Carthage took one last look through the windows. The carnival was gone, and the last of the tents lay collapsed in dark heaps on the ground. Without the bunting, or the electric lights, the cliff would have seemed like it hadn't been touched in a hundred years. The only evidence of them were the long and bald ruts pounded into the hillside.

Carthage said goodbye to Halcyon, and all the opportunity it offered him, and then didn't look back again.

In the dining car, he sat down at the table and took a late supper. He felt suddenly starving, and Dominic served him cold cuts and tea as he watched his copy of the paper and waited for Ms. Belvedere's commentary to appear.

Huxley ate with him, having a one-sided conversation about politics and the magistrates on Helios, and then retired from the table to one of the armchairs but kept talking.

The Principal Star had sunk and vanished into the sea of aether beneath the Isles. Carthage, feeling calm, watched the distant stars flash by as the train curved through a darkened sky.

At some point, he realized Huxley had stopped talking and looked across the car to see that he was asleep. Lightly snoring, arms bundled tightly over his chest.

"Dominic," said Carthage. "You ought to give Mr. Huxley his coat."

"Why?"

The electrical's lack of empathy for basic human conditions often startled Carthage. How could Dominic know so much and yet understand so little?

"Because he looks cold, Dominic."

The electrical tsked, and trundled over to lay Huxley's coat over his crossed arms. In his sleep, Huxley sighed and visibly relaxed.

"Humans are so high-maintenance," Dominic complained. "I don't get cold. Or hungry. I only need my battery charged every night. This company would be more efficient if Mr. Huxley was replaced with an electrical."

"I've considered it." Picking up the paper again, he gave it a light shake to refresh it, but nothing new appeared.

Dominic, refilling Carthage's teacup, observed him. "There you go again," the electrical said.

"I'm waiting for the new commentary to appear."

Dominic dropped two lumps of sugar into the cup

and stirred it for him. "I would think you will be waiting until morning."

Dominic was right. Her review would have to run past an editor first, and everyone was already in bed.

Bed was where he should have been, too. Helios was barely a day and a half away. It wasn't much time to recover, and there would be another show to rehearse as soon as they arrived. But he didn't feel ready for bed.

"Dominic," he said as the electrical started to roll away. "Why don't you sit here and talk with me awhile?"

Dominic obliged, rolling back up to the edge of the table. "What would you like to talk about?" The lights of Dominic's eyes blinked as he scrolled through his memory banks. "I can tell you about the flora and fauna on Helios."

Carthage shook his head.

"How about the history of Helios?"

Carthage sighed. The only things Dominic had to talk about were things that Carthage had taught him.

"What if I told you about Herbert Wooster?"

"Herbert Wooster?" That was a topic that didn't ring a bell.

"Herbert Wooster," Dominic began, "was a dairy baron during the Milk Crisis of—"

Carthage held up a hand. "Thank you, Dominic. Never mind." He rubbed his eyes and pushed away from the table. "I think I ought to retire, anyway."

"Yes, you should recharge."

Carthage stood up and suppressed a cry as pain lanced up and down his legs. It took him by surprise;

he'd experienced little pain on Halcyon. He realized it had only caught up to him now because this was the first time in days he'd been sitting still for so long.

Working his way around the table, he tried to lengthen his stride. All he needed was to stretch himself out again, and he'd be fine.

He crossed the length of the car and had almost passed its threshold into the sleeping car when another jag hit, buckling him. This was worse than pain. It was paralysis.

Catching the gilt frame of the door, he was surprised to feel a pair of hands supporting him. Dominic, who looked up at Carthage under his arm, held a perplexed silence for awhile.

Carthage was relieved as pain returned to his legs. Anything was better than feeling nothing. Still grasping the doorway, he slowly straightened, but he found he had to lean on Dominic.

Together, they limped down the hall. It hurt to put his weight down, especially on his right leg. That one had always been worse.

As they reached the door of his compartment, he leaned a palm on the paneling and took a deep breath. Dominic unlocked and opened the door for him. The rack where he slept was still folded down, and he staggered through the door and straight down onto the bed.

Considering the effort of undressing, he decided he didn't want to attempt taking off his trousers or his shoes. He'd take off his waistcoat and his tie and sleep in his clothes. Or maybe he'd just take off his tie. Now that he was sitting on the bed, he understood exactly how tired he was.

Dominic spoke again and startled him. Carthage hadn't realized Dominic still lingered in the doorway.

"Perhaps," the electrical said helpfully, "you need a new pair of legs."

Carthage, working off his tie, sighed. "I'm afraid it isn't that simple, Dominic."

"And why is that?"

"It's very painful to change out our bad parts."

Dominic tsked again and slowly retreated, closing the door behind him.

"Being human," Carthage heard him say on his way out, "must be so complicated."

★

AN ELECTRICAL UPSET

AINSLEY BELVEDERE, SENIOR CRITIC.

FORCESDAY, 12TH QUARTER-NOCTUS.

HALCYON — I have been in show business for a very long time. It takes a lot to astonish me; although I am occasionally astonished by terrible entertainment, I can't remember the last time I was astonished in such a way that a performance elicited from me a genuine smile. Frankly, I had already written my commentary before I ever attended Mr. Carthage's show. I am pleased (and somewhat abashed) to say that I had to rewrite this column —the latter type of astonishment is what Mr. Carthage and his 'Electrical Menagerie' did to me last night.

MS. BELVEDERE'S COMMENTARY CONTINUED ON PAGE 4A

CARTHAGE FOLDED THE paper under his arm and stepped off the train. The Principal Star was high and warm over Helios, carving Pegasus Park in mid-afternoon shadows.

The park, a massive sprawl of greenery, outdoor theaters, statue gardens and waterwork plazas, was built in the heart of the city. There were landrails laid into the park, which let the performers pull their trains right into camp, and camp bustled now, still being erected by stage crews. Somewhere, iron stakes rang with a peculiar music as they were hammered in rhythm.

Two cars down, Carthage found Huxley fixing his sleeves up higher under his sleeve garters as the electricals unloaded the train.

Carthage opened the paper again, and saw Huxley glance at it then look away. Carthage was puzzled. That was a peculiar response from someone who had been so offended by their omission from the last commentary, but it was also what he'd done at breakfast. After their incredible efforts on Halcyon, Carthage expected Huxley would want to bask in the glory.

The rest of Ms. Belvedere's commentary was as glowing as the paragraph that appeared on the front page. He looked forward to talking with her and thanking her for what she said. He hoped to astonish her again in two days.

Dominic gave a cheerful electronic whistle as he approached. Carthage turned as Dominic rolled over the grass, copper body clanging when it hit a rut. Wincing, Carthage reminded himself, again, to fix Dominic's off-kilter wheel.

Dominic's hand was raised, metal fingers grasping envelopes. "I have the post," he said. "For Mr. Huxley—"

Huxley, who had disappeared into the dark mouth of the freight car, reappeared. "Me?"

"A telegram," Dominic reported, and Huxley sprang from the gangway to claim it. Dominic turned to Carthage with an envelope. "And Master Carthage."

Carthage, surprised, took it. It was cream-colored linen paper, closed with dark blue wax that was stamped with the seal of a Pegasus in flight. He broke the seal and unfolded the letter.

The letter wasn't printed on holopaper; it was real ink. Very expensive copper ink, as a matter of fact. The letters flashed with a metallic sheen as he tilted the letter toward the sunlight.

You and your associate are formally invited to drinks and dancing, 9 o' clock tomorrow evening, to be hosted at Helios Hall. We would also like to specially invite you to perform your practice of illusion for the other distinguished guests, including the Governor of Helios and the magistrates. This is a great honor which we have not bestowed on any other contender. Our governor is particularly excited to see your electrical butterflies, which we read about in the paper. Please send your response via Palace Administration.

Thank you,
Bird Lionguard
Chairwoman,
Helios Committee for Social Endeavors & the Arts

Specially invited? Something fluttered in Carthage's heart — or was it his stomach? He looked up to share this news with Huxley, but Huxley had taken his telegram and disappeared.

This *was* a great honor. But it was not the stage he was acclimated to. This was an invitation into a persistent arena in which the spotlights stayed fixed and the show never really ended. Where there were spectators — and critics — on all sides, with no wings to wait in. This was the *society* stage, an entirely different kind of debut — an invitation to stardom.

He was surprised, after so many years wishing for recognition, how much that frightened him.

He turned to Dominic. "Dominic, run back to Palace Administration and tell them the answer is yes. Huxley will send along a written RSVP shortly."

"Yes?" Dominic, who had not read the letter, didn't seem to understand.

"Yes," said Carthage, and those internal butterflies flustered around again when he did. He slipped the letter into his coat, where it lay snug against his heart. "We're performing at the ball."

9

MASKS

The telegram contained just five words:

WE ARE PLEASED WITH YOU.

It took Huxley twice as long as it should have to dress for the party. He kept pausing to read the telegram again, almost anxiously, as if the ink might fade or the meaning might change.

Apparently Ainsley Belvedere's syndication ran as far abroad as Fallsbright. His father would have opened the paper at the breakfast table, as he always did, and found the review. Over coffee and orange juice, Huxley's parents then shared proud words. Proud enough to send a servant five miles down the road to the telegraph station in Queens Junction. Promptly, so that it reached Helios before he did.

It was a satisfaction without hesitation or doubt.

Dominic's metal fingers clanged as he knocked on the door of Huxley's compartment.

"Yes," answered Huxley, glancing into the mirror to tie his tie.

Dominic opened the door. "Master Carthage is ready."

"Yes, I'm coming." Huxley stuck his tongue between his teeth. It had been awhile since he wore a bow tie.

"Do you require assistance?" Dominic asked.

Huxley turned and bent slightly, obliging.

"You are typically punctual," Dominic observed, tying the bow tie. "But not today. What's wrong with you? Are you cold?"

"Am I... what?" Huxley furrowed his brow, then dismissed it. Fool's errand trying to understand how the circuits worked. He straightened and gave the tie a tweak. "I've just been distracted today."

"By the telegram you received."

"Yes." Huxley shrugged into his coat.

"Was it bad news?" Dominic asked.

"No," said Huxley, and picked the telegram up off the fold-down table by the window. He folded the note in careful quarters and slipped it into his coat, where it rested snug near his heart. "No, it was good news."

"I see," said Dominic, in a voice that suggested he didn't really see at all.

As Huxley stepped off of the train and into the night air, he was just in time to see Carthage stumble and take a knee in the grass. Worried, he moved to Carthage's side.

"What happened?" he asked, and tried to offer a hand of help.

Carthage pushed Huxley's hand away. "Don't help me," he said with a hint of panic in his voice.

Huxley stepped back, bewildered. "Are you alright?"

"I..." Carthage got to his feet without help. He bent at the waist to brush flecks of grass off his knees. On inspection, his trousers still looked presentable. "Aye. I just stumbled, that's all."

Huxley, perplexed, moved away. "We should go," he said. "Don't want to keep society waiting."

★

HELIOS HALL WAS only across the street from Pegasus Park, where the trains were, and it seemed silly to take a cab, but it would have been sillier to arrive on foot to a ball. So they walked from the campground, across a picnic lawn to a plaza where cabbies chatted around a fountain, and Huxley hailed the first cab he saw with matching horses.

The cab driver, taking a look at the way they were dressed, got a gleam in his eye like he expected a good tip and sprang into service.

The matched silver-gray mares carried them down a tree-lined bridle path and out of the park into city traffic. Helios Hall, uplit by columns of electric light, stood like a palace on the intersection. The cabbie, deftly dodging traffic, delivered them to the door at a handsome trot. Huxley leaned to look at the other patrons arriving and saw that the invitation hadn't been exaggerated. Just behind them arrived someone in a four-horse carriage, attended by footmen.

The cabbie opened the doors for them, and Huxley paid him extra. "Double if you're back around at midnight," he promised, and the cabbie tipped his derby hat.

"Aye, Cap! I'll do a song and jig if y'like."

"None of that, now," said Carthage, overhearing. "We're entertainers. Can't have you upstaging us."

The cabdriver roared with laughter. "Entertainers! May stars fall! Are y'anybody famous?"

Huxley exchanged a look with Carthage, and they shared a rare grin.

"I suppose we sort of are," Carthage answered.

The cabbie hopped onto the back of the cab. "I'll be right here," he promised. "Me and the girls."

At the door, a servant in white tails accepted their invitation, then walked with them to the landing of the staircase to announce them. The hall below was filled with a mingling crowd of patrons from Helios and beyond. They paused, lifting their heads, and applauded.

Huxley ran a nervous hand over the star-shaped fob that dangled from his watch chain. He wore cream fall front trousers, a navy tailcoat, and a double-breasted waistcoat with buttons gilt in real gold. He always dressed well, but it had been a few years since he'd been invited to any kind of social event. Ballroom clothes felt startlingly foreign, as did the attention. Having so many eyes on him did not feel exactly pleasant.

Carthage, on the other hand, bristled with new energy. He wore a black coat embroidered with birds and laurels, gloves and a top hat. He swept his hat off in greeting, then, ever the performer, rolled it neatly up his arm and back onto his head.

How could Sylvester Carthage, a man so shy and pensive, be braver than Huxley standing in front of a crowd? Huxley was beginning to understand that bravery was an act. A character Carthage played. Someone much warmer than he really was.

Aware that he was not the celebrity, Huxley waited three steps before he followed. From behind, it seemed that Carthage stepped unevenly as he went down the staircase. Huxley furrowed his brow, hoping Carthage hadn't bent an ankle when he tripped. But it was subtle, and when he looked again, he was sure he'd only imagined it.

Helios Hall was an impressive piece of architecture with balconies and flourished archways modeled in plaster, large electric chandeliers, and a pink marble floor. Frescoes of unicorns graced a trio of domes in the high ceiling. It smelled like champagne and wig powder; there were magistrates in their old-fashioned wigs everywhere.

A trio of them approached Carthage right away. Huxley saw Carthage falter. Speaking face-to-face was different than doing hat tricks at the top of the staircase. Huxley moved, intending to intervene with an introduction. But someone called to him by a name he didn't often hear.

"Arbrook!"

Huxley turned as two familiar faces swarmed him from opposite sides. He felt so displaced by that familiar voice calling his first name that he stared at them instead of acknowledging them.

The man looked at his wife and boomed a laugh. "Would you believe it? He's forgotten us already!"

"Mr. Cabot, of course not!" Huxley put out a hand, and John Cabot gave him an aggressively robust handshake. "The sound of your voice took me right back to Fallsbright, that's all."

"Right back to being switched for eating autumn apples in the summer, by that look," said Mrs. Cabot. The Cabots and the Huxleys owned adjacent properties, and when he was a boy, he'd fairly menaced his neighbors with a taste for unripe apples.

Huxley laughed. "I still prefer mine before they turn too sweet," he said. On Fallsbright, he'd have exchanged kisses on the cheek with her and her husband, but mainlands etiquette had different boundaries. He bowed to her instead.

"How's your father?" asked Mrs. Cabot.

"My father?"

"Well, he'd had his angina just before we left. But that was nearly a month ago. We wondered if he was feeling better."

"Oh, yes." Huxley looked down at his dress shoes, pretending that he already knew this. No correspondence had come to tell him that his father was having chest pains again. "Yes, he's better. He's quite well. What are you doing all the way out here in the Central Isles?"

"Holidaying," said John Cabot. "We've come to visit cousins in Helios. And Sassy wanted to see the Monuments to the National League."

"Sassy's here?" Huxley started to look for her, and his heart lurched when he half-turned to find her already at his elbow.

Too late to run.

"Brook!" she purred, and offered him her hand to kiss. He did, dutifully, and raised his eyes to meet hers.

He paid dearly for those stolen apples. Early in their young lives, Saskia Cabot sighted him over the garden wall and fairly menaced him with a taste for his unripe affection. By the time he became sweet on girls, he was already soured to her.

She had been about seventeen when last he saw her, leggy and round-faced like girls were, but now she was a woman. She wore a ball gown the piercing blue of a Fallsbright flag, choked with dark lace and flounced by what had to be about thirteen underskirts. "However have you been?"

Huxley had spent too much time abroad, ear strained to decipher Carthage's musical rhythm and trilled R's, which could make even a sandwich order sound like a song. Saskia's accent, hard-edged and then drawled at the end like she was trying too hard to be genteel, jarred him. Stars, was that what he sounded like to everyone else?

"I've been just fine," he answered her.

"We read about you in the paper," she said. "Seems you've been more than fine."

Her father nodded in agreement, clapped Huxley on the arm. "We're tickled, son. You've made Fallsbright proud."

Huxley felt a warmth he hadn't felt in months, warmth like a Fallsbright day. His heart ached, a little, to see his old friends here. Even Sassy was a sight for sore eyes — and perhaps warranted a second glance.

"Thank you," he said with a smile. He ran his hand

over his watch chain again, but some of the nervousness diminished within him.

He was beginning to remember what it was like before he was prodigal. When he was still invited to functions and talked about openly. When his mistakes were laughed off as boyhood folly. When he wasn't dismissed out of hand.

He was beginning to remember that he liked it.

The Cabots introduced him to their cousin, the magistrate, who then introduced two barristers and a county clerk. Shortly after, a few chairpeople from the Helios Committee for Social Endeavors & the Arts came over to introduce themselves, and Huxley spent some time trading compliments and polite humor with some local journalists and members of the committee.

He lost track of Carthage completely, and realized only when a clock chimed that it was almost time for Carthage to perform.

They'd re-staged a version of the butterfly spectacle for this venue. Huxley was accustomed to being backstage, with something to do, but this time all there was to do was watch, which left him feeling uncomfortably idle. He turned toward the staircase as someone dimmed the chandeliers and announced Carthage.

Carthage started with the simple apparitions at the top of the stairs, pulling butterflies out of his hat and his sleeves, then borrowed a coin from a man lingering on the landing and changed that into a butterfly, too. The crowd tittered with laughter at the man's look when he never got his coin back. The close-up work on the staircase was misdirection, both to build anticipation and to stall while the other butterflies arranged on the ceiling.

As Carthage descended the staircase and the string quartet swelled, just over Huxley's shoulder one journalist whispered to another.

"Is it me, or is he limping?"

Huxley had been watching the show, but his stare went blank. Was it better to acknowledge the remark and defuse it, or to ignore it? That quandary was a bit like choosing red or black. Luck would spin the wheel.

He decided to ignore the comment, perhaps even deny it if asked. But then the second journalist replied.

"It isn't you. He is."

Huxley turned. "Mr. Carthage suffered a minor fall today." They looked startled, and he realized they didn't know he was standing within earshot of their remarks. He forced a smile, hoping to sound conversational, not defensive. "He'll be more than fine in time for the audition."

Well, now that he'd acknowledged it, they'd be reading about that minor accident for days, but at least it would stave off any gross speculation.

Huxley, distracted, had missed the finale. He realized the performance was over only because there was applause. He looked up as the lights flared and saw the hall filled with a hundred electrical butterflies.

Andromeda Skyhawke stood nearby, staring up in wonder. Along with a gray mask, she wore a gown dyed the understated color of a mourning dove's wing and hemmed with silver embroidery. Huxley realized that he hadn't seen her in the audience at Halcyon — perhaps she missed the spectacle the first time. He watched her, enjoying the smile on her face and wishing she'd seen it in the amphitheater, the way it was meant to be performed.

Andromeda caught him looking at her and gave a slight curtsy. He started toward her, and she moved to meet him. But he was intercepted by Saskia Cabot. Mr. and Mrs. Cabot weren't far behind.

"Just stellar!" declared Sassy, holding a hand up to one of the still-fluttering butterflies.

"Well, aren't we lucky we got to see your show," said John Cabot.

"Everyone on Fallsbright will be so jealous we got to see it first!" his wife agreed.

Andromeda, undeterred by Sassy, closed the distance on Huxley's other side. She was still smiling.

He stepped back to make her part of the circle.

"Miss Andromeda Skyhawke," he introduced her. John Cabot's brow lifted, and Huxley recalled what Carthage said about the Skyhawke family's copper patents and fabulous wealth. The new look of interest on the Cabots' faces suggested the financial boon attached to that surname was not lost on them. "These are old friends and neighbors of mine," he said, "Mr. and Mrs. John Cabot, and daughter, Miss Saskia Cabot." To them, he added, "Miss Skyhawke is competing with us. A talented illusionist herself."

John Cabot kissed Andromeda's hand, and the women curtsied. Sassy had a cool look, but fanned herself anyway.

"Wonderful," Andromeda said to Huxley. "I missed

the show on Halcyon. Be sure to give my regards to Mr. Carthage. His control is excellent. I should like to be that good at close-up magic one day."

"We were just congratulating Mr. Huxley ourselves," agreed Mrs. Cabot.

"This calls for a toast," said John Cabot, and turned toward a passing tray. Andromeda was standing at his hand, and turned with him. As the waiter paused, Mr. Cabot took two glasses of champagne, one for himself and one for his wife.

Andromeda also took a glass in each hand.

Huxley saw Mrs. Cabot and Sassy both look at the second glass and then freeze in anticipation. He paused, hoping Andromeda might turn and hand the second glass of champagne to Sassy.

Instead, she offered the glass to him.

The Cabots' eyes rested on him. Declining the drink would only humiliate Andromeda. But accepting it would make him complicit in the gaffe.

Sassy's brows were high, lips pursed. Someone watching something particularly scandalous. He knew at once that his reputation at home rested on this moment. Sassy would waste no time writing home to tell girlfriends about Andromeda's bold motions; did he really want his name included? The story was sure to circulate back to his parents.

We are pleased with you.

The telegram in his breast pocket weighed like a stone against his chest.

And yet, Andromeda did not appear to realize what

she'd done. A look of uncertainty crossed her face as his hesitation became obvious. That look pained him. He knew what it was like to feel humiliated.

He wouldn't do it to someone else.

He took the glass.

Sassy drew a sharp breath that everyone heard. A glance at her revealed an almost devastated look that made him wonder exactly how far her imaginary designs on him had progressed in the last hour since they reunited.

The Cabots had knowing eyes and false smiles.

Mr. Cabot raised his glass.

"Well," he said. "To young Arbrook. Who seems to have gotten a leg up in the world."

It was a very sly, very subtle dig, but Huxley understood it. He drank to it anyway.

A bell rang, opening the dance floor. Andromeda had a look that said she sensed the cold disposition of the group but didn't understand where it came from.

Huxley cut across the circle and held out his arm. "If you'll excuse us," he told the Cabots. "I owe the lady a dance."

Andromeda, looking grateful for the getaway, seized his arm.

Sassy sniffed, like she might either scoff or cry.

"Of course you do," said Mr. Cabot. "Good evening."

Andromeda grasped his arm tightly as they walked away together. Her touch felt warm. Nervous.

As they reached the dance floor, he turned to face her and took her hand in his.

They were quiet for four bars. She *did* know how to dance. He'd give her that.

"Who are you?" he asked finally.

"What do you mean?"

"You aren't highborn," he said.

"I beg your pardon?"

"You're very good at pretending. Someone obviously trained you in the graces. But you have habits no well-off woman would ever even acquire."

Under the mask, her expression tightened. "Such as?"

"The night we met," he said as he turned her, "you forgot to introduce yourself properly. You swore on the Stars, too, which I have never heard any genteel woman do. You move like someone accustomed to running, and your hand lingered too long on my arm in the amphitheater."

He searched her, but she was silent.

"You shouldn't feel bad, they're small things. I was almost fooled. But then there's what you just did."

"What did I do?"

Then she really didn't know?

"You handed me a glass of champagne."

Her hand tightened over his, anxious. "I appeared ignorant?"

"Not ignorant. Just presumptuous. You seemed to be making a rather assertive romantic overture — marking your territory, I think the other lady might say. When I didn't object, we appeared really rather familiar." He couldn't repress the tug of a smile. "Can I assume that you weren't *actually* making a marital proposition just now?"

"No, no." She let out a breath, understanding. "And I've humiliated you as well, then."

"I think it was implied that I am romancing a woman with more money than me. An implication I don't find humiliating at all — I'd be flattered by a rich wife." The song ended, and he looked at her, serious again. "But you aren't who you say you are. Who are you?"

The ballroom clapped. Andromeda searched him for a moment, and fear crossed her eyes. Then, still holding his hand, she turned and pulled him sharply off the dance floor.

Leading him under an archway, she took him upstairs to a balcony on the second floor. The balcony was dark except for sconces on the wall, and it gave a full view of the dance floor below. Another dance started, and Andromeda turned to face him.

She took off the mask.

Inhaled.

"You're right," she said, the edges of her accent roughening. Her eyes were cast down. "I'm no gentlewoman. I grew up in an orphanage on Celestia — I don't even have a last name."

Huxley crossed his arms. "How, then, did you come to be Miss Skyhawke?"

"The Skyhawkes *do* have a daughter," said Andromeda, "But she's been away from the mainlands for twenty years. I only borrowed the name to use onstage. Sergei knew someone who forged my papers." She fingered the mask and wouldn't meet his eyes. "You have to understand, Mr. Huxley. We lied because we thought it was the only way.

Can you imagine what... what *those* people down there would think if they knew where I came from? When Sergei scouted me, I was running shell games on the sidewalk. I only owned one dress. I knew nothing about being anything decent. He promised to make me a star, and he did. But it was at the price of my identity. Who I was — that illiterate orphan — had to die. I had to be something more alluring. I had to become a *Skyhawke*."

She turned away from him and went to the marble railing of the balcony, looking down at the ladies and gentlemen in their finery. "I know it won't last forever," she said, and the accent slipped further. Took on gritty edges like a piece of rough-hewn wood. "But I sure do like pretending. Putting on pretty dresses. Acting like a lady. I almost start to believe it myself." She sighed and looked down at the mask in her hand. "Then I remember. She's a character. They aren't really clapping for me."

Was that really what she thought?

"Of course they are," he said, joining her side.

Her gaze lingered on the floor, so he moved closer. Her gaze flicked up. She was flushed, sharp lines drawn between her eyes.

"Of course they are. We *all* have smoke and mirrors. We have—" He caught a holopaper butterfly lingering near his hand and flicked it, making the colors on its wings change. "—magic tricks, and technology. Music to make you feel something, and lights to tell you when to feel it. But if I've learned one thing from Sylvester Carthage, it's that none of it matters without *heart*. I've seen your act. You're breathtaking — and that's all you."

She was looking at him like nobody had ever said that before, and the gaze was too much. He turned away and leaned his elbows on the balustrade rail of the balcony. On the ballroom floor, Sassy accepted a dance from a handsome stranger.

"Take it from Arbrook Huxley," he said. "You can fake just about everything in life — except talent."

"Which Arbrook Huxley?" she asked.

He looked at her, surprised. Her eyes were clear and questioning.

"Arbrook Huxley, you-can-quote-me? Or Arbrook Huxley, so nervous he hides a gun up his sleeve?"

Then she *had* discerned it when she grasped his arm in the amphitheater. He flexed his fingers, suddenly aware of its presence. He wore the sleeve gun almost continually, quick-draw mechanism buckled to his arm. There'd been a particularly anxious spell when he'd even slept with it. He barely noticed it anymore. It had become a part of him, a hidden comfort.

Downstairs, Sassy laughed as her partner turned her. She'd be just fine. Huxley wasn't whatever it was she wanted him to be. He'd never been. Maybe somebody else could be.

"I had honors at academy," he told Andromeda. "They gave me laurels for the essay I wrote."

"That's impressive."

"I had a friend rewrite it before I turned it in," he said.

"Less impressive," she conceded.

"When I was in my teens, I rode steeplechase," he continued. "After being weighed for the handicap, I'd change out my iron stirrups for aluminum and my heavy boots for light ones. I still have ribbons hanging up at home — but I didn't win a single one fairly."

Andromeda was silent. She leaned on the balustrade with him. It wasn't very ladylike, but he appreciated it.

He went on. "A few years ago, I got caught counting cards at a casino on Astoria Isle. The casino said they would pay me a lot of money to deal Sixes. Before I met Carthage, that's what I did for a living. I'd count until the odds favored the gamblers, and then I'd reshuffle the deck. It was about the third time a gambler drew on me that I picked this up." He flicked his wrist, and the silver pistol appeared in his palm. It was cool in his grasp. "The only 'magic trick' I know."

He stung all over, but when he risked a glance at her, there was an unmasked pain in her eyes. Not just sympathy. Something deeper. Like what he said meant something personal. He looked away again. The gun vanished back up his coat sleeve.

Downstairs, Ainsley Belvedere, standing by the staircase banister, laughed at something another journalist said.

"I'm twenty-five now," Huxley said, swallowing the rock in his throat. "And I've never accomplished anything except copying the answers without getting caught. All I have is what I hide up my sleeves. And I'm afraid of the day it'll all catch up to me."

"No," said Andromeda, forcefully. He turned to her, surprised, as she went on: "I think you *want* to be caught."

"Why would you say that?"

"You aren't stupid. You aren't lazy. I think you must have thought doing the wrong thing was the only way to be noticed. *Infamy over obscurity*, isn't that what they say?"

She was very close, leaning closer like she was going to take hold of him. Maybe she already had. Some force grasped his heart, pulling him forward. It wasn't entirely pleasant. Like her words were about to rip something right out of his chest. But maybe it was something that needed to escape. He gave her a look that begged her to keep talking.

"I think you did all the wrong things," she said, and dropped to barely above a whisper. "I think you did everything wrong. I think you ruined yourself on purpose. Yearning for somebody to stop you. Desperate for somebody to find you out. Somebody..." her breath wavered. The space between them had somehow vanished. A violin wailed. Huxley tilted his head toward hers. "Somebody who would finally see you and let you..."

The audience broke into applause.

Andromeda inhaled sharply, like waking from a dream. Pulled away. "Mr. Huxley," she said with a wry look. "I don't think a lady should be alone with you in an unlit alcove."

"Good thing you aren't a lady," he said, playful, and reached for her hand, but she moved away.

"Of course I am," she said, and put her mask back on. "Especially to you."

Oh.

Was that really what she wanted?

He stepped back.

Bowed very slightly at the waist.

She curtsied and went downstairs, leaving him alone and feeling that she'd unraveled him. He lingered in the balcony for a few more minutes, trying to collect himself. Like a ransacked trunk of clothes, his feelings didn't seem to fit in the same configuration they did before.

Although they were mixed up, he got them stuffed back in.

He was on Helios, having the adventure of a lifetime. It was too late to take second glances at the past. Too soon to worry about the future. He was at a ball, he was in the papers. He was young, and didn't being young mean living in the moment?

He went downstairs, back to the party. Padlocked his regret, and threw away the key with a glass of champagne.

10

MISDIRECTION

§ylvester Carthage had never been the guest of honor at a party before.

In fact, he'd barely been to parties.

He remembered one of Elys's birthdays — thirteen, wasn't it? He'd been invited down to the parlor to have cake and punch, but he didn't know Elys's friends, and didn't understand the rules to any of their games. But one of Elys's girlfriends had been forced to bring along her eleven-year-old brother.

While the other children played parlor games, the smaller boy sought Sylvester out. He'd been very fascinated by Sylvester's wheelchair and had gotten down to look at the aluminum spokes. Then he showed Sylvester the frog he was hiding in his pocket, and Sylvester held it and identified what kind of frog it was and what it ate.

Sylvester explained to the boy that frogs were happier living outdoors than they were in pockets, and then together they ventured into the garden to let it go. While they were there, they found a nest of worms hatching out of the garden bed, and they collected stones off the path, and then they got into a competition over who could throw a rock the farthest.

It seemed harmless. And they'd only broken a flowerpot that perched too precariously on the garden wall. But when Sylvester's father found them, he was furious. He sent the smaller boy back to the party and took Sylvester inside.

"You're sixteen! And you're playing, like a child, in the dirt? Do you know how you've humiliated yourself?" He scrubbed the dirt off Sylvester's hands, then took him by the shoulders and said, more gently, "You're a young man now. You ought to act your age. Being lame, people will assume you're also — well, you know — *dim*."

Act your age.

He wasn't even sixteen anymore. He was a grown man and a professional. But there were all the rules of high society to remember, and he'd had hardly any practice. People would want to talk, and what was Carthage supposed to talk about?

He thought that men his age probably talked about their wives and the stock market, and young people went on about things like politics and fashion. Carthage didn't keep up with politics, he didn't care what designers were wearing, and he wasn't sure how the stock market worked. Or wives, for that matter.

It was one thing to stand onstage, haloed by stage lights and guarded by smoke. Up close, his sleight of hand would hold up, but the illusion of who he was might not. What if he wasn't what they hoped he was?

Standing on the staircase, it was easy to imagine he was on a stage. Maybe this wouldn't be so hard. Maybe he could get away with a grand entrance, a tip of his hat and a winning smile.

That's right, Sly. One foot after the other.

Even when it hurts. Even when you're afraid.

This won't be so bad. Huxley will do the talking. You'll do the magic.

But a pack of magistrates cornered him the moment he set foot on the ballroom floor. They headed him off so that he was trapped with his back to the staircase banister, and when he turned, Huxley was not there.

"Sylvester Carthage!" said one of the magistrates, and shook his hand.

They looked all the same in their powdered wigs, and they all had long, proper names with multiple hyphens. Carthage scrambled to commit the names to memory, but already couldn't remember which name went with which white head.

"It's a pleasure to have you in Helios," said the magistrates, then looked at him like they expected something.

Well, of course they expected something. He was the guest of honor. He was expected to *say* something. "It's a pleasure to be here," he answered, hoping that would be enough. But they continued to stare at him with their many hopeful eyes. The moment stretched.

Say something. Owt, anything!

"I... I see you're all magistrates, then?"

Like a many-headed beast, they all seemed to answer at once.

Yes, of the High Courts — I am also a circuit judge in the rural districts — Yes, Forstyle-Harms and I sit on the bench under Magistrate Tennings-Proctor — Are you interested in the law?

There was a long pause, and Carthage realized one of those was a question. "Oh, me? Not at all."

The following silence vaguely stung. Carthage felt his heart go into his throat. They'd offered him compliments, and he'd trampled an obvious invitation to offer compliments back.

"Of course, I mean..." What would Huxley say? "I don't have the stomach for it. I tried to read the Six Treatises when I was a boy, and it put me to sleep."

Was that better, or worse? He wasn't sure anymore. By the silence that followed, maybe it was worse.

"Of course, the law is important," he tried to correct. "And the magistrates — what the magistrates do..." He felt warm and slightly sick. *The show must go on.*

Sometimes a trick went poorly, and the audience saw your mistakes. But there was no running offstage. There was only blustering through it. He tried to do that now, but he wasn't sure what he was saying anymore. As he listened to himself talk, the strains of cello coming from his left seemed to slow to a pained whine.

"It was the language of the Six Treatises, I think, and... I did a lot of reading as a boy. It was just — I spent a lot of time indoors, I did a lot of reading. I was an avid reader, but it was all the lengthy precedents. Too high-minded for a common man, I think."

"Well, that's an awfully postmodern notion," said one of the magistrates. "The Treatises have served this monarchy, and its 'common man', for hundreds of years. Could you clarify what you mean by that?"

Could he clarify what he meant? He wasn't even sure what he *said*. He was being looked at now like he was standing in the box in the high courts for a cross-examination.

"No," he stammered. "I — I'm... forget what I said."

His pulse pounded so loud he was certain everyone could hear it. He was so warm that his starched cuffs and collar burned him. This wasn't what he was supposed to be. This wasn't who he *wanted* to be. And a bad performance on *this* stage could mark a man for life.

Coming here was a mistake.

"Excuse me," he said, and bolted between two of the magistrates without really making eye contact. The ballroom was a tangle of people, and every single one of them looked at him as he hurried across the floor.

All he ever wanted was to be seen, but now all he wanted was to be forgotten again.

Cool and fresh air drew him under a low archway and plunged him into an open courtyard on the backside of the hall. The sky was clear and the Stars all stared as he escaped the ballroom and pulled a breath of cold air.

The courtyard felt it was faintly spinning. He staggered against the white trunk of a birch tree and vomited into the hedges.

Two young men, putting out cigarettes as they went past, saw him. One of them laughed.

"The party started without us," he said to his friend.

"Stage fright," said the other, and sounded more sympathetic.

But Carthage wasn't afraid of the stage. Onstage, the narrative was in his hands. He edited out the bad parts and rewrote the ending. On the stage, he was the master of his own reality, and he could be anybody he wanted to be.

Out here, somebody else was telling the story. The awful parts were uncensored.

The ending was uncertain.

Maybe it had been better to be small and hidden away.

Maybe he'd been better off behind a window.

He paced the empty courtyard, stomach churning, until it was time to perform. Then, relieved to have something constructive to do, he tidied himself and went back inside for his act.

The dimmed lights were a comfort as he stood once again on the staircase. The audience laughed when he palmed a coin from a bystander, and his rattling heart steadied. It was so much better to be laughed *with* than *at*.

This was easy. This was even fun. He could do this. His butterflies brought a thunder of applause, and his raging stomach tempered.

He was swarmed again when the performance was over, but this time, his head was on soundly, and he remembered what to do: misdirection.

People wanted to introduce themselves, and when

they did, he'd ask if they wanted to see a trick. He didn't have to talk about anything important. He had patter memorized, it was all part of the show. He went from patron to patron, barely seeing them. Not even trying to remember any names.

He relaxed further as he got gasps and smiles back. The fear melted away, like snowflakes on a kindling furnace. People gushed about his butterflies, which still lingered on columns and chandeliers. Sometimes people wanted to understand how a trick worked, but he smiled and pressed a finger to his lips. His profession was to trade in secrets, and that made everything easier. Nothing had to be real. It only had to be convincing.

He only had to be convincing.

And people *were* convinced. He saw it when he looked at them. That willing repartee between performer and patron that demonstrated respect.

He remembered doing street magic, watching people walk by and sometimes even roll their eyes, as if they were too good for it. He'd come so far since then. These people were more than entertained. They clung to him like he was some imported thing. They hung on his words. They *liked* him.

No matter what happened after this, he was vindicated. No matter what happened at the audition, or beyond. He always had this moment. The pleasure of *being* and *doing* growled in his chest. This was what he was meant to do — as God hung the Stars to shine, so The Almighty had also fixed something burning inside Sylvester Carthage. He'd never been more alive.

Neither had his dreams. Once fixed like a far-off place, known only to him on maps, his dreams of the royal palace now stood visibly on the horizon.

Huxley finally turned up, a glass of champagne in hand. Carthage, feeling especially friendly, was glad to see his companion.

"Where have you been?" he asked.

"Nobody," said Huxley. "I mean, nothing." He swiped a petit four off a passing tray and stuffed it in his mouth as if silencing himself.

"I wasn't sure," said Carthage, and clapped a hand on Huxley's arm, "but I'm glad we came."

Huxley looked at the hand on his arm. "Have you been drinking?" It was muffled around a mouthful of cake.

"No, I haven't been *drinking*." He didn't like the way alcohol mugged up his thinking. Huxley knew that.

"You just seem..." Huxley washed his cake down with a drink and gestured like he didn't know what to call it. "Really, you know..."

"I feel happy."

"That's the word," said Huxley.

Bird Lionguard, head of the social committee, came over to introduce herself. She had a warm smile on her face, like she already knew them, and addressed Carthage directly. "Mr. Carthage," she said. "It's such an honor to have you. Thank you for accepting my invitation. I speak for the committee when I say that your presence does not disappoint. In fact, I'd say that the papers hardly do you justice! Thank you, also, for the wonderful bouquet."

He tipped his head. "The bouquet?"

"The arrangement was beautiful. As were the kind words that accompanied it."

"The..." Carthage started. Standing just behind her, Huxley nodded frantically. "*Ah.* I'm glad you enjoyed it."

They lapsed into silence. She glanced at the dance floor, and they listened to the music together.

Ms. Lionguard adjusted her shawl and looked back at him. "Have you found Helios to be hospitable?"

"I'm afraid we haven't had the chance to see much of it," said Carthage.

"I've found it to be pleasantly warm," answered Huxley. "This is my first time here. I'll say, this hall is something else."

But Ms. Lionguard was looking at Carthage. Smiling. Expecting something. What?

"Can I show you something remarkable?" he asked, ready to show her a trick.

"Oh," she said. "I'm afraid I should move on. I have a hundred more guests to greet. I just wanted to... well, stop by to thank you. I really was quite taken with your show."

She exited, and Carthage turned to Huxley. "What have I told you about forging my signature when you send gifts?"

Huxley was agape. "Why didn't you dance with her?"

"Dance?"

"She was practically *begging* you to ask!"

"I..." Carthage felt himself flush. "She wasn't."

"She was! It's not too late. Go catch her."

He shook his head. "No, I... I don't know how."

"You don't know how to dance?"

"I don't know how to *ask*." The dancing itself would be a secondary hurdle.

"Don't know how to...? Hold my drink." He shoved his glass into Carthage's hands. "I'll *show* you."

Huxley caught up with Ms. Lionguard, smiling. Carthage lingered at his back, a safe distance away.

"Ms. Lionguard," Huxley said. "You're terribly busy. But I was wondering if I might steal just one dance."

She gave a polite look of sympathy. "I really mustn't," she said. "I couldn't possibly neglect my other guests."

"Of course," he replied. "Next time, perhaps."

"Ah, so *that's* how it's done." Carthage said as Huxley rejoined him.

"Well, in horsemanship, we'd call that a refusal. Sometimes, you know, you don't go over the ditch, you fall into it. It's not the end of the world." He took his drink back and got a momentarily morose look. "Then, sometimes, the horse bucks you off and tramples you on her way back to the barn. That's fine too. You'll be fine."

"Anyway, I was right. She didn't want to dance," said Carthage.

"No, she didn't want to dance with *me*." Huxley shook his head. "You need help. I should help you."

That was terrifying. "No, no, I—"

"*Oh.*" Huxley seized his arm, indicating another woman. "There. That's Katrina Belladonna. She's a singer."

"And?"

"*Talk to her.*"

"I don't know anything about her — what am I supposed to say?"

"Give her a compliment," said Huxley, and shoved him toward her. "Be yourself."

Be yourself?

If only it were that easy.

"Ms. Belladonna," Carthage said, and his stomach dropped as she turned to him.

"Mr. Carthage," she said, eyes lighting up. She had creamy brown skin, a green dress, and a soft mouth. A compliment? She was beautiful, but he couldn't possibly just say that. He scrambled for something else to say.

"I understand you sing," he said.

"I do," she answered with an amused look. "I understand you perform illusions."

"I do," he confirmed.

The moment stretched. Huxley chimed in.

"I believe Mr. Carthage was hoping to ask if you might privilege him with dinner and a private concert aboard his train tomorrow evening," he said.

"Oh?" Her brows lifted. "Well, I—"

Carthage, horrified, turned on Huxley. "*No.*" Then he turned back to Ms. Belladonna. "No. No. I couldn't possibly inconvenience you. It was nice to meet you — thank you. Good evening."

He pulled Huxley away, leaving Ms. Belladonna to stare after them with a perplexed look.

"No, no, *no,*" Carthage said. "I'm not — that was far too forward! Almost indecent."

"Would you calm down? What's the worst that could happen?"

"She could say yes!"

"She could say *yes*?"

"And then I'd have to entertain her. *Alone*."

Huxley stared at him.

"You're right," he said finally. "You're completely right. When you put it that way..."

"Huxley..." Carthage warned.

"It's too much for a man to bear," Huxley went on. "In fact, I can hardly stomach it."

"Huxley."

"That you might be forced to entertain her... over dinner... the *inhumanity* of it! Will the heavens shrug at such injustice? The horror! The indecency!" He grasped helplessly toward the ceiling. "Stars above, is there truly *no other way*?"

"Huxley."

"My greatest condolences, poor martyr — shall I pen the epitaph now?"

"Huxley—"

"Here lies Sylvester Carthage, *dead of having dinner with a beautiful woman*."

Carthage pushed Huxley away and turned, making eye contact with a woman as she walked between two columns. He straightened his tie and looked at her. She wore a shimmering blue-green gown that matched her eyes.

"My lady," he said, and her stride faltered. "Your dress — it..."

Be yourself.

"...it reminds me of the way sunlight hits the sea on a clear day."

She blinked, considering that compliment, and a pink flush tinged her cheekbones and the tips of her ears. She smoothed her skirts and gave a shy smile. "Thank you," she said, curtsied, and then hurried off like a smitten schoolgirl.

Carthage turned to Huxley.

"Did you *see* that?" Huxley crowed and feinted a punch toward Carthage's ribs. "You made her *blush!*"

Carthage grinned fiercely.

"Now, go ask her to dance!"

"Oh no. No no."

"Okay," said Huxley, calming down. "Okay. You're not there yet. We'll get there."

THE CABDRIVER WAS waiting when they finally left the ball and came down the long set of steps.

"I'm sorry," said Carthage as he got into the cab. They'd kept him waiting a half hour. "We'll make sure you're taken care of."

"No worries," said the cabbie with a grin. "Was it a stellar good party, then?"

"Oh," said Huxley, lifting a hand. "You have *no* idea. Say, where are the Monuments to the National League? Is it far?"

"Fifteen minutes by trot," said the cabbie.

"Good," said Huxley, and peeled a few notes out of his pocketbook. "Here's an advance."

Carthage leaned out of the cab. "It's past midnight, Huxley. We've got rehearsal tomorrow."

"It's our only chance to see Helios," Huxley argued, clambering into the cab. "Listen, you can't watch life through a window!"

Pierced by that seemingly innocent phrase, Carthage looked at him.

Wasn't this what he wanted when he was a boy? To see the world? He'd never been on Helios before — why wasn't he the one begging to see the rest of it? He remembered the way his heart beat faster every time he unlatched his window. Every time he opened a book.

And now, here they were, holding the keys to the world. His heart beat so fast it threatened to race right out of his chest. He felt like he did the day of Elys's thirteenth birthday, escaping the parlor and running away into the garden. He stood up and leaned out. "Show us the scenic route. We want to see the sights."

"Aye," said the cabbie, winked and slapped the reins.

"If Sassy gets to see the Monuments to the National League," Huxley declared, although Carthage had no idea who Sassy was, "so do we!"

THE DRIVER MADE good on that order. He showed them the whole of the city, including the Monuments, and it was two or three in the morning by the time he returned them to Pegasus Park. Walking down the bridle path, the horseshoes rang against the cobblestones.

In the cab, Carthage tried to teach Huxley a card trick.

"Okay, okay. Alright." Huxley still seemed confused despite repeated demonstrations.

Carthage couldn't help but laugh.

"I feel like — I think you're laughing at me," said Huxley.

"No," Carthage denied. "You make it look so easy."

The cab halted, and the cabbie jumped down to open the door. He'd taken them right up to the train. Huxley got down and fanned the deck of cards.

"How about it?" he said. "If I can guess which card you picked, will you waive the rest of the fare?"

The cab driver got a knowing look. "Sure," he said. Obviously indulging.

"Alright," said Huxley. "Pay close attention. Watch closely. Blink and you'll miss it. Pick a card."

The cabdriver showed his card to Carthage — the five of stars — then Huxley returned it to the deck, reshuffled and cut the deck with one hand. Carthage bit a lip to keep from laughing. It looked fine, but it was already bust.

"Is this your card?" The ace of hearts.

The cabdriver shook his head, also trying not to laugh.

Huxley pushed the deck of cards back at Carthage and took out his pocketbook. "Next time, I need a plant," he grumbled, and paid the cabbie, who tipped his hat at them and drove off into the night whistling.

"You need *practice*," Carthage answered as they went up into the train. The lamps were on in the dining car, and Dominic greeted them by taking their coats.

Carthage reshuffled the deck, savoring the sound the cards made as they arced together in his palms. They

MOLLIE E. REEDER

were his favorite Empire Standards, printed on a soft, matte paper and backed in royal blue. Huxley watched him shuffle, the same intent gaze he had that first day they met.

Carthage had not seen Huxley manipulate cards until tonight. He could deftly cut and shuffle like any good card dealer, and Carthage thought he might take to sleight of hand — but only if he would apply himself to it. "It takes time to get good at something."

"Well," said Huxley, and broke his gaze away from Carthage's hands. "You *are* good. And so was the show tonight."

Carthage straightened the edges of the deck and put the cards back in their tuck box. He relished the woody smell the cards had, like an old book. A cheap deck, but the one he'd been carrying in his coat the longest. The deck had gotten too marked by wear to use in performance. But he liked to practice manipulations with these cards, and sometimes play solitaire.

He folded the tab under to close the pack. He wasn't sure why, but the thought he might be able to teach Huxley something excited him. He looked up.

Huxley had turned away, headed to the next car.

"Huxley," said Carthage.

Huxley turned, and Carthage tossed him the deck. Huxley caught it and looked at it in surprise.

"There are no shortcuts," Carthage said. "Don't give up."

Huxley swallowed as he grasped the deck of cards. Carthage thought it would be hard to give those precious and familiar cards away, but some look in the young man's eye — something like nobody had ever said that before — made it easy.

"Do you think there's hope for me yet?" Huxley asked. Carthage wasn't sure what that question meant. It seemed like it was part of a conversation they hadn't actually had.

"Sure," said Carthage. "I started off just like you. Of course, you know..." He grinned. "I was nine."

"Oh, shut up." Huxley waved him off and turned for the sleeping car.

"Do you remember where you sleep?" Carthage called after him.

"I'll find it," Huxley called back.

Carthage stood for a few moments, unmoving. Then he realized Dominic was staring at him.

"What are you doing?" Dominic asked.

"Just..." Carthage wasn't entirely sure how to express it. Perhaps there weren't always words for things. Maybe there were moments that no author could exactly bottle up inside a book. "Just remembering the way this night feels. Just saving it for later."

"Was it a good night?"

"It was..." Carthage considered. "One of the best nights of my life." He drew a deep breath and forced his tired limbs to move toward the next car. "Goodnight, Dominic. Wake me up in the morning."

"It *is* the morning," said Dominic.

"Well." Carthage winced at that. "Wake me up *later* this morning."

ONE-WAY GLASS

Carthage's mind woke up before the rest of him did. Thoughts circled like starlings with bits of silver in their beaks, flashes of things that didn't quite yet make sense. It was an idea, looking for a place to land.

There was no chasing an idea down. Move too quickly, and it might startle and fly away permanently. The only way was to be still and quiet. Lying in bed, half-awake, fingers laced over his stomach, he kept his eyes closed and waited for the idea to settle on a conscious branch.

It alighted at the front of his mind. Perched on his tongue.

Projectors.

Bolting out of bed, he slapped his notebook open on the table. He stood over it, writing, and he'd turned the page before there was a soft knock at the door.

"Master Carthage," Dominic said.

"I'm awake," Carthage answered over his shoulder. He shut the notebook and moved to get dressed. This would be a full day of rehearsals.

Dressed and shaved, he took the newspaper with him and came out of his compartment to find Dominic changing a light bulb in one of the lamps. "Is Huxley awake?"

"No," Dominic said. "He turned over and called me a *jalopy,* which I don't think was meant to be very kind."

Carthage went to the next compartment and tried the latch. It was unlocked.

Drawn shades kept the compartment dim and gray, and Carthage almost tripped over a trunk hiding in the darkened floor. Huxley was asleep face-down on top of his rack, still dressed from the party down to his shoes.

Carthage whistled and hit him with the rolled-up newspaper, eliciting a muffled retort.

"Who are you," Huxley slurred as he lifted his head, "and why are you in my room?"

"Listen, I've had an idea." Carthage snapped his fingers like they might generate sparks. "Just now. About projectors."

Huxley, groaning, rolled over and dug his knuckles into his eyes. "What time is it?"

"Already eight o' clock, and we've got rehearsal." Carthage pulled the tab on the shades, letting the light in. Huxley buried his face in the crook of his arm as Carthage went on. "I've just had this idea, about projectors. It's a vanishing act. Using the sphinx illusion. We'd need a projector — no... we'd need two. And a pane of one-way glass... are you listening to me?"

"Something about projectors."

"*Two* projectors. And a pane of one-way glass."

Frustration crept in. The party had been a grand time. But they weren't here to have parties. They were here to work — and win. They weren't going to win by sleeping in. "Come on, Huxley. The day's still young, and we have rehearsal!"

Huxley remained recumbent. "Why... *why* are you in such a good mood?"

"Because I've got good sense," Carthage muttered on his way out. "And I'm not hungover."

★

CARTHAGE READ THE morning edition while he wolfed down a piece of toast on his way across the lawn to the tents. It happened that a gossip columnist had been in attendance at the party, and he'd written an expose. Carthage thought he shouldn't read it, being that it was rag journalism, but a picture of him accompanied the article, and the temptation was too great.

The journalist began with a bitter history of social politics on Helios, which Carthage skimmed. Apparently two magistrates were barely speaking and had almost come to blows over punch, and rumors swirled that someone on the social committee wanted Ms. Bird Lionguard's chair position. The journalist complimented the catering and the band, and name-dropped a few VIP guests. Carthage's eyes settled as they reached his own name:

HEADLINING THE EVENING WAS MR. SYLVESTER CARTHAGE, who performed for patrons with an abridged presentation of his act featured last week on Halcyon. I was disappointed that Mr. Carthage did not preview any new material here in Helios... is it possible Halcyon was a high point for the Electrical Menagerie? We will find out at the audition tomorrow.

Mr. Lior Bonaventure wore horsehair bracelets and a smart navy tailcoat tailored by Derby and Winehouse. A sturdy man of few words, Bonaventure was tight-lipped about his upcoming audition, but did promise that he would take his audience on Helios to 'new heights'. He is currently this reporter's favorite to win the competition on Celestia.

Mr. Alastair Hemlock did make an appearance but, true to his moniker of 'The Silent Man', declined to interview with me. He was observed leaving early in the evening and there are rumors that he attended a private party upmarket. It is suggested the guest list of this private soiree included controversial names in business and politics — names I don't dare run in this column, but you may use your imaginations.

Miss Andromeda Skyhawke, wearing surprisingly understated colors, arrived with no escort but was witnessed in a rather cozy colloquy upstairs with a competitor, Electrical Menagerie producer/manager Mr. Arbrook Huxley. I can verify this rumor personally, as I was the one who witnessed it. Sources close to Mr. Huxley indicate there may be an attachment between the two, and one can only wonder if such a star-crossed romance can survive the heat of competition. Trouble may already brew as Mr. Huxley and the lady did not speak to one another again after said private palaver in an upstairs balcony.

Keep your paper fresh, for I am currently investigating an even more scandalous secret which may reveal shocking facts about one competitor's true identity. Expect that exclusive report in tomorrow's edition.

FOR MORE ARTS & ENTERTAINMENT, SEE PAGE 3

"Huxley," muttered Carthage, and tossed the crust of his toast aside for the birds.

Dominic, rolling alongside him, offered him a thermos of tea. "What about him?"

"We ought to *leash* him, that's what." He accepted a drink of tea as they ducked into the tent. Slapping the paper down on a bench, he took off his coat and began planning his choreography.

Huxley was along a few minutes after, with a cup of coffee in hand.

Carthage picked the paper up off the bench and turned to him. "Did you have a..." He looked at the article to remember what the journalist called it. "A 'cozy colloquy' with Miss Skyhawke?"

Huxley paused and looked at him. Steam wicked from his cup. He'd carried one of the good teacups off the train.

"Did I ... do what now?"

"Were you fraternizing with the woman in some way that might have been perceived as romantic?"

Huxley opened his mouth and pulled a long breath. Carthage recognized the Huxley stall. That was as good as a yes.

"*Was* it romantic?"

"No... or... hmm..." Huxley paused to take a drink, then shrugged. "I don't know."

"Huxley!"

"It was complicated."

Carthage shook his head. "You're out of your depth."

"Excuse me?"

"This woman is far too calculated to fall for compliments."

"What are you so worried about?"

Carthage held up the paper. "This. This is *exactly* what I was worried about. You were just trifling, and now there's a scandal."

"Alright, first — this is only a *scandal* if you're ninety years old, a nun, or Sylvester Carthage. Second, have you forgotten that we're here to generate press?"

"I'm here to *win*," Carthage said. Some part of him stung, and he wasn't sure why. "Isn't that why you're here?"

"I'm here to save the company from bankruptcy," Huxley answered. "And I'll take any press I can get. You don't have to like it. You can cling to your creative integrity. But your show is worthless without marketing. I'm supposed to worry about the money. You should be *thanking* me — I've gotten us in the paper twice."

They both fell silent. Birds sang morning songs in the trees, and some roustabouts chanted nearby. Dominic creaked quietly as he looked between them.

"Twice?" Carthage asked.

"Did I..." Huxley's eyes darted to the left. He lowered his cup. "Is that what I said? It's not what I meant."

Some force threatened to buckle Carthage. He wanted to sit down, but anger held him up. Another heavy length of silence passed before he worked up the strength to press the issue.

"Huxley, did you have any contact with Ainsley Belvedere before the show on Halcyon?"

"Just... briefly."

"Did you, in any way, persuade her to write a favorable review?"

Huxley answered with silence.

Carthage took a step toward him. "Did this *persuasion* involve any kind of gift?"

"Yes, alright?" Huxley raised his hands in surrender. "Yes."

"A monetary gift?"

"Yes."

"A bribe."

"No, it—"

"Yes, Huxley! It's called a *bribe!*"

Huxley seemed at a loss. He said nothing.

The implications of it hit Carthage like a fist to the heart. Huxley *paid* her to enjoy the show?

Every ounce of confidence he felt soured at once into

shame. Embarrassment washed over him, and a dark cloud rolled behind it.

He was a *fool*. A failure. And who else, besides Huxley and the critic, knew it? Carthage was not only a fraud, he was the last to know it.

An electrical butterfly landed on his hand, blue-green wings shimmering as they waxed and waned. He dashed the butterfly to the ground and stepped on it.

Its mechanism crunched. The battery whimpered.

Huxley, taken aback, stared at it. So did Dominic.

Carthage straightened his tie, the lapels of his coat, and his hair. "I need two projectors and a pane of one-way glass."

Huxley looked up. "Now?"

"What else would I mean?"

"I thought we were going to rehearse."

"I need them *for* the rehearsal. For the finale."

Huxley took his book out from under his arm and looked at the script. "Aren't you doing the hatbox for the finale?"

"I've had a new idea this morning. It's better than the hatbox."

Huxley stared at him. "The audition is *tomorrow*. You can't change the act now."

"We'll rehearse all night."

"The night before an audition?"

"It's fine." Carthage spread his hands, as if that might demonstrate his fitness. "It's not a problem."

"I really don't think that's a— "

"The hatbox is *trite*," Carthage interrupted. "It doesn't live up to what we did on Halcyon."

"Okay." Huxley held up a hand. "I need time to find projectors. I'll have to ask around. Give me an hour." He turned and ducked back out, seeming eager to leave on an errand.

Carthage turned around to see Dominic stoop down to pick up the crushed butterfly. Irreparably destroyed. Dead. Dominic cupped it in his metal hands, staring at it as if trying to make sense of it.

"Why did you do that?" he asked Carthage. "You built it — why would you destroy it like that?"

"Huxley was a mistake," said Carthage. "I shouldn't have trusted a partner. And never a *boy*. Lovesick, reckless, covetous — and that profane mouth! But *bribery*? And of course, he knows better! What's so difficult about being decent?"

"I will tell you a fact," Dominic said. "Humans are afraid of pain."

"That's not a relevant fact, Dominic."

"But of course it is. You said it yourself, two nights ago on the train. Perhaps Mr. Huxley is just afraid."

"I didn't say that — what are you talking about? Afraid of what?"

"Don't you remember?" Dominic discarded the mangled butterfly. "It's very painful to change out your bad parts."

★

HUXLEY DID, TO his credit, come through with two projectors. By the time he returned, Carthage had already choreographed the trick, and then spent several hours programming the projectors and trying to get the positioning right. After only managing one or two run-throughs, it was already early evening and the alloted time for their dress rehearsal in the big top.

The act was in no way ready for its dress.

"I can still see the gimmick," Huxley called. He sat in the stands, watching from the vantage of the audience. "There's a seam of light around the edge, especially when the picture turns toward you."

"I'll fix it," Carthage said, and went to adjust the gamma of the second projector, thinking it might minimize the telltale halo that formed at the hologram edge. "You just bother with light and sound."

For the rest of the dress rehearsal, they worked separately. It was not so much a dress rehearsal as it was a rough draft. The lights came up and down, out of time with Carthage's blocking, as Huxley taught the lighting cues to the lighting electrical. Just when Carthage had gotten his new effect working correctly, they were booted out of the big top and back to their own tent. So much for a full dress.

In their private rehearsal space, they had to get the projectors staged, again. Carthage programmed this change with the technical electricals while Huxley paced back and forth, running his hand repetitively over his watch chain and looking at the watch itself too often as the band played a song that sounded completely wrong.

"That isn't right," Huxley told them. "That's the wrong key."

"It's what the music says," answered Blackjack, the fiddling electrical. He held the sheet in his blue fingers.

"Well, the music is wrong," Huxley said. "Don't you have ears?"

The electricals seemed confused. They *didn't*, technically, have ears.

"The music says—"

Huxley snatched the sheet out of Blackjack's hand and scribbled over the key signature. "Just play it in major!"

The band, after a few moments of transposition, restarted the piece in a major key instead. Carthage, feeling warm, stripped off his coat. This act required him to hit his marks exactly or else gaff the trick. Sawdust stuck to his trousers, and his knees complained. He bent over and grasped them. The heat of his hands only halfway settled the pain.

"Dominic," he called as softly as he could over the blare of the band. Dominic bent, too, making himself eye-level. "Can you fetch me an aspirin off the train?"

"Yes, of course."

Seeing Dominic go, Huxley, who was rubbing his temples, called out over the music. "Dominic, fetch me an aspirin from the train!"

Post-aspirins (and sandwiches, which Dominic brought without being asked), they went until one or two o'clock in the morning. They did not talk except to bark feedback across the ring at each other.

By the end, Carthage thought the act had actually shaped up into something presentable. But he found himself also miserable, inside and out. He did love this work so much, even the grueling parts, but tonight his legs wailed in complaint and his heart was made of lead. Even playing the music in a major key couldn't lift the spirit of misery off of the whole company.

Perhaps Huxley felt the same, because he slapped his book down and worked off his tie. "That's it," he said. "We both know it isn't right. But we've got a few hours tomorrow before the audition. If we skip the other performances, we can fit in another run-through."

"Fine," agreed Carthage, and that was their goodnight.

Huxley left, and Carthage went after him, limping under the Lesser Lights.

THE AUDIENCE — and the judges — audibly gasped as the electrical beast swiped its paw. Its steel claws, polished to a gleam, slashed inches from Carthage's coat. He shouted and cracked the whip in his hand, feeling sweat break out under his collar and the brim of his hat as he leapt.

The audition was going well, he thought. He had all of the front row set forward in their seats. There was still time to bust it, though. This was not a simple effect, and he'd had so little time to rehearse.

The electrical beast gave a loud, electronic snarl, its mouthful of silver teeth glinting under the hot lights. Carthage taunted it with the whip, daring it closer as it batted at him with powerful paws. He could hear a bearing in its right forelimb sometimes click. That would need looking after.

Snarling, it reared up on its hind legs. The yellow bulbs set into the sockets of its tin skull blared red, and a small voice on the front row cried out a warning as it lunged for Carthage again. He jumped out of its way, snapping the whip overhead with a pleasing crack.

The electrical hissed, metal joints whispering as it sank into a crouch. Then, roaring into the air, it sprang upon him. The crowd gasped again, and a lady screamed. Carthage fell back, opening his watch as the beast fell upon him.

With a flash of light and a roar so loud it shook the tent, the beast was gone.

The crowd rumbled with delight, and Carthage snapped his watch shut. Shaking it once, he jumped up and held it to his ear — then opened it, cautiously.

The watch snarled, and with a chagrined look, he snapped it shut again right away. The crowd hollered.

"It's true what they say, then." He put the watch away in his waistcoat, winking to the front row. "Any problem can be tamed, with *time*."

Somewhere, somebody laughed, and a chorus of applause almost drowned out the music as the electrical band started back up.

He swept off his hat and took a bow, heart surging on the wave of applause. Other electricals came out to finish the final musical number and take their bows.

As he passed from the spotlights to the dark, his gait faltered. But he made it almost all the way through the curtain before he buckled.

Huxley, standing just offstage, tried to catch him and mostly failed. Carthage ended up on his knees and one hand, Huxley holding just one arm, which was unhelpful and somewhat painful.

"Stars. Are you alright?"

Carthage didn't answer. He grasped Huxley's sleeve, the only thing he had to anchor himself, and tried to pull himself up. He only managed to pull Huxley off-balance. He fought rising panic. He couldn't bring his feet back under him.

Dominic appeared on his other side, and together he and Huxley picked Carthage up and set him down on a crate.

"What happened?" Huxley asked.

The band was winding to an end. It was final curtain, and Carthage was supposed to go back on to take bows.

"I have to go back on," he said, and tried to stand up. He'd taken a single step when he started to buckle again; Huxley and Dominic caught him quicker this time. They eased him backwards, back down.

"You can't go on," Huxley said. "You can't even walk."

"The electricals won't know when to exit without me," Carthage said, feeling panicked. They were supposed to stand on their marks until he came out and finished his bow. If he never appeared, they would stand there indefinitely. That would be a strange and profoundly awkward ending to what had otherwise gone off like a miracle.

"I'll take care of it," Huxley answered, and reached toward a hat rack for a spare hat.

"Huxley, wait—" Carthage didn't get the chance to finish. Huxley was already moving out and through the curtain, barely making it into the ring before the cue was missed. It wasn't going to look right for the stage manager to take Carthage's place. It was as good as telling the audience that something was wrong.

On the other side of the curtain, the crowd applauded one last time. It was polite, respectful clapping reserved for a producer, not the performer.

Any frustration Carthage might have felt faded as he reconciled that Huxley did the right thing. Moving quickly had saved them the misstep of dead space in the ring. The show had to go on.

Even, it seemed, *without* him.

CARTHAGE, STRONGLY DECLINING Huxley's determination they should call a doctor, went back to the train to sleep instead. It was what he really needed. A doctor could do nowt for him, except maybe prescribe him drugs he didn't like to take.

Lying down on his rack, he fell into a restless cycle of dreams in which he relived the audition repeatedly — but something different went wrong each time.

By the time Huxley knocked on his door, it was dark past the window, and he had a hard time remembering which version of the audition actually happened. But he felt more than a little better. From the lesser light outside, he'd been asleep for several hours. He still ached, but putting his feet on the ground promised he could walk.

"Aye?" he asked when Huxley knocked again, more urgently. "It's open."

Huxley appeared, seeming just as tired and disheveled.

His tie was loose, and his hair was mussed from wearing a hat.

"Sorry I didn't wake you," he said. "They've read the results."

Carthage straightened. "And?"

"We were advanced to the final round," Huxley said. A look of relief flickered over him, but he didn't seem to have the energy to smile. Then the relief passed. Something anxious in its place.

"The final audition..." said Carthage. It didn't feel real. Perhaps he was still too tired.

"Except they've suspended the results," Huxley went on, "pending a hearing."

"What? A hearing?"

"It's Bonaventure. He was eliminated, but he contests it — he says someone poisoned his horses."

THE TENT THAT housed contest administration was abuzz with heated voices, even on approach. As Carthage entered with Huxley, he saw that the foremost of these voices belonged to Lior Bonaventure, who stood before the judges' table, holding a wilted sprig of leaves and white buds as if it were the exhibit in a trial. Alastair Hemlock was there, along with Miss Skyhawke and her manager. Lord Protectorate Vicewar stood near the judges with his hands behind his back.

"Three of them colicked the morning after the party," Bonaventure was saying. "It was only the dilution of the water in the trough that none of my poor horses were killed!"

"There's dogbane all over this park, Mr. Bonaventure," said the principle judge.

Bonaventure showed them the stem of the weed. "Cut cleanly with a pair of shears, you say?"

The judge took the sprig and examined it, frowning.

"I've been the favorite to win this competition. It's in all of the papers. Someone clearly had a mind to end my chances." Bonaventure turned to face his fellow contestants, a cold look of fury. "And the monster is present in this very room."

The principal judge conferred for a moment with his fellow administrators. Then, turning back to the competitors, he took off his spectacles and sighed.

"This is most distressing. Having examined the evidence, we must concur there may be foul play involved. A truly disturbing crime, to taint the water supply of God's creatures! As you know, Our Celestial Lady's birthday is in just a few short days. But until this matter can be brought to rest, the contest must be postponed."

A wave of disappointment rippled across the competitors.

The judge tapped his spectacles on the table in front of him. "Unless, of course, there is something anyone wishes to disclose?"

Carthage saw Miss Skyhawke shoot Huxley a certain look, but he wasn't sure what it meant until she opened her mouth.

"Mr. Hemlock," she said carefully. "I would hardly dare to accuse you. But — on the day the light fell and nearly killed me — it comes to mind that Mr. Huxley caught you sneaking in through the back door of my rehearsal just minutes before the calamity happened. Could you, perhaps, lend some explanation?"

Hemlock, who was sitting in a chair across from the judges' table, turned his derby hat over in his lap. "Well, I... but I told him—" He turned to Huxley. "I *told* you. I was only coming to borrow some spirit gum."

"You did beat a rather hasty exit when I uncovered you there," said Huxley.

"I..." Hemlock looked around the room to find everyone staring at him. His pale face took on an indignant flush, the first hint of color Carthage had seen in him yet. "What possible motive would I have for sabotaging anyone?"

"Perhaps a political one," Carthage murmured.

Everyone looked at him.

Huxley glanced at Carthage. Knowing agreement passed between them.

"We suspect," began Huxley. It seemed hard for him to say. "Well, there is reason to think that Mr. Hemlock subscribes to Terraformist ideals."

Vicewar drew a sharp breath and stepped forward. "Whatever gives you such a suspicion?"

Carthage answered this time. "Mr. Hemlock possesses a manifesto — which we glimpsed entirely by accident."

Well, *almost* entirely by accident. Carthage's conscience winced at that white lie. They had, in fact, been somewhat snooping when they cracked the blank pages.

Hemlock gave a scoff that sounded strangled. "This is bosh. I won't sit here and be persecuted." He got to his feet, making a move for the door, but Huxley and Sergei headed him off from either side.

Vicewar closed the distance, circling like a falcon sighting a mouse. Hemlock, seeming to sense his own defeat, turned away from the door and back to face the Protectorate and the judges.

There was a long and heated pause.

"I am a Terraformist," Hemlock said finally. "It's true. And I won't hide anymore. This is precisely the kind of oppression the Terraformists oppose." He gave Carthage and Huxley a searing glance. "A state in which citizens are turned against one another by false constructs like 'class' and 'authority'. I am a performer, yes, but a performer's *greatest* calling is upon the world stage. Answering that call, I entered this contest to gain audience with the regents and the Future Queen, in order to make a bold and overdue *demonstration* for the common man."

Contest administration looked alarmed at this confession, even though Hemlock was currently hundreds of miles away from the Future Queen.

"Have any of you here taken time to read our party positions? What I serve is a more enlightened age. The corruption of authority will destroy this world unless we rise up to overturn the institutions that shackle us to our baser selves. We will never be better men so long as priests and protectorates exist to debase us." Hemlock was turning from white to red with passion. "Yes, I'm a Terraformist, and proudly! But you won't get any confession of wrongdoing from me, for I've done *nothing wrong*. I have only tried to save you from yourselves."

"In fact, Mr. Hemlock," said Vicewar, "it seems probable that you *have* done wrong. I'm intrigued to note that the only two acts which have not suffered misfortune are Mr. Carthage's and yours. Do you have any alibi for the night when Mr. Abernathy died?"

"I was in my tent, of course. Probably reading. Are you suggesting I killed Abernathy? You said yourself what happened to him was an accident."

"And we've determined you were present when the light almost fell on Miss Skyhawke."

"I've explained *that* incident more than once."

"Mr. Bonaventure," said Vicewar. "When do you suppose the dogbane got into your water trough?"

"By my reckoning," answered Bonaventure, "it was sometime in the night — while I was at the party."

Vicewar's hands were tucked behind his back, but his eyes were sharp and keen. "I seem to recall that you left the party early, Mr. Hemlock. Do you have an alibi for your whereabouts once you left?"

"I..." Hemlock paused. Some of his fervor faded. "No."

"If you refuse to provide an alibi, I shall have to assume wrongdoing. Do you wish to name someone to confirm your alibi?"

Hemlock's gaze and his mouth hardened. The sunken eyes were dark and firm. "No."

Vicewar sniffed and straightened. "Very well, then. You'll be coming along with me for further questioning."

Hemlock was arrested peaceably, but he gave Carthage and Huxley a cold look as he went by. "Queen's men," he said. "I hope you're pleased with yourselves."

Carthage didn't feel very pleased with himself. Huxley looked downright sick.

The judges also looked perturbed. "Please give us privacy for a few moments while we discuss this turn of events," they said, and the competitors exited into the lesser light.

Walking across the lawn, Carthage gave a long sigh.

"What's wrong with you now?" Huxley asked.

"Everything," answered Carthage. "But mostly that rumors imply Alastair Hemlock was at a Terraformist meeting the night the horses were poisoned. He can't give an alibi without outing other prominent party members."

"Then he's innocent," Huxley said.

"I'm not sure about that. He's an anarchist, salted with the vocabulary of equality to make him more palatable to reasonable minds. As is the whole party." Carthage wondered if this might offend his young companion, but Huxley just frowned as if he wasn't sure what to think.

"Mr. Carthage? Mr. Huxley?" It was the principal judge. "If you would rejoin us inside."

★

THEY FOLLOWED THE judge back inside, but Carthage was surprised to find that none of the other competitors were there. Instead, two chairs faced the judges' table.

"Please," said the judge. "Have a seat."

Carthage unbuttoned his coat to sit down. He felt suddenly conscious of the state they were in. He'd thrown water on his face and run his fingers through his hair to reset the side he'd slept on, but he doubted he was his most presentable.

Huxley, perhaps having the same thoughts, fixed his tie. The judge looked up and seemed to interpret this gesture as something guilty.

"Are you nervous, Mr. Huxley?"

"Just flashing back to all those schooltime memories of sitting in the Vicar's office," Huxley ribbed.

The judges looked wan, and didn't laugh.

"As you know," began the principal judge, "it was our intention to send three acts to the final audition on Celestia. Given what has recently been revealed regarding Mr. Hemlock, he has been ejected from the competition. We have therefore readmitted Mr. Bonaventure in his place. The lady advances with him, of course."

There was a feeling of dread in the room, and Carthage caught himself tilting forward. "All good news," he said. "We look forward to competing against both of them on Celestia."

"Ah, but there is now of course the matter of *you*." The judge was leaning across the table on a folded newspaper, and tapped it now. "Given what has just come to light in the evening edition, this hearing is to determine whether or not your act should be allowed to advance."

Huxley rose from his seat and reached for the paper, which the judge handed over, then sat back down. As Carthage glanced at the headline, his empty stomach constricted.

It was an old photo, blurry around the edges — how had they even managed to find it? A family standing on a lawn before a great house. The father, his hands on the shoulders of his eldest daughter. The mother, holding the hands of two more sisters. And a teenage boy — lanky, nearly gaunt, smiling with pensive eyes as he grasped the silver wheels of his chair.

CANNONGATE CONSPIRACY? asked the headline, and the subheadline elaborated: *Did Sylvester F. Cannongate take alias 'Carthage' to conceal ugly past, or present trouble?*

This expose had landed the gossip columnist on the front page — above the fold. Carthage tried to read the article, but Huxley turned it over before he could. All Carthage glimpsed were the ugliest words:

Invalided childhood —

Near-death experience —

Family ruin —

Confirmed, recently suffered a fall —

Huxley's fingers were tense. He had to be shocked, but he looked straight ahead at the judges and remained remarkably cool.

Carthage looked at them, too, and also tried to remain cool. "I already disclosed to the Lord Protectorate the discrepancy between my birth certificate and passbook names," he said.

"But you didn't disclose your medical history."

"I don't see how it matters."

The judge pursed his lips, as if Carthage was being stubborn. "It was noted you didn't take final curtain today. Was there some issue?"

Carthage's hand lingered on his knee, finger tracing the seam of his trousers. "I *really* don't see how any of this matters."

The judge turned now to Huxley. "Mr. Huxley, answer

honestly. Given the observation you've had of his fitness, can Mr. Carthage continue to compete?"

"I don't think I understand the question," Huxley stalled.

"Alright," said the judge, playing along. "I'll elaborate. Do you think your companion, if granted the honor of performing for Our Celestial Lady, would be able to fulfill the obligation without impediment?"

"I am not his physician, nor his mother, nor his nanny," Huxley said. "He can answer that question himself."

The judge turned back to Carthage. "Will you submit to examination by a physician?"

"Absolutely not," said Carthage. "I won't be looked over for *blemish* like a lamb at market."

"You're both being very obstinate," said the judge. "You aren't giving us many options."

"There is only one option," said Carthage. Feeling threatened, he was filled with uncommon boldness. "And that is to judge me on the merit of my audition — as you promised to do."

The judge looked at his fellow judges. Sighed in defeat.

"You are, in fact, the best audition we saw all day. You may not confess this to your competitors, but certain members of this panel have advocated your merits ardently already. I do believe that Our Celestial Lady would simply adore you, your tricks, and your delightful creatures, and might even find some common ground with..." He paused as if he thought he were about to say too much. Shaking his head, he gave them a thin smile. "I suppose there's nothing else I can say, gentlemen. Except, perhaps — break a leg on Celestia."

★

THERE WERE NO congratulations as Carthage and Huxley returned to the train. In the dining car, Huxley picked up their copy of the paper, shook it, and continued to read the article without sitting down. Dominic served tea and then disappeared without a word.

Carthage, unsure of what to say, was glad for the silence. He collected a cup of tea, folded his coat over his arm and started for the next car.

"No," said Huxley, and slapped the paper down on the table. "You aren't running away from this."

Carthage turned back.

Huxley pointed at him. "I took my scalding. Now you'll take yours."

Carthage still wasn't sure what to say. But if yelling at him would make Huxley feel better, then he'd stand and take it.

"Is this true?" Huxley asked.

"Aye," said Carthage. "I was Cannongate, until the family was ruined."

"You know that's not what I'm talking about." Huxley put his face in his hand for a moment, as if hiding some expression. When he looked up, there was only fury. "We shook hands. We signed a contract. A six-month tour — and you didn't think it was worth mentioning that you have remittent sweeps?"

"I don't have sweeps," Carthage said. "I *had* sweeps, I was cured when I was twenty-one."

"You must be kidding," Huxley said. He pointed to the paper. "Is this true? What it says about the fire?"

Carthage's eyes stung and his throat tightened. He was barely able to consider that day without reliving it. His coat was still folded over his arm, and with his other hand, he fingered the lapel. "I don't know what the article maintains," he said. "But yes, there was a fire. I was twenty-six. It brought down the house and half the estate before they contained it. We lost everything that day. It crushed my family with shame."

"A fire that nearly killed you."

"I suppose..." Carthage hesitated, resisting the phrasing. "It might have killed me, had I not been rescued from the house."

"And you couldn't save yourself, because...?"

"I..." Carthage's voice felt raw, just the way it did that day, screaming for help. Heat licked all over him. He closed his eyes, unable to face what was coming for him. "I couldn't walk."

"That is what I would call a remission, Mr. Carthage. I would not call it *cured*."

Carthage opened his eyes, and his mouth. But Huxley wasn't finished.

"Do you grasp, in your..." he flexed his fingers, trying to drag up something forceful enough, "*crooked little mind*, that I have staked my *entire life* on you? And you really couldn't bother the courtesy of being honest? What if we got halfway through the tour and you couldn't perform? And what if the judges are right? What if you can't perform on Celestia? I left everything behind! I'm on the line for every penny I have. I have no family left, and no friends—"

"I'll be fine," Carthage started, talking over him, "I overworked on Halcyon and haven't been able to—"

"I could lose *everything*!"

"I *never* breached your faith!" Carthage didn't like being shouted at, and found himself shouting back. "When have I *ever* let you down, *Mr.* Huxley?"

This did quiet Huxley, but it didn't quiet Carthage. "It's more than I can say about you," he said.

"*Me*?" Re-ignited, Huxley got an incredulous look. "All *I* do is my most stellar to make *you* look good! Tell me, please, what I ever did to let you down."

Something Carthage had been holding back for the past day — maybe longer — roared up. The heat that threatened him now swallowed him whole. He hurled his teacup down and shattered it on the floor.

"You didn't *believe* in me!"

He heard the pitch of his own voice. Pained. Not the ferocious way he meant to say it.

Huxley stared at him for a moment, wavering between expressions. But the expression that lingered the longest seemed to resemble fear.

Fear?

"It's a good act," said Huxley. "That whole happy-color-funtime thing you do. Butterflies and flowers. But there's a hidden darkness to you I think almost no one has ever seen. You have a false name. A hidden past. A disease you never told anyone about. You like to talk about religion, and tradition, and morality. What is it you're asking me to *believe* in?"

Stung, and suddenly ashamed to be standing over the shards of a broken teacup, Carthage loosened his posture and softened his voice. "Huxley—"

"It says there was an investigation. The abiding protectorate-inspector called it *suspicious circumstances.* Neighbors said *arson.*"

"That's gossip — not journalism," said Carthage.

"You were alone, that's what it says. Everyone else had gone to town for the parade, even the staff. But you came back, alone. You were the *only* one in the house when it started. You were the *only* one questioned."

"Huxley—"

Huxley held up the paper. "Did you start this fire?"

Carthage ran his tongue over his teeth. "There were no charges made."

Huxley lowered the paper. There it was again, in his eyes — unmasked fear. "That isn't what I asked," he said.

Carthage shook his head and took a step forward, trying to close the yawning distance between them.

But Huxley stepped back, and his left arm tensed. "The Protectorate said something. It's been nagging me — ours is the only other show that hasn't been sabotaged. Everyone was at the party two nights ago, but you left for at least forty-five minutes. After we arrived, we were separated and I looked for you. I know you stepped out."

"I went into the garden for fresh air," Carthage said.

"The day the light fell, you left pictures and went back to the train alone. And the night Abernathy died — I invited you to dinner, but you said you had work to do. I didn't see you again until he was dead."

Carthage, floored, could only stare at his companion.

"He'd provoked us just an hour before. You and I had more motive than anyone."

"You can't really believe I murdered Silas Abernathy. Huxley, listen to yourself. You *know* me!"

"I *don't* know you!" Huxley clenched the paper in his fist. "I don't know anything about you. I didn't even know your *name*."

I don't know you?

Carthage had just finished complaining to Dominic that he didn't want a companion. That taking Huxley along had been a mistake. Huxley was right — Carthage never wanted closeness.

So why did it hurt so much to hear that?

The following silence felt like the enclosed space after a performance. Cloudy and too quiet.

"The fire was an accident," Carthage said finally.

Huxley, seeming humbled, rubbed his eyes like he was coming out of some kind of stupor. "I... I'm..." It seemed like he was trying to apologize for something, only didn't know how. Carthage understood. He felt exactly the same. Huxley, seeing Carthage put on his coat, settled for a question instead. "Where are you going?"

"To the nearest telegraph office," Carthage answered as he fixed his collar. "I have to wire my sisters and apologize. They'll be waking up to the headlines in the morning."

12

RUNAWAY THINGS, II

Huxley sat in a chair in the dining car and didn't move for at least half an hour. Dominic came in, trundling about like he always did, as if nothing was wrong. Took out a silver dustpan and a small broom. Swept up the pieces of the broken teacup, and then began to dust the furniture.

Huxley felt strange, as if he'd become a part of the decor. But he didn't get up.

"Are you still alive?" Dominic asked him finally.

"Am I alive?" Huxley turned to him. "Yes, I'm alive. Why would you ask that?"

"You were uncharacteristically motionless and quiet. I thought you might be dead."

Huxley blew air through his teeth. "Did I make a terrible mistake, Dominic?"

"The probability is high. But you'd have to be more specific."

"Thanks a lot."

"You're welcome," Dominic said without a trace of irony.

"I suppose I didn't mean it," Huxley went on. "I can't really fathom Sylvester Carthage bashing anyone over the head. He'd have to ask their permission first." He pushed himself out of the chair, regretting his accusations.

He had shouted, from the cracks of his own broken heart, that he didn't *know* Sylvester Carthage. But that wasn't totally true. Perhaps he wasn't quite sure what Sylvester Carthage *was*. But he did know what Sylvester Carthage *wasn't*.

Carthage held nothing but gentle wonder for the world and its inhabitants. He didn't sneak up behind people in the dark. He didn't sabotage, tamper or bribe. To suggest otherwise was nothing short of what Huxley was sure that newfangled psychotherapist his parents had forced him to see once or twice during adolescence would call "projection".

Sylvester Carthage was not a cheat.

Pacing to the other side of the car, Huxley leaned to look out the window and glimpsed a figure headed back toward the train. His mouth ran dry. He felt contrite, but he also felt angry. What was he supposed to say when his companion returned?

Favoring flight over fight this time, he decided his best recourse was to make himself scarce. He was about to leave the dining car and hide in his compartment when somebody gave a polite knock on the door.

Huxley turned back. That wasn't Carthage.

He answered the door to find Andromeda Skyhawke standing on the railroad ties and holding a bottle of wine.

She seemed hesitant, and there was a moment of silence.

"Are... you alright?" she asked at last.

"Am I alright?"

"You look like you've been run over by a train," she said.

"Oh," he said, and scrambled to rake his fingers through his hair and fix the tuck of his shirt.

"No, no..." She bit her lip. "The look on your face."

"I was just..." He looked around, like the right words might appear. "I was just... you know."

Of course not, but she was polite enough not to press the issue.

"Well," she said, hesitating. Her eyes flicked away. "I know I last left things somewhat... awkward. And, since we've both had the happy news of traveling to Celestia... I wondered if it was too late to take you up on your request."

"My... request?"

"Dinner," she said, and mustered a shy smile. "Strictly personal, I think you promised. I brought a bottle of something to celebrate."

He was not quite in that particular gear, and stared at her just a moment too long.

She blinked, lowering the bottle of wine behind her back. "I... never mind. It was a bad idea."

"No, no." He descended one step as if he might catch her before she got away. "Please, come in."

She seemed now torn. "I shouldn't be here... I should just—"

"Please," he said, and hoped he didn't sound as

desperate as he felt. "I've just been sitting here by myself. A little dinner and conversation is exactly what the doctor ordered. Come on, come aboard."

He offered her his hand, and she mounted the train and entered the dining car.

Huxley was now glad Dominic had been tidying only moments before. The electrical had changed the crumb- and-coffee spotted table linens, organized the reams of schematics Carthage left strewn on an end table, swept the floor of dirty tracks, carried off the coat that had been lying over the back of a chair, and somehow even managed to make the place smell vaguely floral. Closer inspection proved that scent was fresh-cut flowers in all the vases.

The train looked decently presentable, not like two bachelors lived on it. Huxley was relieved.

"Please," he said. "Take a seat. Allow me just a minute."

He left her sitting in an armchair and went into the next car, where he found Dominic changing his bedsheets.

"Psst," Huxley hissed, undoing his tie as he entered the compartment.

Some metallic part in Dominic's head clicked as it turned to look at him.

"Miss Skyhawke is joining me for a meal," Huxley said. "What can you whip us up for supper?"

"Well," began Dominic, in what already promised to be an unhelpful response. "I haven't had a chance to visit a fresh market in days. I was going to fix bagels and lox with pickles and capers... that face you're making, what does it mean?"

"Dominic, it occurs to me that you are at a significant disadvantage in life."

"I am?"

"You were programmed by Sylvester Carthage. Listen, Dom, new rule. If I ever bring a friend aboard the train, *never* try to serve her pickles and lox. Those are, absolutely, the least charming foods I can think of. Don't you have anything less... abrasive?"

"Given that I don't eat foods, I'm not sure if I may judge which ones would be considered abrasive. Perhaps a bit of charcuterie? I have some hams, a Brie, a liver pate and a bit of vegetable terrine leftover from yesterday."

Huxley changed his shirt, which he now noted smelled like stress and secondhand cigarette smoke, for a fresher one. "That'll have to do. Perhaps some honey and jam, too."

"Shall I open the marmalade your mother sent you?"

Huxley pulled his braces over his shoulders and paused. He'd been saving that for some time. Who knew when he'd get a care package again?

Then again, what was he saving it for? There surely wouldn't be a day any more tumultuous — or victorious — than today.

"Why not," he answered, and buttoned up his new floral waistcoat.

"Very good," said Dominic, and started to wheel away. "I will serve the meal shortly."

Huxley caught him before he could get all the way out the door. "Hang on," he said, and with his elbow buffed away a scuff on Dominic's copper forehead. "There," he said. "Now we both look like the gentlemen we're supposed to be."

DOMINIC CAME THROUGH with supper, and Andromeda smiled at him as they were served.

"He's so very charming," she divulged to Huxley as the electrical returned to the kitchen. "So much personality in the manner and the face. Not like the ones we have running our train. And the butterflies, too. Mr. Carthage has a way of infusing things with character and life."

"Hm, well, he *is* a character." Huxley took a swallow of wine to wash anything further out of his mouth. It tasted expensive, heady with blackcurrant and aged woods, with a bitter and perplexing finish. "What is this? It's got some note I can't place."

She gave an embarrassed look. "I'm afraid I know nothing about wine," she answered honestly. "I think it was a *Briard* something-or-other. It had lions on the label. I chose it because it looked expensive."

How foolish of him. Of course. "Tell me about your upbringing," he said.

"Oh," she said, turning a napkin over in her lap. "You don't really want to hear about that."

"I do."

She looked out the window for a moment. "I suppose the answer is that I didn't have much of an upbringing at all. I lived in a girls' home for my first fifteen years. It was hard, but the friendships I had were sweet. And the things I learned were invaluable."

"What kind of things?"

She looked at him and gave a thin smile. "How to palm a coin. How to speak politely for extra servings. How to mediate with enemies. How to do without. All things that I find serve my current role well — except, perhaps, that last one. It is so jarring, when you've had nothing, to suddenly have *something*. And a bit frightening."

"Frightening?"

"When you have little, you have little to fear. The more gains one has, I am learning, the more one may lose."

"What will you do when this contest is over?"

"I suppose that depends on the outcome."

"Either way, surely your manager will take you touring? Or find a theater to host you in one of the cities?"

At the mention of her manager, her eyes dropped. "Perhaps," she said.

Her sudden smallness turned Huxley's stomach. "Do you... have a good relationship with him?"

"I have only ever been a means to his end," she answered. "I suppose I should be grateful for the opportunity he gave me. But I do grow tired, lately, of feeling like a commodity."

"I see."

"Enough about me. I haven't known anyone from Fallsbright. Tell me about *your* upbringing."

"Well," he said. "I grew up on an orchard, riding horses and climbing trees. I had a governess until I was twelve, and then I went away to academy. I rode horses competitively for the school team, and I used the tree outside my dormitory window to sneak out at night. So, my rustic childhood served me well."

She shook her head at his mischief, but she was smiling. "What do you miss the most?"

"It's higher, of course, than the mainlands. I miss the warmer climate terribly. I miss the straightforward way people talk about things, and that men and women are more readily permitted to be friends. But, the *most*? Ugh, absolutely the food."

"You don't appreciate our fine cuisine?"

"Everything out here seems to come pickled, canned, or formed into a loaf." He held up a forkful of liver pate. "Even the meat."

She laughed.

"I'd kill for a real meal." He hesitated to confess this, but couldn't hold it back. "I've been awfully homesick."

"What about you?" she asked. "What will you do when this contest is over?"

"I wish I knew." He sighed and took a drink. "The future of my company is unclear. I suppose, like you said, that it depends on the outcome."

She was silent. Of course, that was an awkward topic. Their futures rested on defeating one another. He thought he should change the subject again, but confession poured out of him.

"We were nearly bankrupt before we joined this competition," he said. "We staked this train to the bank just for the capital to enter. And now — well, he's been angry at me, and with what's in the papers, I'm fairly cross with him."

"He didn't tell you his history?"

"No," said Huxley. These were not the things he was supposed to tell a rival, but it was a relief to say them.

"Well," she said. "It makes me sorry to think of you two parting ways. The Electrical Menagerie is something magical, and I have a feeling that it wouldn't be half itself without one or the other of you."

He put a wedge of apple in his mouth so that he wasn't forced to agree or disagree. Especially because he thought he would be forced to agree.

"There's something I've been wondering," she said. "And it's forward, but I thought there's no harm in asking. How did he do the trick today? The disappearing beast?"

Huxley laughed, thrilled by her boldness. "It'll take more than a *Briard* something-or-other to get me to tell you that."

She smirked at him as she spread a bit of marmalade over a cracker. "It was worth a try."

Dominic came to attend them, and Huxley looked out the darkened window. The electric lights were pleasantly dimmed, but still too bright for him to make out anything in the glass beyond his own reflection.

"Dominic, is there any sign of Carthage?" He'd been out awhile, but perhaps he'd come back quietly and entered through the rear of the train.

"No, sir. Shall I bring on coffee and marzipan?"

"Oh," said Andromeda, getting a giddy look. "I do love marzipan."

Huxley sent Dominic back to the kitchen to serve coffee and turned back to Andromeda.

185 •
. * ⋆

"Let me tell you a ruckus story about marzipan," he said, and put Carthage's absence out of his mind.

13

THE TRESPASSER

Carthage, not wanting to walk very far, took a cab instead to the nearest telegraph office. It happened to be in the bottom floor of the post office, and the postmaster was already in bed, but he got up to send Carthage's messages anyway. Two to small parishes on Atlas, where Carthage's younger sisters had settled with their husbands, and one to Elys, in the city.

YOU WARNED ME, he said to her, without explanation. The others might wake up to it, but Elys kept current with the news and she'd have seen it as soon as it broke.

AM SORRY. STILL YOURS. SLY FOX.

He wondered, as the postmaster took his slip of paper and sat down to tap the letters out, what it was like to read everyone else's personal correspondence. Perhaps it might appeal to a voyeur, but Carthage felt horrified by the idea. Too many secrets, he thought, were pinging across the wires and the relay stations in the sky.

And secrets were a heavy thing.

After riding to the park, he did not feel like returning

to the confinement of the train. Instead, he sat down in one of the nearby fountain plazas, where winged plaster horses reared over cherubs spitting water into the basin below.

The park was active, even at night, and a couple strolled through the willow trees, holding hands. Another man passed by, walking an enormous dog off-leash, which stopped and stuck its head over the rim of the fountain to drink from it. A protectorate, patrolling the park, saw this and scolded the man into putting the dog back on its lead.

Thoughts had circled Carthage like birds for days. There were too many of them, and too loud, that flock of starlings contesting for a single branch.

He closed his eyes, trying to settle them.

Seeing the patrolling protectorate made him think of Lord Protectorate Vicewar, which turned his mind back to Alastair Hemlock. Somehow, even that dark topic was a welcome diversion from the other things weighing on him. His remarks to Huxley, the beginning of a revelation, had been interrupted when the judges called them indoors. But he'd been saying something important.

Alastair Hemlock hadn't poisoned the horses. Of that, Carthage was almost sure. He'd been to an illicit meeting instead.

But if Hemlock was innocent, then which person was guilty? It seemed improbable that Bonaventure would harm his own horses — or risk losing them by orchestrating a stampede the night Abernathy died. They were his livelihood, but even more, he was a decent man with a clear kindness for animals.

Process of elimination left only Miss Skyhawke, but the evidence didn't add up there, either. Carthage didn't think she was strong enough to kill Abernathy with a blow to the head, and she had an alibi with Huxley during every misfortune.

Of course, there was one more suspect party. Ever-present, but so quiet he seemed almost invisible. The lady's manager, Sergei.

What did the papers say? That Miss Skyhawke arrived 'unescorted'? Carthage didn't recall seeing Sergei at the party at all. And he'd arrived to the scene of Abernathy's death last.

But if he was tampering with the contest to gain an advantage, what purpose might he have had in dropping a light on his star's head?

... Of course, the light hadn't nearly fallen on the lady's head. It had nearly fallen on *Huxley*. Huxley, who had the misfortune of standing in the wrong place at the wrong time. Perhaps the light wasn't meant to fall on anyone at all. Sergei would have known the lady's blocking. The light that dropped was well away from harming her. And it succeeded in detracting suspicion.

After all: what purpose would anyone have for dropping a light on his own star's head?

Carthage opened his eyes.

If nothing was done, the falsely-accused Hemlock might be tried for Abernathy's murder. And the true killer would not just get away. He might get all the way to the palace.

Carthage wanted to warn Vicewar, and got up from the bench, but hesitated. Already, one man had been arrested on Carthage's word. He felt responsible for what became of Hemlock, and it seemed rash to do that again. What he had against Sergei was compelling, but circumstantial. There was a slimy sense of dread in the hollow of his stomach, like biting into a rotted apple core. Something that suggested he was close to an ugly truth.

What he needed was evidence.

He walked from the plaza back toward the camp.

He'd gone to his compartment on his way off the train to pick up a cane he'd kept for many years. It was good, cut from walnut with a brass handle that carved away at the end like a lion's maw.

He didn't enjoy walking with it — he thought it made him look infirmed, and he felt ashamed to look infirmed. But he was glad for it now as he crossed the wide lawn, as he was able to lessen the pain on his worse side. The darkness, he thought, concealed his broken gait.

Approaching Miss Skyhawke's train, which was parked parallel to his but on the opposite side of camp, he worried he'd run into either Sergei or the lady. But there was no sign of them. Perhaps having a late dinner somewhere else.

One car was evidently the lady's, even from outside — he could see the lacy window dressings. It appeared she had an entire car to herself. The one prior to that appeared to be a passenger car, sans the finery in the windows. Carthage seized the handrail and mounted the steps, trying the latch on the door. It was locked.

He went then toward the locomotive, finding another car which appeared to be a dining or a lounge car. This one was unlocked.

He considered turning back and fetching Huxley. It seemed better to go about something like this together. And Huxley, surely, would know a thing or two about trespassing.

But he still hesitated to return home after everything that had transpired. He still wasn't sure what to say. And, although he'd begun to become dependent on having a companion, what if that partnership had already collapsed? Being on his own had never stopped him from mustering the courage to do whatever it was that needed to be done.

He entered the train alone.

His blood quickened as he stood for a moment, letting his eyes adjust to the dim light. It was only a train, but it had the spooky feeling of something unnaturally empty. This was a lounge car, but it seemed surprisingly spartan. There were sofas along the walls, and newspapers on a low table. It did not exactly feel like a home, the way his train did living with Huxley.

Crossing over to the next car by its interior gangway connection, he was glad to find the interior door to the next compartment unlocked. This, as he suspected, was Sergei's private compartment. There was an unmade bed and a writing desk strewn with papers.

Glancing once out the window to make sure no one

was approaching the train, Carthage leaned on the cane and rifled through the papers.

Most of them were receipts. There were top-down drawings of the venues, and Carthage forced his eyes away from a diagram that demonstrated how Miss Skyhawke's transformation into a live bird was done. He wasn't here to spy on her, and he only cared to understand how something worked if he could figure it out himself.

Concealed by a slough of papers was a black book. Carthage flipped this open. It was a portfolio book, filled with pages and photographs, and the writing was in Alsatian, full of beautiful and distinct loops. He couldn't read Alsatian, but turned the page and found a picture of himself stuck to the next page. There were bulleted points alongside his photograph. One was his date of birth, and another said, in the common Imperial tongue, "Atlas Isle".

Was Sergei researching him?

He found Huxley on the next page, annotated with similar information. There was a sentence circled toward the bottom, which appeared to have been written after. It had a heavier, almost angry hand. The only familiar word was "Andromeda".

The rest of the book proved to have notes taken on all of the competitors, including photographs and clippings from the newspapers. It appeared, that on each competitor's page, Sergei had recorded when their rehearsals were.

That was not wholly criminal, Carthage reckoned,

although seeing his photograph pasted into the book and scribbled on like a science experiment unnerved him.

Then noticing a drawer in the desk, he tugged it open. Inside, there was a bottle of some clear liquor with a handwritten label and a cork top. He could smell something stringent, as if perhaps it had at some point spilled.

Abernathy reeked like swill.

Remembering Huxley's words, he worked the cork off and smelled the contents. It burned with the repellent odor of petrol, a smell that lingered on his tongue as an unpleasant taste. "Reeked" was certainly the right word.

What had happened that night Abernathy died? Did Sergei kill Abernathy and pour this moonshine down his throat as part of a staged accident?

Noticing something else at the back of the drawer, Carthage bent to look closer. It was a small black box, which he picked up with his handkerchief to examine more thoroughly. The box was small enough to fit in a man's pocket. There was a copper coil at one end, and a binary switch with one side marked, warningly, with red tape.

Carthage had tinkered a bit with short-wave radio, but he'd found the technology fiddly and hadn't pursued it very far. This switchbox appeared to be some kind of experimental radio-controlled trigger — but what for?

Deeper in the drawer was a matchbox, and Carthage looked inside to find a set of small, paper-wrapped charges, which reminded him of the crackers children liked to set off during festivals. He probed one to find that it had a length of wire running along the inside of the wrapping.

The switchbox had to be a remote detonator for these small charges. That was fascinating. Carthage had to bury wires so that Huxley could detonate the pyrotechnic blast caps backstage using a hard-wired switch, and a radio remote made much more sense. But why were these instruments concealed in Sergei's desk?

Beneath the box of charges were some loose sheets of paper, which Carthage took out to examine in the low light. These were also written in Alsatian, but mathematics were a common language. He couldn't read the notes, but he understood the gist of the accompanying equations.

Sergei, using physics formulas, seemed to be trying to figure out how much explosive to pack into one of the charges. There were a few bits of work crossed out — failed attempts. But there was nowt to indicate what he'd been using this for.

The drawer seemed empty, but Carthage, following instinct, thrust his hand toward the dark recess at the back. His fingers brushed something metallic, which he withdrew.

It was a C-clamp, the kind used to hold electric lighting overhead. But it had been broken in half by some force. The severed ends were melted and warped as if by high temperature — perhaps by a small explosive charge.

The arithmetic on the loose papers now made more sense. There was a calculation of time — how long it took for the clamp to fail — and a bit of work that seemed to estimate what the safe distance was from the falling light itself.

This was what Sergei had been working on. A way to fake an accident during his own rehearsal. He'd rigged his own light to fall and triggered it remotely.

A bolt of adrenaline passed through Carthage's chest. The falling light had been on a *trigger*, not a timer? Then Huxley hadn't just been standing in the wrong place at the wrong time — Sergei had seen him underneath the rigged light and put a hand in his pocket to press the switch.

Vicewar needed to examine this evidence for himself. But Carthage would return to Huxley and warn him first. It was clear neither of them were safe. He shut the drawer and turned to go.

Sergei was behind him.

He hit Carthage with an unforeseen right cross that knocked Carthage back against the desk, blinded by a flare of white spots in his vision. Sergei, wordless, pounced on him and pinned him down on the desk, heavy hands wrapped around Carthage's throat.

Panicked as thumbs dug into his windpipe, Carthage pried desperately at Sergei's grip with his free hand. Then, realizing he still held his cane in the other, turned the handle about and wielded the lion's mouth against his attacker.

Sergei's grip loosened as he reeled away, and Carthage stumbled from the desk and bolted for the door. He only had to get off the train.

Sergei chased him through the doorway into the

lounge car, and Carthage turned, unwilling to have his back to his attacker. The big man was pale with stress, and blood trickled from cuts over his eye and the corner of his mouth.

Sergei said nothing as he advanced. Carthage, taking a halting step backwards, looked for some secondary weapon. But there was nothing — not even a lamp to pick up. Closing the distance, Sergei lashed a kick at him, and Carthage swung the cane at Sergei's ear. The man had been in more than a few fights. He was quick to dodge, and then struck out, connecting the heel of his boot with Carthage's knee. A deliberate act to cripple his opponent.

Carthage could not suppress a cry as he buckled.

14

VERMILION

"And that's..." Huxley waved a hand. "That's sort of how I was terrified of owls for at least six years."

Andromeda laughed.

They hadn't left the table. The marzipan story had turned into another story, and then another, although it seemed they were getting progressively more embarrassing as they went.

Dominic cleared the table quietly, taking away the silver coffee service.

"I'm actually kind of *still* terrified of owls," Huxley said. "But I've never told anyone that."

"No?" said Andromeda.

"No, of course not. It's a sort of feathery woodland creature. It isn't a masculine thing to be terrified of."

"Well," she said with a smile. "Then I suppose it's a sort of secret we share now, isn't it?"

Dominic took away the coffee cups and the pot of sugar.

Andromeda reached across the space where the sugar had been. Put her hand over Huxley's.

"Perhaps," she said, "you could tell me another secret."

"Another secret?"

"I would so much like to know how it's done," she said. "The disappearing beast."

"It's projectors," said Huxley. "And a pane of one-way glass."

"Of course," she murmured to herself. Her hand retracted.

"Mr. Huxley," Dominic was suddenly there, grasping Huxley by the sleeve. "You should say goodnight."

"Say goodnight?"

"Yes, to the lady," said Dominic, and looked at her. He still held Huxley by the sleeve. "It's time to say goodnight."

"But we're having so much fun!" said Andromeda. "Dominic, why don't you run back to the kitchen and put on more coffee?"

"No," he said. "It's very late. It's time for you to leave."

"Listen, electrical," said Andromeda. "You must do what I say."

"That is incorrect," answered Dominic. "I must do what my operators say."

"Dominic," said Huxley. "You're really being rude. Go back to the kitchen."

Dominic looked at him, and his eyes flickered as if there was about to be some kind of computer error.

"No," he said. "I can't do that."

"*No?*"

The electrical had never told Huxley no before. As far

as he understood, it was not even possible for Dominic to say no.

"I may not do anything that endangers you," Dominic answered.

"Endangers me?" Huxley wanted to be angry at Dominic for defying him, but he'd never exactly noticed how funny Dominic looked. So round and shiny, with his twinkly lights for eyes. What a silly little electrical man! Huxley laughed instead. "I can't say goodnight yet. I haven't even kissed her."

Dominic's grasp tightened, now on his arm. "Mr. Huxley, something isn't right with you. Can't you tell?"

Something isn't right with you.

Now that Dominic mentioned it, Huxley *didn't* feel exactly right. Maybe not quite *wrong*. In fact, he felt quite good. But not really *right*. The room was sort of jumbling around like a kaleidescope, and had he really told her how Carthage's trick worked?

He wasn't exactly sure why he did, except that she had asked him and it seemed natural to answer honestly.

His smile faded.

"I'm sorry," he said to Andromeda, whose smile also waned. "Excuse me. I... I think I've had too much to drink."

He put a hand on the table to steady himself as he stood up. The paisley wallpaper seemed to be crawling, and everything shifted hard to the left. He staggered down to the rug, seizing the tablecloth with him as he fell. Their glasses, sliding off the table, crashed to the floor.

"Something is very wrong," came Dominic's voice from above. If it were even possible for his electronic voice to sound alarmed, it did. "I'll get help. I must find Master Ca*rrrrrrrrr...*" The voice deepened then died.

Huxley looked up. Andromeda grasped Dominic's battery in one hand. She'd pulled it out of the back of his head to turn him off.

Huxley's broken wine glass pooled at his left hand. Too much to drink? He'd only had a glass or two.

Dominic was right.

Something was very wrong.

He didn't think he could walk, so he crawled a few inches across the carpet. Andromeda's shadow fell over him.

"What's wrong with me?" he asked, fighting panic.

"You'll be alright," she said as she managed to lug him halfway up from the floor and into an armchair. "In an hour or two. You've just ingested something the Alsatian secret police invented during their last war. A tonic used on enemy spies so that they tell the truth. It's quite safe, with no lasting effects."

"You..." He stared up at her, unable to fathom it. "You *poisoned* me?"

"You must understand," she begged, taking his hand. "Only *one* of us could ever win. And I tried to tell you. I told you from the very beginning that you would be disappointed in me. I warned you that I would be single-minded. I even confessed, at the party, that *everything* I am is an act."

An act.

He thought of her standing on the tracks, holding a bottle of wine. *"I brought something to celebrate,"* she'd said.

"You tricked me?" He was feeling muggy and having a hard time accepting it.

Her apology, her invitation to dinner, her shy smile. It had been a lie? Had she only *feigned* interest in him for the last hour? He remembered the look on Carthage's face when he learned the critic had been paid to praise him, and suddenly understood.

Andromeda tightened her grip on his hand. "There is *nothing* for me if I don't win. Sergei wants only one thing from me, and that is for my talents to deliver him to the palace. It is the single purpose of the very existence of Miss Skyhawke. When that purpose is over, so is she." Her breath caught. "And I'm not ready for her to end. Don't you *understand*?"

"You don't want me to *understand*," he answered. "You want me to *approve*. And I can't."

She released his hand, bitterly. "Of course not. Now I know where you come from. If you fail, at least you may go crawling home to mummy and daddy. You're afraid of humiliation, but you know nothing of survival."

"Andromeda," he said, and pitched forward. It was the closest he could come to standing up. The patterns on the carpet seemed to be swimming, and it gave him a sickish feeling. "What have you done? Are you a Terraformist, like Hemlock?"

She shook her head, firm. "Sergei is, but I am nothing — not Terraformist, nor Monarchist. Politics are a luxury. Most of us are preoccupied with just surviving."

"And Silas Abernathy...?" Huxley searched her, too frightened to ask the question.

She took a breath at the implied accusation. "Abernathy was a terrible man. He learned about my orphan upbringing and tried to *blackmail* me — as if tragedy is something to be *ashamed* of. But Sergei killed him instead. I didn't know it until you and I found Abernathy dead. You were there — you saw my horror. Surely you know I had nothing to do with any murder."

"I trust *nothing* you say now," Huxley said. "I trust no glance, or familiar touch, and certainly no smile."

She looked stricken, as if he'd stood up and backhanded her.

"You want it both ways," he went on when he saw that look. He could taste the bitterness of his own voice — or maybe it was the aftertaste of poison. "You want me unsurprised that you are a liar. But you also want me to believe you."

"I'm not the only one who wants it both ways," she said, regaining a defiant look. "You want to play games — you want to keep secrets. You're indignant that I tricked you into dinner? That I tried to learn your secrets? But it's what you did to *me* the night we met. Wasn't it your intention, from the very beginning, to find some *use* for me?"

"I... I..." He stammered deliberately, trying to hold off the answer. But it blared out of him. "Yes."

"And you really thought I'd be *foolish* enough to let you kiss me?"

Foolish?

"No," he said. "I *never* thought you were foolish. In the balcony, you showed me who you are, and I showed you who I am, and that, for me, marked the end of any 'game'. I liked you the most in that moment when you had nothing to offer me except your honest companionship. I... I..." Now *he* felt foolish, saying it aloud. His head ached. "I thought you might kiss me because you felt the same way."

That disarmed her. She seemed pained as she looked down at him. But there was still some sharp edge to her.

"I will ask you one question," she said finally. "And you will answer truthfully. Then we will *both* know. If you answer correctly, I'll know there is something for me to hold onto besides this contest. I'll know it's not too late to turn back. Here is the question, sir — one question to save us both: if you had to choose. If you could only have *one*. Would you have me, or this contest?"

"I—" He dug his fingers into the upholstery of the chair. Words swam through his mind, the words he wanted to say and the words he *wanted* to say feeling jumbled up. His mind reached forward. But it was his heart that answered. "If I could only have one — it must be the contest."

The pained look hardened. "Arbrook Huxley," she said, "I liked you better when you were a liar."

He felt ashamed, but didn't know what else to say. And he was afraid to open his mouth. What else might it reveal that even he was not ready to learn?

She bent down to eye level. Grasped the arms of his chair. "Tell me," she said. "The master code for the electricals."

The master code for the electricals?

Vermilion.

"I—" He shook his head. "I can't tell you—"

"Tell me, Huxley. What is the master code for the electricals?"

Vermilion.

"Why?" he managed to ask. "I can't tell you that it's... it's... I'm not supposed to tell you—"

"What is it?"

Vermilion!

"V—" he bit off the word and pulled a ragged breath. "I can't — it's — I can't tell you that it's—"

She took his face in her hands and looked him right in the eye. "What is the master code for the electricals?"

Lie to her! Something in him screamed.

"*Vermilion,*" he answered instead.

She turned her back on him.

Someone came up the steps and through the door — Sergei, who shoved someone else down into the other armchair.

Carthage. He was alive, because his head moved. But he seemed half-conscious and then didn't move again.

Alarmed, Andromeda went over and put a hand on his arm. "What... what did you do to him?"

"He was spying on me," Sergei said, and spat at Carthage's feet to curse him. "Did you do what I told you?"

"Vermilion," Andromeda answered.

Sergei laughed and looked at Huxley. "You were easy, then. When I was in the army, they trained us to survive weeks of interrogation. You would be shot by your own captain for giving your secrets up over dinner with a *woman.*"

Huxley didn't respond.

I have a gun.

He wanted to say it aloud every time it ran through his mind. As if there was no barrier between his mind and his mouth. He bit his tongue instead, willing himself to just remain silent.

He didn't totally trust himself to aim, but some of the coherence was coming back to his limbs. When Sergei turned his back, Huxley would shoot him.

I'll shoot you.

He bit his tongue harder.

Sergei located the panel on the wall that summoned the electricals. The stage crew had already finished loading the train, and they were charging in the freight car. The engineering crew that ran the train was also dormant until they were ready to leave, but Sergei pressed the button that woke them up.

The four locomotive electricals marched into the dining car to answer the call.

These electricals were not a lot like the performing ones, and certainly not like Dominic. They were simple, almost binary in their function, with little more than the basic intelligence needed to perform their duties. They didn't even have names, just their jobs painted in dull gray on the shoulders.

Sergei turned his back on Huxley.

Huxley tensed, but before he could draw the gun, Andromeda pinned his arm down to the chair. By the look on her face, she knew what he intended, and she gave a warning shake of her head. She didn't announce the gun to Sergei, but she'd saved his life. She would not let Huxley shoot him.

"Vermilion," said Sergei, forcing the word through his heavy accent. The electricals all went dark, then their eyes blinked back up. Pulsing. "I am your new operator. Give me administrative access."

"Granted, operator."

"Override all previous operators."

"Confirmed."

"Your new master control is my voice," Sergei said. "I order you to erase all other passwords."

"Confirmed."

Huxley's heart already rested low, but now it sank lower.

Sergei went on. "This train will depart in four minutes. You will take the F Line at Junction Five. You will take this course at seventy-five percent speed. These passengers will stay down for their own safety. If they get up—" here Sergei pointed to Carthage and Huxley. "—you must make them sit back down."

"Yes, Master," said the conductor, and tipped the tin hat that was built onto his head. He, the engineer and the fireman went to the locomotive. But the trainman stayed in place. Watching.

At some point, Carthage had wordlessly opened his eyes. He now shut them again.

Andromeda released Huxley, freeing his gun hand. But now she stood with her back to him, blocking Sergei from his line of fire. "You promised you wouldn't kill them!"

Sergei's boots thumped as he closed the distance. "It's too late for feeling bad," he said. "You have a bargain to hold up."

"We *both* do! I said I'd get you to the palace — but *you* said you wouldn't kill them!"

Sergei seized her by the arm. "*I* won't," he said as he yanked her to the door. She had little choice but to go with him as he dragged her like a doll behind him. "They will just have a sad *accident*."

Then they were gone.

The engine fired, thrumming the floor, and the whistle blew to clear the tracks. The train hissed, then shuddered as the brakes disengaged. There was a jolt as she rolled forward, and the whistle blew again as she picked up speed and headed across the park.

The tents flashed by, and then the trees. The clacking of the wheels increased against the landrails. Then there was a slight thump as the train hit the skyrail junction.

They changed headings and ascended, up and winding through skyscrapers, passing billboards and windows lit with electric lights. Huxley already felt ill, and the incline was making him railsick.

Carthage didn't stir again, and Dominic, powerless and slumped, seemed forgotten in the corner.

The train picked up speed, brushing the bottom of the clouds, and Helios vanished below.

Huxley shut his eyes.

They'd done it. The Electrical Menagerie was invited

to the final audition. They were due on Celestia tomorrow morning.

Instead, the mutineered train carried them skybound to an unknown destination.

15

THE F LINE

Carthage gasped, startled, as he woke up. He sat straight up in the chair, lashing out a fist that connected with nowt but air.

"You're fine," came Huxley's voice from nearby. "You're just punchy, take a breath."

Pulse hammering, Carthage tightened his grip on the arms of the chair and pulled his legs underneath him. He was aboard the train, although he couldn't recall boarding, and Huxley sat across from him.

His limbs and airway were taut with adrenaline, as if he'd just been running, and the sky was dark. Nothing made sense, and he started to push himself out of the chair to get a better grasp on the situation.

An electrical — one of *his* electricals — appeared over him and shoved him back down. It was the charcoal-colored electrical trainman. He was supposed to be in the locomotive. His amber eyebulbs glimmered at Carthage as he spoke.

"Passengers must remain seated," the electrical intoned. "For safety."

Carthage remembered a dream he'd been having — one about the electricals taking over the train.

Then, he remembered it wasn't a dream.

"I was getting nervous," said Huxley. "I called your name a few times, and by the way you just muttered at me and didn't wake up, I was starting to worry. What happened?"

It was beginning to come back. The darkened train. A fight with Sergei. "I think I was kicked in the head by an seventeen-stone Alsatian."

"Well, by the look of him, you gave as good as you got." Huxley paused. "Well, obviously not quite *as* good, since you lost. But I'm really very impressed. I would not have had any money on you at all."

"Thank you?" Carthage looked past Huxley, out the window.

They were skybound. The night was clear, and distant stars flicked by. Something unpleasant surged up within him, and he started to stand up again. But a glance at the trainman stayed him. "Huxley, I'm sure we're in mortal danger."

"As am I," said Huxley. "And if we're going to die, there's something I have to confess."

"Now is not the time," said Carthage.

"I really have to," disagreed Huxley. "It's just that I really thought you were boring and arrogant. But it turns out that you were right about more than one thing. So maybe you are a bit boring, but there is something admirable about your prudence. Because, tonight, I have been betrayed by a woman you warned me about."

"Well... alright. But perhaps we should focus on escaping."

"You're something else, you know that, Carthage? I really envy you. You're very talented, and I especially admire how collected you are in a crisis. Except for that time you broke a teacup on the floor. That wasn't very collected."

"Huxley... what's wrong with you?"

"I was spiked with a truth serum which seems to have drastically lowered my inhibitions." Huxley raised a confident hand. "But it's alright. I think it's wearing off."

"I'm quite certain it's not," said Carthage.

The train juddered, and they both flinched.

"We've got to get off this train," murmured Huxley.

"Please remain seated," the trainman reiterated, taking a threatening jolt forward.

The working electricals were tall, and stronger than any man. But maybe — together — they could overpower the trainman. Each of these electricals had a battery in a housing at the back of the head. One of them only had to reach it.

Carthage looked meaningfully at Huxley and tapped the back of his neck.

"The—" With some effort, Huxley seemed to stop himself from responding aloud. He nodded instead.

Carthage pointed at him and then counted off on his fingers — One. Two. Three.

On three, Huxley sprang from his seat and swerved under the mechanical arm that swung for him.

The trainman whirled on his omni-directional caster,

grabbing Huxley by the shirtfront. Carthage leapt to his feet, staggering, but staying himself.

"Passengers must remain seated." The trainman lifted Huxley in a powerful grasp — all the way off his feet. Huxley gave an audible yelp as he left the floor. "For *safety!*"

From behind, Carthage yanked off the plate covering the battery and pulled the battery out of the electrical's head.

"Please sit do*wwwwwwwwn*—" The bulbs went dark and the arm dropped, loosing Huxley to the floor.

"One down," said Carthage as Huxley got to his feet. Together, they moved toward the locomotive.

Three more.

Sneaking out of the dining room and through the kitchen, they caught another electrical — the conductor — entering from the locomotive. Carthage yanked Huxley backwards, out of the narrow corridor and into the kitchen pantry, as the conductor rolled past.

When he'd passed between the curtains that separated the kitchen from the dining room, they darted back out and to the fore end of the car, hurrying now. It would take the conductor a matter of moments to discover the trainman deactivated.

"Do the electricals know how to reactivate each other?" Huxley asked as they approached the locomotive.

"I don't think so," Carthage answered.

"That's not the answer I was looking for."

Unlike the couplings that joined the other cars, which were enclosed by gangway connections which allowed passengers to cross between cars without exiting into open air, the coupling that hitched the locomotive to the rest of the train was uncovered. Passing from one to the other meant crossing between two open platforms.

Wind snapped their coats as Huxley hauled open the door. Across the platforms, inside the locomotive cab, stood the engineer, helming the many wheels and dials that controlled the train.

In a lead-lined boiler compartment on the other side of that wall would be the fireman, who stoked the train's engine with stardust. The only way to reach him would be to follow a precarious walkway that skirted the exterior of the train, past the engineer's cab and through a hatch into the belly of the locomotive.

Carthage looked down. There was nothing but sky beneath them as the train sped along its route, except for the faint line of red-gold heat that appeared where the wheels touched the invisible rails. A gleaming thread suspending the train and all its passengers in the empty sky.

Huxley indicated that Carthage should go into the cab and deactivate the engineer — thereby volunteering himself to make the daring catwalk into the engine room to deactivate the fireman. He crossed the gap between platforms by leaping it and then took the railing in hand to follow the outside edge of the train.

Carthage, taking a breath and muttering a prayer, leapt after him. It jarred his knees, but he stuck the landing on the locomotive platform with a grimace, crouching instinctively in case the electrical engineer heard his approach and turned. But the roaring wind and the chugging of the acrid, star-powered engines concealed his approach as he slid open the cab door.

The engineer watched the dials, preoccupied, and Carthage reached to quietly take a screwdriver off the cart of tools by the door. He'd get the battery out even quicker with something narrow to pry off the little hatch.

Creeping up behind, he raised his screwdriver toward the tin plate.

The engineer's head spun one hundred and eighty degrees, all the way around to face him.

Carthage, startled, staggered back. He remembered only then that he'd installed a gimbal that turned three hundred and sixty degrees so that the engineer could look out all the windows without wheeling around.

He now regretted that decision.

"Mutineer!" said the engineer.

Carthage pointed at him with the screwdriver, backing off. "No. I am your operator."

"Mutineer!" the engineer repeated, and turned his whole body around to seize Carthage.

"I'm not the mutineer," Carthage said through gritted teeth, grabbing an exposed pipe to anchor himself as the engineer tried to drag him toward the door. "*You're* the mutineer!"

"I am the engineer," the electrical said, and Carthage lost his grip. He rammed the screwdriver into the electrical's left eye, shattering the bulb and blinding that side.

"Please desist." The engineer turned his head to

compensate for the blinded eye as he continued to drag Carthage toward the door on the side of the cab — the door that opened to nothing but sky. "I must eject you from the train."

"This is *my* train! I'm your operator!" He couldn't reach the battery. He used the screwdriver again, trying to find a vulnerable seam along the electrical's head. But the engineer was strong enough to hold Carthage with one hand as he yanked the side door open with the other.

A fresh gust of cool night air hit Carthage from behind, and he reeled as he found himself too near to the threshold and at the mercy of the rebellious engineer.

Spreading his legs to anchor himself, and throwing an arm against the doorjamb to brace, he tried to gouge the electrical's other eye with his free hand.

"Don't do that," the electrical complained as they wrestled in the doorway. "Please exit the train!"

Huxley reappeared on the platform.

"Huxley!" Carthage shouted, sensing he was close to losing his place in the door.

Huxley's left hand flicked like a striking asp. Something gleamed in his palm, and there was a bang and the sharp sting of stardust — a lighter and brighter note than the smoke pouring out of the engines. The engineer's grasp faltered, and he spit sparks out of his mouth and ears. Then he slumped over.

Carthage, steadying himself, looked at the hole in the electrical's head, then back at Huxley, who still held a pocket pistol in his hand.

"You— you— since when have you carried a *gun?*"

"Always," answered Huxley.

"Well, why didn't you use it *sooner?*"

"I've only got two bullets," Huxley said. "And there were four of them, I thought... oh. There were *four* of them." Just as the door on the other platform opened, he turned, raised his arm, and shot the electrical conductor.

Then he turned back to Carthage. "There," he said, and seemed pleased with himself. "*Waste not, want not.*"

Carthage pushed the damaged engineer out of his way and crossed over to the charts on the table. Huxley, alongside him, wiped frost off the muzzle of his gun as Carthage flipped through the sky charts.

They departed Helios, which had several junctions... Carthage consulted the spherical compass mounted on the wall. The train had an ascending northwest bearing.

That meant they weren't on the A or B Lines which ran directly into downtown Celestia. Either of those would have been beginning to bear descending in order to meet the landrail junction at the edge of the isle.

That meant — he followed the only remaining skyrail route, a bold yellow line printed against matte blue, with his fingertip.

"We're riding a terminating line," he said, sounding more calm than he felt.

"We're..." Huxley jolted and pushed Carthage's hand out of the way to see for himself. "A *terminating* line?"

The architects of the skyrails relied on the natural corridors of magnetism that curved like river tributaries across the sky. But sometimes these magnetic tributaries, rather than reconnecting with land, eddied in the sky and terminated. If a rail line couldn't be anchored to land with artificial poles, it had to be abandoned.

Carthage looked at the train's gauges, wrapping his fingers around two wheels. They were traveling at seventy-five percent power. "How far away from Celestia does the line end?"

"Two miles," said Huxley as he consulted the chart. Then, he moved toward Carthage with sudden intention. "We've got to pull the emergency brake!"

Carthage turned and caught him before he could lay a hand on the brake. "Don't!"

"We're going to *crash*. We've got to stop!"

"Do the math," said Carthage. "The train is traveling at seventy-five percent speed. We departed—"

"An hour and a half—"

"An hour and a half, at seventy-five percent—"

"Ninety miles—"

"And the length of the line is—"

"Stars," said Huxley. He came to it quicker, and paled. "We don't have *time* to stop."

They stood in a paralyzed silence for at least thirty seconds.

"There's only one thing to do," said Carthage, and turned to the helm. "Increase approach vector."

"Did you just say we should *speed up toward our doom*?!"

Carthage flicked a switch, then pulled a lever. The train gave a subtle groan. "The rails terminate before the edge of the isle. We won't have enough momentum to *crash*. We're going to *fall*."

Spiraling out of the sky, beyond the reach of land,

straight down through the fumes of the aether sea and into the star-specked vacuum beneath it. That was *not* how Sylvester Carthage wanted to die — irretrievably cast out so that they couldn't even bury him.

That was not how he *would* die.

He hauled on the wheel and heard the stacks vent overhead, pulling more air into the engine.

"Even if we jump, the escape packs don't have enough fuel to carry us two miles from the end of the line to safe ground. Our only hope is to increase the train's speed and use inertia to ride it as far as we can before evacuating." He put a hand on the throttle and looked over at Huxley, who was silent. "Do you trust me?"

Huxley visibly swallowed. He had that wan look of someone young forced to confront their mortality for the first time. "Yes," he said. Then he gave an unexpected laugh. "It *is* wearing off," he said, with relief. "That was a lie!"

Well, for once it was a lie Carthage would accept. Perhaps they were not in confidence, but they were in agreement.

He laid the throttle as far as it would go, and the train growled as they accelerated toward the end of the line.

WITH THE TRAIN'S throttle set, they went back into the coaches to retrieve their bail-out kits. As Huxley went to fetch those, Carthage attended to Dominic. The electrical sprang to life somewhat violently when Carthage replaced his battery.

"*Rrrrr*thage!" he exclaimed, as if he'd been mid-sentence when he'd been turned off. There was a pause as he computed. "I seem to have missed something."

"It's alright," said Carthage, and clapped a hand on the Dominic's head. He was glad to see all three of them back in one piece. "We're all alright. But we're bailing off the train."

"Oh dear," answered Dominic. "How inconvenient."

"I'll say," muttered Huxley as he reentered the car, holding a kit in either hand.

Carthage's stomach dipped as he took the sturdy handle of his kit in hand. They hadn't, actually, ever done an evacuation drill. They'd only read the instruction manuals and practiced putting the packs on. At the time, it had seemed all very straightforward and academic.

It didn't feel so academic anymore.

The packs themselves had brass housings and were quite heavy due to the internal components. Carthage checked the date on the tag and was relieved to see they'd been inspected recently. Huxley must have taken the kits into a shop while they were in the Southern Isles.

Slipping an arm through one of the straps, and then the other, Carthage hefted the pack onto his back. The mechanisms inside rattled as he pulled the shoulder straps to tighten them, raising the pack so that it didn't list too low on his back. Huxley was fumbling, and Dominic had to help him buckle the strap that went across his chest.

Running a hand down one of the shoulder straps, Carthage locating the metal tug that marked the end of his ripcord.

His pulse quickened in anticipation of having to pull it.

They were reaching the end of the line. He could tell because the rails were beginning to glitch. The train wheels thrummed, and the dirty china rattled on Dominic's serving cart. A tremor violent enough to knock them all off-balance told Carthage there was little time left.

"We have to be ready," he said, as Dominic checked the fittings of his pack.

Huxley went to the door and heaved it open, hitting them with a violent gust of air. The train was still accelerating, headlong into the wind. Visible sparks jumped from the wheels beneath them.

Ahead and below, snowy clouds obscured Celestia. Was there *owt* down there? The isle was completely shrouded. How were they to land in safety if they couldn't even see where they were going?

The train shuddered, as if pained, as the rails gave way to gravity. Carthage's equilibrium lurched as inertia took hold — pulling them all hard and down.

They were still skybound, but now the locomotive was nosing down, crashing toward the clouds. Its headlamp sliced the gray fogs, and the couplings groaned as gravity seized them.

Huxley staggered back from the doorway with an irrational look.

"This train is *everything* I have," he said, and tried to turn back. "I can't. I won't! There's another way!"

Carthage seized Huxley's hand and planted it over the

ripcord. "Pull your cord!" he commanded, and shoved Huxley backwards, over the threshold and off the train.

Then, turning, he motioned to Dominic. "Dominic, come! We'll jump together."

Dominic came close. Carthage reached to grasp the frame of the door as the train howled and furniture began to slide sideways. "Now, Dominic!"

"No," said Dominic.

No?

"I may not do anything that endangers you," said Dominic. "Our combined weight will consume too much fuel."

Carthage clutched the doorway as paintings fell off the walls and his bone china teapot smashed against a window. The train was listing, hard — falling, now, and taking him with it. His electricals were all in the cargo hold, plunging to the ground. Blackjack, and Jasper, and Marietta, and all of the electrical beasts. Everything he'd built. Everything he had.

But Dominic? Dominic was his oldest and most trusted thing. His closest companion. He wouldn't. He *couldn't.*

"Dominic," he commanded, clinging to the doorway of the dying train as the night air clutched at his back, "I order you to jump with me!"

"It's alright," said Dominic, and laid a comforting hand on him. "I've just learned a trick for this."

And then he pushed Carthage off the train.

It was surprisingly nonviolent. For a moment, Carthage was looking up at the shadowed train, the glimmering of Dominic's electric eyes the only thing he fathomed out of the darkness. Descending backwards into the sky was almost peaceful.

Then gravity wrapped its fingers around him, and the wind screamed into his ears, and the air raked its teeth over him. And then he was no longer *descending*. He was *plummeting*, off the train and down into the churning of the clouds. His hands groped toward the vanishing dreams that plummeted with him. Eyes fixed into a smoldering sky that drew further and further away.

By the waning light of Veris, Sylvester Carthage fell out of the sky.

He plunged backwards into the clouds — frigid clouds wet with precipitation that stung him — and only then had the presence of mind to put a hand on his ripcord.

He rolled over midair as he yanked it, deploying his wings. The lightweight battens snapped out, and the wind caught the canvas stretched between them. Snug against his back, the engine in the pack purred as it turned over, and he felt the heat of it even through his clothes.

Suddenly accelerated by the jet pack, his wings sliced through the clouds, and he tilted them down and forward, trying to orient toward what he thought was land.

The clouds parted abruptly to reveal a looming, jagged mountaintop, and Carthage veered hard to avoid clipping its rocky face. Wind rattled the battens, and he fumbled to remember where the brake was.

Land — sharply outcropped with snowy rock — was rushing to meet him, and relief at seeing the isle beneath him transformed into the fear that he would crash into it.

Below him, he glimpsed a trail of light like a firefly. Huxley. The light faltered against a patch of stark white snow as Huxley crash-landed.

Overhead, something wailed. Carthage looked up in time to see that he was on a collision course with the train, which fell headlong like a dying dragon, cars kinking midair. A coupling snapped with an audible crack, and now the train was falling in two pieces.

Locating the braking cord, he choked his engine hard. The train soared overhead as he lost acceleration, and he heard it crash into the mountainside just a split second before he smashed into a drift of snow.

There was a terrible noise, cold, and nowt but white as he flipped over more than once down a slope. His engine was still burning, but wheezed out as snow jammed up its intakes and damped the stardust, and then his wings snapped violently as he rolled over on them. With a final cough, his pack gave out, and then he was lying facedown in the snow.

He didn't think he'd been lying there very long, and it was only when he felt warm hands on his back that he realized how cold he was. He had to have been lying there longer than he thought.

"May stars fall," Huxley said. "Please don't be dead."

Carthage breathed and rolled over.

Huxley, crouching over him, exhaled and made the liturgical sign of gratitude — the kind they taught to choir boys — heavenward, something Carthage had never seen him do.

Carthage began to pry the straps off of himself. The

broken batten of one wing was digging him in the ribs. The heavy clouds overhead began to spit small flakes of fresh snow down at them.

"Where is the train?" he asked as he crawled out of his broken wings. He hurt all over, but it seemed nothing was broken.

"Just yon," said Huxley, pointing. "Down the ridge."

Carthage climbed to his feet, and they clambered ungracefully through leg-deep snow to the edge of the ridge. Celestia was a lower isle, nearer to the cold aether sea than it was to the star-warmed sky, and the region was swirled with frequent fronts of even colder air. Apparently, they'd landed in such a storm.

The very short hike was exhausting. By the time they reached the ridge, Carthage wanted to lie down and sleep, maybe forever. Crosswind, blowing at them from the shallow pass they stood over, cut him to the bone. His clothes were damp, and his fingers and toes were numb.

The train, wrecked against the mountainside, was crumpled over in the pass. The ridge was steeper than Carthage expected, and he looked for an easy way down. They desperately needed dry clothes and something to start a fire with, which they'd find in whatever was left of the train.

"There," said Huxley, and indicated a better, snow-softened path that could take them down the ridge.

They walked halfway down, then the path unexpectedly steepened and they more or less slid the rest of the way.

The snow was shallower at the bottom, which let

them walk instead of wade, and that was a relief. Huxley was limping after his landing, and Carthage didn't know how long his own legs would hold out. The train, so close, beckoned them.

Not only that, it looked mostly intact. It had fallen in two pieces — the locomotive and the dining car; the sleeping coach, cargo, and the caboose.

The locomotive was smashed beyond recognition, and most of the cars were rolled over, but cargo and the caboose were crumpled but intact. Perhaps the electricals had survived, and perhaps they could even salvage parts of the train.

But a burning odor paused Carthage, and he put out a hand to stop Huxley in place.

"The engine is burning," he said. "If the stardust catches—"

The locomotive exploded before he could finish the thought.

They ducked, covering their heads as shards of it rained the pass, air glittering with combusting stardust and flaming debris.

When it seemed safe to look at it again, what was left of the locomotive still smoldered in littered pieces.

He didn't think anything would explode again, and straightened with a sinking heart. Something about the engines blowing had a terrible finality.

Their train was destroyed.

Huxley stood and just stared at it, hands on his head. He looked a bit as he did the night Abernathy died — distant, and almost confused.

But Carthage staggered toward it, climbing over rocks as he went. He forgot all his physical pain, knifed instead with desperation. Dominic had been aboard the dining car, which was half-buried in the snow, scorched by flames that licked about its wheels.

"Dominic!" Carthage called, and heard his voice break.

An electronic whistle rang from underneath the crumpled car.

Carthage, slipping to his knees on the wet ground, got down to find Dominic's copper frame pinned under the heavy corner of the train car. The electrical's body was broken open to show sheafs of aged wiring inside, and the eyes flickered.

"Dominic," Carthage repeated. "It's alright, my friend — I'll get you out."

"*Alpha, Alpha, Nine...*" There was an unnatural sound that sounded like an error. Then the eyes flickered again. "Master Carthage," Dominic said. "You survived."

"I did," breathed Carthage. "So did Huxley. You saved my life, and I'm going to save yours."

"I have a failing component — serial number Alpha, Alpha, Nine-Six..."

Carthage tried to pry Dominic's head open, but jerked his fingers back. Dominic was hot as a kettle, so hot that steam rose from the snow underneath him.

Carthage tried desperately again, this time with his hand wrapped in the damp handkerchief out of his pocket, and managed to access Dominic's internal components.

High heat had melted the coating of the most sensitive wires, and the motherboard — the brain stem of the electrical man — slowly warped. Sparks arced between two diodes at irregular intervals.

"Dominic," said Carthage, and racked his brain. What could he do? This wasn't fixable, but he had to *try*. "Dominic, you can't — *please*. Just hang on until I can get my toolbox!"

He started to get up, but Dominic lifted a hand and caught him, pulling him close again. "I'm failing."

"Dominic," said Carthage. "You... you can't. You are — you always have been — my best friend."

"No," said Dominic. "I have been your greatest illusion."

"My...?"

"I am only electrical," said Dominic. "I am only what you have made me to be."

"Dominic," said Carthage, stung. "But you're entirely more than that!"

"I don't understand you," continued Dominic. "Although I have tried, I have been a poor companion."

"Dominic — *no*. You have been my very *best* companion."

"You have taught me so many things. Now, I will tell you what I learned. You need a companion who is more than just what you make him to be. A companion who can surprise you. A companion filled with ideas you've never had. One with all the same feelings. You need a companion who is permitted to tell you *no*. You'll be alright, Master Carthage." Dominic's eyes flickered.

"The other human will take care of you now — and you must take care of him, since he's so afraid. I know what being afraid *is*, but I don't know what it *means*, and that's the problem with an electrical man. You, Master Carthage, you're more than electrical. You're more than imaginary. You're *human*."

Carthage shuddered as he exhaled. He interlaced his flesh-and-blood fingers with Dominic's copper ones, watching the lights of Dominic's eyes fade. It smelled like solder and burning wires.

"Thank you," he said, "for your service."

Dominic gave a cheerful whistle. "My pleasure, Master Ca*rrrrrrthage*..." The voice deepened and died, and the bulbs went out.

Snow fell.

Carthage stood up and turned around.

Huxley was sitting on a rock, unmoving, not even a shiver, staring at the wreckage of the train. Or perhaps the wreckage of his life.

Dominic was right. Carthage knew exactly how that felt. He stumbled through the snow and sat down alongside Huxley.

It was only them on this wild and desolate mountaintop, a hundred miles from the depot where they were supposed to be arriving to fanfare and parades. Nothing applauded but the creaking limbs as wind moved through the trees. Nobody watched except the Stars and God.

Carthage became aware that they had not actually spoken — not properly — since that fight on the train so much earlier. That seemed like a lifetime ago. As did his anger. It was hard to be angry at someone when they were the only thing you had left.

He thought about everything that had happened since then. Huxley, bravely venturing alongside the train — without being asked. Huxley, quicker than Carthage had ever been with numbers, an unexpectedly sharp shot, and keen on all the details Carthage overlooked.

Attentive, and reliable, and never lazy — careful even to make sure the bail-out kits were regularly inspected.

More than a partner, Carthage realized, or even a companion — almost what you might call a *friend*.

"The day the estate burned," Carthage spoke finally, "I stayed home alone. We had just gotten electrical lighting — we were actually the first house in the parish to have electricity. I decided to install voice control to the manor switchbox, which was not something I'd done before. Fiddling with the breakers, I overloaded the wiring and started an electrical fire." He rubbed his hands together, looking off.

"Elys, my sister, was in town with a young man, but she got a funny feeling. Her escort refused to leave the parade early, so she walked all the way home alone. Trusting only her instinct. And when she arrived, the house was already engulfed in flames.

"She found me succumbed to the smoke on the floor, and by one of those miracles of tragedy, was able to drag me out the kitchen door to safety." He shook his head.

"My other sisters were fortunate to find decent marriages. They took new lives and new names. But Elys became our matriarch instead. When I failed to restore the family fortune, she went to work. She is the only one who keeps the Cannongate name, and bears every ounce of shame carried with it. She was the one at my father's side when he died penniless, and she nurses my old mother even now. I often wish..." he swallowed. "I often wish that I could be more like her."

It was unclear if Huxley even heard any of it until he answered. "Why are you telling me this?"

"Because I have never told anyone else. And I think that you, of all people, deserve to know something about me that no one else does." Carthage looked at him, but Huxley's gaze was still set ahead, on the train.

"You're a remarkable young man," said Carthage. "I don't know if anyone has ever told you that."

Now Huxley looked at his hands.

"I know that *I* haven't," Carthage went on. "But it's true. Perhaps I haven't even realized it enough. And what I should have said, about the journalist, is this: I have higher expectations of you than that, because you're *better* than that. Do you understand?"

"Yes," said Huxley. "I'm sorry." He turned, finally, to look Carthage in the eye. "And I *do* believe in you," he said. "I have ever since I saw you looking like a downright grifter on an intersection corner. I believed in you when you said we should stake the train on this contest. I even believed in you when you wanted to learn a new trick the day before an audition."

"I suppose you rue all that," said Carthage, washed with regret.

"No," said Huxley, and looked again at the smoldering train, and didn't look washed with regret at all. "No, I still believe in The Electrical Menagerie. And I still believe in Sylvester Carthage — or Cannongate, or whatever the falls your name is. We had a starsfelled good show, partner... it's just a shame it had to end like *this*."

The wind gave a gust that swirled snow around them, reminding Carthage that they were still in grave danger. "We must salvage any dry clothes we can," Carthage said, pushing himself up from the rock, "and start a fire immediately."

"I'm quite warm," said Huxley, although he was damp and specked on the head and shoulders by snow.

"An ominous sign," said Carthage, and hauled Huxley to his feet. "You and I still may not survive this ordeal."

16

THE HEADLINE

The sleeping car was listed over on one side, snow sloughed around it in drifts. Huxley, with Carthage lending a hand, managed to open the side door, and as they crouched over it, Huxley peered into the darkness of the coach. The opposite wall was now the floor, and it was too dark to see very well.

He climbed through to dangle, then dropped the remaining distance. It was only a few feet, but he misjudged in the dark and didn't quite stick the landing. Something crunched under him, and he must have made an audible complaint because Carthage leaned over the doorway with a worried look.

"You haven't broken something, have you?"

Huxley grasped to identify whatever it was he'd landed on. Then, holding up a shard of it, he laughed. "Just a lamp."

Carthage was silent for a long moment. "I really liked those lamps," he said.

"Well, I'll be more careful," said Huxley, and tossed the piece of it over his shoulder with a crash.

He was in the vestibule at the fore of the sleeping car, and had to climb over the wall of his own compartment. The narrow corridor of the coach, turned sideways, was too cramped for him to stand up as he crawled over the horizontal door of his compartment and turned the latch.

The door fell open with a bang, and he peered in at his own room.

Everything had been upended into a heap onto what was now the floor, such a dim jumble he could barely make anything out. He dropped down again into the compartment and began to feel around in the dark for the trunk where he kept his clothes.

It was too dark to tell if whatever he changed into exactly matched, and also too dark to see if he was as patterned with bruises as it felt he was. But the clothes he'd been wearing were stuck to his skin with melted snow, and he was glad to peel them off.

Then, using the top end of the rack where he slept to climb back through the door, he went next door and tried to get inside Carthage's compartment. The door was locked, and he crouched over it and kicked the latch until it gave.

This compartment was a hundred times worse. He realized that it had probably been wrecked *before* the train crashed and rolled over. Carthage was many things, but tidy was not one of them.

When he'd recovered whatever he could from the car, including extra coats and blankets, he kicked through one of the exterior windows in the narrow corridor and climbed out that way. The lesser light on the snow was almost blinding compared to the near-total darkness on the train.

The caboose was almost fully intact, and Carthage had gotten the back door open so they could get inside. Then he'd stolen a snatch of flame from one of the still-burning pieces of wreck to start a fire in a brass drum.

Using an open window to vent the smoke up and out, they fed the fire with bits of paper and the legs of Carthage's workbench. Feeling unnerved about having an open flame so close to the barrel of pyrotechnic stardust, they rolled the sealed barrel outside. The car warmed up to the point of nearly hot, although flakes of snow still drifted in from the open window overhead.

Dry, warm, and relatively safe, Huxley curled up under a blanket he'd stolen off his bed and shut his eyes.

Would anyone ever find the train, so high up in the mountains at the very edge of the isle? It was cradled by the land, nestled in this hidden pass. Even a solar ship soaring low might miss it, particularly as falling snow continued to bury the colors of the train. What would Huxley's parents do if he never returned home?

He must have been skipping in and out of sleep, because for a few moments, he *was* home. Sleeping downstairs in the study. A fire purred in the fireplace. There were voices in the hallway.

But one thought interrupted this dream, then presided over him the rest of the night. It was not exactly his most rational thought, but it was his most fervent one. Fallsbright, and fantasies of being far away, vanished.

We're going to miss our audition.

★

It was fully daylight by the time Huxley woke up all the way again. His back ached from something funny he'd been lying on — a windowpane, he discovered.

He sat up and found Carthage still sitting over the fire, holding a curtain rod for a poker and hooded under a wool blanket. He looked like some kind of witch, but Huxley was too tired to laugh about it.

As the snowstorm continued outside, too cold and too blinding to venture out, they sat there nursing their bruises for more than half the day. Neither of them said it, but there seemed to be an expectation: they were now overdue. There would be an inquiry, and shortly someone would come looking for them.

Surely, someone was looking for them?

They had never really talked about anything but the company, but there was no company of which to speak anymore. Huxley could not really bear to sit up on the mountainside, possibly for days, in the agony of silence. But it was Carthage who seemed even more desperate for conversation.

He began to ask questions he'd never asked before — did Huxley have brothers or sisters? What were his parents like? Did he have friends back home? And, with peculiar specificity: "What was it like going to school with other boys?"

So Huxley told him about school, the funny and the shameful — when Marion Merriweather thought he was dying because he swallowed a watermelon seed, and also when Eugene Gatwick convinced Huxley to smoke his first and final cigarette behind the chapel. Wick had laughed at him when he'd thrown up, so Huxley had shoved him, and Wick had shoved him back, then they both were sent into the Vicar's office, except that it was Wick with a cigarette case in his blazer, and the Vicar had been so blustered by it that Huxley was dismissed entirely without punishment.

"Did you have many fistfights?" Carthage asked him.

"I suppose the regular amount," answered Huxley. "Didn't you?"

"No," said Carthage, with a wry look. "Most people won't fistfight anyone in a wheelchair."

"Right," said Huxley. "What about that, then?"

So Carthage told him about the house where he was born, and the room that consisted almost his entire world for nearly twenty years.

The very thought of it made Huxley's skin crawl, but Carthage described that house almost lovingly — the high and arched windows that faced the green hills, the rosy wallpaper in the hallways where his sisters were scolded for etching their gaining heights in pencil, the many books he had in his room, and the memory of listening to the girls talking to one another as they fell asleep on the other side of his wall.

He learned illusion from a book with a purple cloth binding that had been in the downstairs library and had an inscription on the bookplate addressing it to his father from a distant uncle. The book was unread and forgotten until he discovered it there and claimed it for his own bookshelf. It was called *Fantastic Things Revealed*, and he said that it saved him.

"Saved you?" asked Huxley.

"I was nine years old," said Carthage, "And I was not just losing my legs, but also my hands. I could barely grasp a spoon anymore. But I was so enamored by those Fantastic Things, I had to try. I started with the simplest effect in the book. And the practice became a therapy that recovered the use of my hands."

"Which trick was that?"

Carthage waved his hand, and a coin appeared.

As afternoon dawned, the storm broke, and they ventured back out into the snow to see what kind of supplies they could scavenge from what was left of the dining car.

The answer proved to be very little. One end of it had succumbed to the exploding locomotive, bursting the kitchen to pieces and destroying everything in what used to be the pantry. Huxley was especially mournful to find that his coffee had burned up.

Sticking out of the snow, however, he did find a single whole container of kippers, which was dented but still sealed, and certainly edible. Well — as "edible" as pickled herring could ever be, anyway.

Carthage recovered something else. The holopaper. One corner was singed, but it survived. He refreshed it with a crisp shake, then stood and stared wordlessly at the headlines.

"Everything alright?" asked Huxley.

"No," said Carthage. "We're *dead.*"

"What?" Huxley crashed through a particularly deep slough of snow to see for himself. The lettering on the damaged paper flickered, fizzling at the edges, and gave him a headache when he looked at it.

FATAL ACCIDENT CLAIMS ELECTRICAL MENAGERIE

CALLUM EDISON, STAFF WRITER

SUNDAY, 15TH QUARTER-NOCTUS

HELIOS — The private train carrying Messrs. Sylvester F. Carthage and Arbrook Q. Huxley of the Electrical Menagerie has been declared lost-a-sky by the Railway Commissioner. The train was due this morning on Celestia Isle for the final round of the royal competition, but never arrived. When the train was noticed to be overdue, an inquiry was launched on Helios Isle, from which it last departed. Said inquiry was headed by Lord Protectorate Miles Vicewar, who had this to say:

'Multiple witnesses place the train departing from the landrail junction at Pegasus Park around ten in the evening, and further investigation confirms that the train could have only left Helios traveling the A, B, or F lines. Having ruled that the train did not make it to Celestia on the A or B lines, nor was it stranded along one of these routes, I must conclude that the train took F at the junction.'

The F line out of Helios is a terminating skybound line which was aborted by architects twenty-five years ago when it failed to anchor on Celestia. The Lord Protectorate confirms that the switch is clearly marked and absolves the Railway Ministry of any negligence, raising mystery about what exactly happened last night when the train left its station.

This tragic development comes only hours after the secret identity of Mr. Carthage/Cannongate was revealed by a Times reporter, calling into question if there is any correlation. All the Lord Protectorate was willing to state is that 'some sort of compromise in judgment occurred, but it is impossible to speculate if the accident resulted from human error, malfunction of the electrical crew, or self-infliction.'

Sylvester Carthage/Cannongate, 44, was a royal citizen born on Atlas Isle. Arbrook Huxley, 25, was Fallsbrighton. Their survivors have yet to comment.

"Impossible to speculate!" shouted Huxley. "Well, they're *speculating* that we're dead!"

"*Human error?*" Carthage was seemingly somehow more upset by that than any of the rest.

"I can't believe none of our loved ones made any commentary about us!"

"*I* can't believe the Lord Protectorate would go and just declare us *dead!*"

They looked at each other, angry, but then the scowls faded.

"We're dead…" said Carthage, and got a blank and frightened look.

Huxley, too, looked around. Suddenly feeling very small in the shadow of the mountain. "Nobody is coming?"

Wind howled through the pass.

"Our would-be murderers have gotten away," said Carthage. "And what is the endgame?"

"Andromeda implied that the single purpose of her guise existed to get them inside the palace."

"Alastair Hemlock took the fall for the sabotage, and the investigation into our near-death is already closed. Nobody knows there is any remaining conspiracy, except—"

"You and I," finished Huxley.

Carthage pressed his mouth into a grim line. Huxley crossed his arms against the cold, and the weight of these revelations.

A moment passed. Then Carthage spoke again.

"Whatever's at stake, the life of Our Celestial Lady rests on it. As does the whole Empire." He folded his paper under his arm, taking an entirely different posture. "We must escape this contemptible slope in order to save our Future Queen."

Well, alright, but there was also another point, one that motivated Huxley with more significance. "It seems we must also escape this contemptible slope in order to save *ourselves.*"

★

THEY CLIMBED UP what Huxley thought was some kind of game trail, out of the pass and over another ridge, to survey the interior of the isle. Grasping against the rocks at the edge of the mountain, they looked down at Celestia below.

There were no cities and no palaces visible from here. Just miles and miles of rock-studded snow that gradually descended into the lowlands.

"How big is Celestia Isle?" Huxley asked Carthage. He wasn't very good with his mainlands geography.

"Five hours across by landrail."

Well, that wasn't good news. They weren't on a landrail. They were on *foot*.

Huxley looked at his watch. It was late in the afternoon. "In order to stop the final audition, we'd have to get to the Capitol City before nightfall."

"We can't make the audition," said Carthage. He had recovered a book from his workshop, which he took out from under his arm. Huxley saw that it was an atlas. Carthage turned to a dog-eared page and tapped a map of the isle. "The Capitol City is too far away."

"If we can't stop Andromeda and the Terraformists before the final audition, I'm sure they'll win. And then they'll caravan directly to the palace."

"You're right." Carthage held the book open toward him, showing a gold star printed in the middle of the map. They were high in the Wolfsheads, and Carthage's finger rested on the royal parish of Starborough, just beyond the foothills of the mountains. Closer than the Capitol City. "We'll meet them there."

"Of course," said Huxley. "We only have to reach the palace in time to warn the Palace Protectorate."

Carthage clapped the book shut and tucked it under his arm, staring off in the distance as if he could see the palace right there.

"But the princess's birthday is in just a few days," said Huxley. "How will we ever make it down these mountains in time? It's an impossible distance to walk."

Carthage turned to him. "Nothing is impossible, Huxley. Not with a little imagination and the Grace of God."

"Alright... shall we *imagine* ourselves walking to the palace?"

Carthage turned and looked down into the pass. Huxley looked too.

"Don't you see it?" asked Carthage.

Below them, the broken bits of train lay sprawled like a mechanical carcass.

"Our livelihood and dignity wrecked atop a mountain?"

"Look closer, Huxley. Look at what we have!" Carthage grinned. "We have everything we need to build something *new*."

17

THE MIGHTY ENDEAVOUR

Carthage stared down into the belly of the freight car, where the electricals had been charging when the train went aground. He was glad to see that the electricals looked salvageable, albeit banged up. But when he sent Huxley down into the car to try and turn some of them on, they discovered that none of them had much power.

Carthage went into his overturned workshop and began to collect miscellaneous parts — whatever seemed interesting. Huxley, standing beside him, held out his arms as Carthage shoved things toward him.

"What are we making?" Huxley seemed perplexed.

"I don't know yet," said Carthage. He took the journal out of his coat and thumbed through it. "Sommat to get us down the mountain and across the snow. Help me find a pencil."

They dug around until they located a pencil, which was broken in half. Carthage ducked out the horizontal doorway and stood in the snowy pass, calling on his mind to settle.

You have everything you need. What is it you want to make?

He wasn't sure. He was cold, and tired, and his legs ached. His batteries depleted, like the electricals in the hold. Wind snarled through the pass, battering the tails of his coat.

Imagination, that fickle thing, only wanted him at inopportune times. It did not like to come when called upon. Now, when he needed it most, it betrayed him. His life now depended on dreams.

But didn't it always?

He closed his eyes and saw himself — his smaller self — sitting with a hand pressed against the window.

What is it you want to make? He asked that younger, and somehow wiser, version of himself.

"Something Fantastic," Sylvester said, with a purple book open in his lap. "A creature to cross the mountain gaps, just like we read in the stories about the Rajah's mechanical army." The boy's eyes were agleam with childlike faith. "Don't you remember?"

Carthage opened his eyes, suddenly excited.

"Do you know how the snowshoe hare hops across the snow and doesn't sink?" he asked Huxley.

"Is this some kind of riddle?"

"His very large feet." Carthage snapped his fingers. "I know what we're building, Huxley! An electrical beast to overcome the snow... but how will we power it? We have no electricity."

"We have stardust," said Huxley. "A *lot* of it."

"Of course. Brilliant, Mr. Huxley. We don't *need* electricity! We have everything to build a combustion engine. Do you think you remember where you left your jet pack yesterday?"

"I think I could find it," said Huxley, and seemed to come alive with a shared excitement. "Unless the snow has gotten too deep."

"Can you climb back up the ridge and try to find them both?"

"Of course," answered Huxley, and moved to go. Then paused and turned. "But, to be clear, are we building a rocket-powered *hare*?"

Carthage laughed. "Of course not. We're building a rocket-powered *elephant*!"

CARTHAGE, USING THE broken nub of pencil, drew his schematics while Huxley climbed back up the ridge and looked for the abandoned bail-out kits.

Carthage was glad, rummaging through his cast-about workshop, to locate all the tools he thought he would need. There was still petrol in the tank of his cutting and welding torch, and for finer soldering with his soldering iron he thought he could borrow electricity from the batteries in the electricals. He took up the cutting torch and a mask and went outside.

He was cutting the pistons and wheels free of the train axles when Huxley returned with both packs.

"Very good," Carthage said, lifting his mask to examine them.

"What are you doing with all that?" Huxley indicated his dismantling of the wheels.

"The train's wheels will turn inside the beast's belly,

powering the pistons in its legs," answered Carthage. "Why don't you find a screwdriver and get those housings open?"

Huxley obeyed, although with a look that suggested he'd never used a screwdriver before.

They worked for hours. Mercifully, the sky was clear and the mountaintop warmer than it had been when they crashed. Carthage showed Huxley how to use the cutting torch, and Huxley, openly gleeful at having been upgraded from a screwdriver to a torch so quickly, spared Carthage the manual labor of hauling the tanks for the torch on his back as he climbed, reached, and crouched to cut parts of the train into pieces.

Meanwhile, Carthage pulled the jet pack magnetos and spark plugs out of their housings and used them to create a new ignition, which he mounted between a set of great steel ribs.

Then, salvaging a timing belt from a bin in the workshop, he fitted together gears and cogs with pins and rods, some of which he borrowed from the electrical performers in the hold.

Eventually, finding it too dark and too cold to keep working, they finished and retired. Crawling back into the respite of the caboose, they split what little food they had — a cannister of kippers — then went to sleep.

In the morning, Carthage found Huxley had climbed back into the sleeping car to fetch a compass he had somewhere in his compartment. Taking Carthage's atlas he mapped a route down to Starborough, and also calculated how much fuel it was going to take to get there.

Carthage took a circuit board and soldered the elephant's brain together. He needed a small motor, secondary to the engine powering the legs, to move its auxiliary systems. He could have taken the motor from any one of the electricals, but he returned to Dominic and opened up the copper body. Dominic's motor — his heart — would now be the elephant's heart, and it would carry them down the mountain.

Then he and Huxley worked together on the timing of the engine. Huxley, who proved to be some kind of human adding machine but did not seem to realize there was anything unusual about it, did the math as Carthage called out numbers.

It was all in the numbers. How long or short did the belts need to be? How hot would the engine get? How much force did the machine need to be propelled?

It took them the whole day to get it firing properly. The Principal Star fell away behind the mountains, and the Lesser Lights flared in a darkening sky. They were lost on a foreign mountain, facing an unknown future. But none of this felt unfamiliar at all. This was only the production of their grandest — and perhaps final — show.

With combined strength and a pulley for the magic of leverage, they tried to raise the skeleton of their electrical elephant to its piston-powered legs.

It was well after dark, and Carthage found himself failing. The elephant creaked as it began to rise, then heaved as it fell over again.

Carthage faltered, staggering down to his hands and

knees in the snow. He heard Huxley panting behind him, and a moment of silence passed.

I'll never make it.

He remembered the many times he had whispered that to himself, and all of the times he'd been wrong. Now, though, he wasn't so sure. He was many years and many miles from that night in his bedroom when he crossed the insurmountable gap between the bed and the bookcase to reach his book about the castle. Years and miles away from the animal menagerie painted on his wall — those imaginary voices that whispered faithfully back to him whenever his strength failed.

I'll never make it, came the thought once more.

"Come on," said Huxley, and pulled him to his feet. "We can do it together..."

Together.

Perhaps he really couldn't — not alone. But he *wasn't* alone. Not this time.

"... *if* you'll pull your weight this time," ribbed Huxley.

Carthage gave an exhausted laugh as they grasped the ropes again.

"Three... two... one!"

Huxley was right. Together, they raised the elephant out of the snow.

Its legs moaned as the weight settled, and the light glimmered on its silver back. Just standing there, even with nowt to power it, the beast seemed almost alive.

It had been such labor Carthage actually felt the chill of sweat down his back.

"This might just work," he said as he leaned his palms on his knees to rest.

"What happened to imagination and faith?" asked Huxley. "Of course it will work. Look at those two pedigreed gentleman that built it."

THEY ROSE JUST before dawn — bless the Lamb, the air suggested another clear and warm day. In the predawn light, they collected what little of their belongings they could salvage and tethered them to the elephant's back. Huxley stood back as Carthage fed the engine with stardust then turned the ignition.

The engine roared, and Carthage felt the heat even standing alongside it. Hopefully the beast wouldn't get so hot it became impossible to ride on.

There was a chugging as smoke vented from the elephant's mouth, and then the engine generated enough energy in the batteries to turn on the elephant's brain.

The yellow eyes blinked on. The gears in the neck grumbled as the motor turned over, and the head wagged. Its large feet stamped with a slight shriek of metal grinding metal, and its trunk, which Carthage had articulated with ball bearings so that it could seize and clear branches and other obstructions, swung back and forth.

The train had borne a metal plate stamped with the manufacturer's name, which Huxley had located in the wreck and fixed between the beast's eyes, so that its forehead now read "Endeavour".

"He's alive!" shouted Huxley.

Endeavour, black and silver with flashes of blue where he was welded together from parts of the train, had red drapery thrown over his back for a saddle, and the gold cord that tied the drapery back fixed to his tusks as reins.

Endeavour was not the most sophisticated thing that Carthage had ever made, but he was a beautiful creature in his own terrible right, and at dawn — on his back — they left the mountaintop and set off for the palace.

18

TWO PROTECTORATES

Huxley, Carthage, and the electrical elephant joined the road into Starborough sometime around dusk. The roadways were congested with traffic — matching horses and expensive coaches. These had to be the royal guests arriving for the princess's ball.

Huxley was almost giddy. Here was a road, a town — people! He wasn't going to die at twenty-five, forgotten in the wilderness. He forgot how tired and how hungry he was, satisfied entirely by the sight of good, old-fashioned *civilization*.

A pair of white horses shied as Endeavour overtook them, and a young man in a powdered wig leaned so far out of the coach he almost fell onto the road.

Huxley went to tip his hat, then realized he wasn't wearing one, so he pantomimed it instead. The gentleman just gaped at them as they stomped into town on a valiant electrical elephant that jangled with salvaged parts and breathed plumes of star-scorched smoke.

Starborough was a wealthy suburb of Celestia which

still retained much of its original architecture from two hundred years ago. The unevenly cobbled roads and quaint high street with steeply gabled roofs looked like a picture out of a children's storybook.

People leaned out, over their window boxes and terraces, to look down at Huxley and Carthage as they arrived. Others, standing on corners, openly pointed at them like they were the masters of a parade. Drawing out of town, they followed the long road to the palace.

Huxley was already planning the telegram he was going to send. It would be costly, but it would be worth every letter.

HELLO MOTHER. HELLO FATHER. AM NOT DEAD. AM VERY MUCH ALIVE. THANKS FOR ASKING. ACTUALLY RESCUED MYSELF SINCE THERE WAS NO SEARCH PARTY. ALSO THWARTED PLOT AGAINST CROWN. HOPE YOU ARE WELL AND NOT STRANDED ON A MOUNTAINTOP AWAITING A COLD AND BITTER DEATH. MISS YOU. LOVE YOU. WILL VISIT SOON.

He meant it. But first he planned to eat a meal, or maybe six meals. So perhaps civilization was not entirely satisfying. Because he also wanted a rare steak, a loaf of bread, an entire blueberry pie, and three pots of the hottest coffee this rock of ice called an isle could muster.

The palace grounds lay beyond a gated archway. It was darkening now, and the courtyard inside the walls was lit by gas, not electric, torches.

The palace itself was hand-laid stone, with many spires and green-painted shingled parapets. Light flickered behind stained glass windows, and fresh snow began to powder the eaves.

There were palace protectorates checking invitations and identities at the gate, but two mounted guards trotted their horses down the road to intercept the elephant before Carthage and Huxley could even reach the arches.

"Identify yourselves," said one of the protectorates.

"Sylvester Carthage," answered Carthage, putting a hand to his chest in introduction. "This is my associate, Mr. Huxley. We must see Lord Protectorate Vicewar."

"Let me see your passbooks."

"Well... see," said Carthage. "We don't have any identification."

Their passbooks had been with the rest of their paperwork, and most of it had burned. That was going to be a headache. But Huxley couldn't fathom that they weren't recognized. "We're the Electrical Menagerie. We were *just* in the paper. It said we died, but we didn't. As you can see."

The mounted protectorates exchanged a look.

Carthage seemed to be getting impatient. He looked up at the palace, hands tightening on the elephant's reins, as if he were thinking about stomping right through the blockade. "We *must* speak with Vicewar. The Future Queen is in grave danger."

The protectorates sat up straighter. They wore pistols on their legs, and the one to Huxley's right had his hand very near to his gun. "What makes you say that?"

"There's a Terraformist plot," Carthage said. "The

illusionist performing tonight is not who she claims to be."

"And you're Sylvester Carthage," the protectorate said, like he was talking to somebody crazy.

"Are you listening? If you don't heed us, the Future Queen is as good as dead!"

Huxley thought that might have been the wrong thing for Carthage to say, but he couldn't get those words out before the protectorates seized them from either side and yanked them to the ground. He found himself face-down on the road, tasting the iron remnants of horseshoes and... well, he didn't want to think about what else.

"Listen, you," said the protectorate that was now sitting on Carthage. Huxley could see them between the legs of the elephant. "Threats against Our Celestial Lady are a capital offense."

"It wasn't a threat!" Carthage blared. The righteous indignation was somewhat lost by the way he was muffled from being pinned to the ground. "It was a *warning*!"

"Whatever you'd like to call it," the protectorate said. "You're coming in until we can sort this out."

He whistled for some backup, and Huxley was yanked to his feet and frisked.

"We're not *assassins*," said Carthage as he was shackled. "We're entertainers!"

As he said that, the protectorate searching Huxley yanked Huxley's sleeve back to reveal the gun hidden up his arm. There was a sharp intake of breath from the assembly of protectorates.

"I'm a *paranoid* entertainer," Huxley elaborated as

they stripped him of his gun and shackled him too. Their poor elephant was also taken away, in another direction.

"Be kind to Endeavour!" Carthage called to the protectorate that wrapped a chain around the elephant's legs.

The protectorates marched Huxley and Carthage together down the road, past carriages and coaches waiting to be admitted. At the gate, Huxley found himself once again drawing alongside the fancy coach with the white horses, except this time on foot.

The same young and dandy gentleman stuck his head out with a smirk, but Huxley had the final comeuppance as he was walked past the checkpoint while the gentleman was forced to produce his papers.

In the courtyard, they were taken down a set of steps that led underground. Huxley was in front, and heard Carthage give a pained gasp as he came down on the steps.

"May we walk a bit slower?" Carthage asked.

Huxley wasn't sure if the protectorates escorting Carthage slowed down. The two escorting him did not. They rounded a corner into a rather ugly, gas-lit room that was made of whitewashed bricks. There were desks stacked with paperwork, and flags on the walls. Past this room, through a locked door, they entered the palace jail.

Most of the cells were already occupied, and many of the occupants were dressed in party clothes. What were all these people doing here?

One well-dressed man wailed. "My invitation is hardly a forgery! I demand to speak with a regent at once!"

Of course. A royal ball could only have the singular effect of bringing every freeloader, con artist, and downright lunatic out of the woodwork to crash it.

"I promise!" cried another, grasping the bars as the protectorates dragged Carthage and Huxley past. He was stocky and middle-aged, with a sort of silly look. "I'm Sylvester Carthage. My death was faked, and I must see the princess!"

"I'm Sylvester Carthage," Carthage said, indignant.

"*I'm* Sylvester Carthage!" the man insisted.

His companion, a very wiry and horse-faced young man, nodded vigorously. "And I'm Arbrook Huxley," he said in the worst impression of a Fallsbright accent Huxley had ever heard.

The protectorates threw Huxley and Carthage in a cell alongside their impersonators and locked the door with a clang.

Carthage gripped the bars. "Lord Protectorate Vicewar. Please. He's got ginger hair and a mustache. Call him here, and he will positively identify us. That's more than these impostors can promise."

Huxley looked at the impostors, who certainly looked to be lacking confidence at their ability to pass in a lineup.

The protectorates didn't answer, but exchanged low words. Then they left.

"We had photos in the paper!" Carthage shouted after them.

"Although," said Huxley, looking down at himself. They were ragged, spotted with oil and soot, coats torn and trouser cuffs frayed, with black fingernails and cuts on their knuckles. Neither of them had seen a comb or a razor in days. "I suppose we don't exactly resemble our photographs."

"You ought to get washed up if you're going to try impersonating gentlemen," said the Fake Carthage, as if offering some trade secret. "And put on some respectable clothes. Nobody would ever believe you were us!"

Carthage ignored them, clinging to the door. Huxley paced.

After a few minutes, the door at the end of the hall opened again. Somebody strode down the aisle of cells, wearing a snow-dusted cape and carrying his cap under one arm. One of the arresting protectorates followed him.

"Lord Protectorate," Carthage cried, and released his white grip on the bars. "I've never been so happy to see you."

Vicewar stopped in front of the cell as Huxley joined Carthage's side.

"Something terrible has happened," continued Carthage. "Which we may only disclose in confidence."

Vicewar turned to the other protectorate and indicated he wanted privacy. The other protectorate stepped back a few feet. "What is it?" Vicewar asked, quiet.

Huxley lowered his voice to answer between the bars. "Miss Andromeda Skyhawke and her manager tried to kill us. As you can see, we survived. But we believe they plan something against the prin— Our Celestial Lady, I mean."

Alarm crossed Vicewar's typically steady face. He

took a slight step back from the bars and turned to his subordinate.

Huxley readied to be released.

"You said these two were apprehended at the gate?" Vicewar asked instead.

"Yes, sir. The Fallsbrighton had a sleeve gun."

Vicewar turned back to them, a cold look. "I don't know who you are," he said, and reached suddenly through the bars, seizing Carthage by the lapel. Carthage gripped the protectorate's hand defensively, and for a moment they only stared at each other. Vicewar's eyes narrowed. "But you really have some nerve."

A stunned moment passed. Of course the Lord Protectorate recognized them, even scuttled as they were. They'd been traveling together this whole time. Why would he act otherwise?

"Vicewar," said Huxley. "Of all the things I thought you were, I never thought you were *corrupt*." Heat flushed his cold limbs as it dawned on him. "But of *course*. It was you who overlooked Abernathy's murder as an accident. Who barely investigated the sabotage. Who arrested Hemlock on circumstantial evidence. And who declared us *dead* with no proof at all!"

Vicewar took a step back, releasing Carthage.

"I've never seen these two before in my life," he told the other protectorate. "We'll have to sort out who they *really* are after the ball — along with the rest of these charlatans."

"Vicewar!" Huxley called after him, but the Lord Protectorate didn't turn. Huxley banged a fist on the bars.

"Boy howdy," said the Fake Huxley from the cell next door. "Ain't this a downright pickle."

"I don't sound like that!" Huxley said. "And I'd *never* wear a paisley vest with *striped pants*!"

"Serves you right for impersonating us," said the Fake Carthage.

Carthage turned, annoyed. "If you're Sylvester Carthage, why don't you do some magic?"

"If *you're* Sylvester Carthage," blustered the Fake Carthage, "why don't *you* do some magic?"

"Alright," said Carthage, waved a hand, and produced a brass jail key. "Oh!" he said, like he hadn't expected it there. "Look at that."

The impersonators gasped and recoiled. Even Huxley was startled. Vicewar must have transferred the key to Carthage under the guise of grabbing him through the bars. But why?

"He's a witch," said the Fake Carthage, backing away from the bars.

"On Fallsbright, we get all our medicine from witches," the Fake Huxley added.

"We do *not*," said Huxley as Carthage reached through the bars and put the key in the lock. To Carthage, he lowered his voice. "Why would Vicewar condemn us and then help us escape?"

"I don't know," said Carthage, pulling a face as he leveraged the key in the lock from his odd angle on the wrong side of the bars. "But I always believed Vicewar was a good man. Perhaps there are forces working beyond his control."

The lock banged, and Carthage and Huxley slid the door open just enough to slip through.

The impostors, realizing that their rivals were now escaping without them, rushed to the dividing bars and began to shout.

"They're escaping!" Fake Carthage yelled.

"Let us out!" Fake Huxley added.

Other prisoners, seeing the jailbreak, shouted too. But the jail had already been too loud, and the warning was lost as Carthage and Huxley escaped down the hall through the opposite door.

This door emptied them out into a narrower hallway, and they went through another door to find a locker room at the end.

"Ah-ha," said Huxley, and stripped off his tatty coat. "Should I say it's time for our costume change?"

"I'd say it's far overdue," Carthage answered as he similarly undressed.

In moments they'd put on pressed trousers with stripes up the legs, clean shirts and navy coats with gold epaulets. There was a sink with plumbing, and Huxley scrubbed the grit off his face, then raked wet fingers through his hair to set it.

He turned and looked at Carthage, who was also combing his hair with his fingers, tucking stray bits behind his ears and under the protectorate's cap he wore.

"Look at us!" said Huxley. "We're rather dashing in uniform, aren't we?"

"That may be generous," Carthage answered, and tossed him a cap and a wool cape.

They escaped from the locker room into another tunnel, heading toward a hard chill that suggested they were nearing an exterior door. That turned out to be true. This tunnel had a set of stone steps leading up into the courtyard.

Carthage put his weight on a hand rail as they ascended. At the top, in the dim glow of the courtyard, he exhaled.

"Huxley," he said. "If we survive this, I think we should take a holiday. Someplace warm where I can rest my legs."

"Wait here," said Huxley, and left him under a gas lamp, darting across the massive courtyard toward the palace steps. There was a circular bridle path with a fountain in the middle, and carriages disembarked passengers at the steps then pulled away, between another set of arches, toward what was probably a livery.

Huxley reached the steps just as a coach arrived — a familiar coach with white horses. A footman sprang from the coach and opened the lady's side first, offering her a step stool and a hand.

Huxley went to the off side and opened the door for the gentleman, who thrust out a fur-trimmed greatcoat, top hat, and walking stick for Huxley to hold. The footman came around just in time to help his lord out of the carriage as Huxley stole off.

Carthage was leaning heavily against the lamp.

"Here," said Huxley, offering him the walking stick. He then threw the hat and greatcoat over the hedges.

Carthage took the walking stick with gratitude, but

then gave Huxley a suspect look. "Just how many ill-gotten skills do you have?"

"Well," said Huxley as they set off together across the courtyard to infiltrate the palace, "how many do we need?"

DREAMS

The palace was far bigger than Carthage ever conceived it could be.

Yes, it was four hundred rooms. That fact existed in his mind, letters on a page. But the magnitude of that was impossible to grasp until you were standing at its belly.

While the royal guests were welcomed at the grand set of doors in the front, Carthage and Huxley entered quietly through what looked to be a service door to the south. They found themselves bursting over a threshold into the palace kitchen, and they were at once transported as if they'd fallen through a portal in some fairytale.

Outside, it was cold and dark, but the sprawling kitchen glowed yellow with electric light and the ambient warmth of stoves and ovens. Downstairs staff, all dressed in matching blue aprons, scurried to and fro — stuffing birds with chestnuts, scattering flour and rolling dough, stirring pots of gravy and roiling cream — as chefs in white caps called out to their sous.

One of the chefs snapped his fingers at Carthage and

Huxley when they almost collided with a woman carrying a tray of scones.

"This is a kitchen," he cried. "Not a garrison, Protectorates!"

Huxley raised his hands in apology as they dodged the cooks.

Carthage, remembering suddenly how very little he'd eaten for days, felt his mouth water. The kitchen smelled like his childhood home did on holidays and during the festivals. The sharp scent of fresh herbs, yeast bubbling and rising, and waterfowl with skin crackling in the oven as it cooked.

A baker, wheeling an enormous six-tiered cake, blocked the door. Carthage and Huxley came up short.

Even incompletely decorated, it was the most beautiful cake Carthage had ever seen. The frosting was ballerina pink, piped lavishly with off-white and dusted with something that made it glimmer. The fragrance of sugar and strawberries was so powerful he could taste it.

The baker left the cart and the cake in front of them and walked away, toward a countertop where several other bakers were modeling roses and birds out of sugar paste and gold leaf.

Huxley's hand darted out, finger aimed at a scallop of frosting. Carthage slapped the hand away.

"What are you *doing*?" he hissed.

"I'm *so* hungry," Huxley said.

"You can't steal food from the Future Queen's table!"

"It's not *stealing*!" Huxley hissed back. "My tax dollars paid for that cake!"

"Well, your hands are filthy!"

"*Fine.* I won't touch the cake." Huxley turned around and seized two cross buns that were cooling on a nearby tray, then stuffed one in his mouth and darted around the cake for the door before there could be any further protest.

Carthage, feeling suddenly too faint to resist, murmured an apology to God and the Queen as he also took a bun. He thought both Graces would permit it, given the circumstance.

Exiting the kitchen, they found themselves in a long corridor lit by gas chandeliers. The walls, paneled in wood and painted white, had paintings of birds at regular intervals.

"Where do we go?" Huxley asked as he put the second bun in his mouth.

Carthage rubbed his head. Once, he knew the entire map of the palace. He'd spent hours studying it. But that had been so long ago. They were downstairs, just outside the kitchen, which meant the grand ballroom was to the west — or was it the east?

He took a bite of the bun he had in his hand. It was warm and soft, with the perfect firmness to the top, so that it had just enough bite. There were raisins in it, and bits of orange peel, and perhaps cinnamon. Not too sweet, and complemented by just a hint of icing.

"Oh," he said. "That's the best thing I've ever eaten."

"I'll say," said Huxley, who licked his fingers. "I could eat a dozen more." He turned like he intended to go back into the kitchen and do just that, but Carthage caught him before he could.

"West," Carthage said. "Through the ballroom. Let's go!"

They followed the paintings of the birds, hooked a corner and went together through a pair of brass-gilt double doors.

This ballroom made Helios Hall look like the downstairs dance hall in a gambling den. It was twice as large, with the ceiling of a cathedral and solid gold chandeliers cast to look like lions holding flaming crowns in their mouths.

The ballroom was being dressed for dinner, staff setting white linen tables with china and gold flatware. An almost overwhelming fragrance of roses filled the room from bouquets on every table and the pink rose garlands draped from the balconies and staircase banister.

Carthage skirted the dinner setting, leading Huxley under the stairs to a door almost hidden in its shadow.

This service door carried them up a winding flight of steps, and Carthage was relieved to have the walking stick as he ascended them. Small, star-shaped windows offered short glimpses of an intensifying snowstorm as they climbed.

They emerged on a second story, through another door into a grand and luxurious hallway lined with portraits of past monarchs. A large picture window at the end of one hall showed the grounds behind the palace, although it was impossible to see anything beyond the darkness and the falling snow.

It felt very quiet here, in contrast to the bustle and noise downstairs.

"Where are we?" Huxley whispered it, as if they were in a church or a museum.

"This is the outer residence," said Carthage, faintly lightheaded to say it aloud. If they were caught and found impersonating protectorates here, where visiting dignitaries and diplomats slept, he was sure they'd be shot.

Where the corridor teed at the large window, Carthage peered around the corner. But this corridor terminated with a set of double doors — probably someone's quarters — which had a pair of very decorated protectorates standing watch outside it.

He drew back, shoving Huxley back with him before the protectorates could spot them.

Huxley gave him a nervous look. What now?

Carthage pointed back the way they came. If he wasn't mistaken, they could go back downstairs and take a slightly longer route around the ballroom and up one of the main sets of stairs.

But as they reached the door in the paneling that concealed the staircase, voices and the thumping of boots carried up the staircase and through the door. Someone was coming upstairs, and the subtle jangle of the gait, as well as the fact they were using a service staircase, suggested it was two or more real protectorates.

Trapped.

Backing off from the staircase, Carthage went to the

MOLLIE E. REEDER

nearest door in the corridor and tried the latch. Locked. Huxley went to the next, but the result was the same.

Carthage struggled to recall what was behind the doors. He closed his eyes, calling to mind the tri-folded map in the center of that pop-up book he loved so much.

The first and second doors were parlors, for dignitaries to read or entertain during long stays in the palace. But those rooms weren't used much, and probably kept locked unless they were requested by a guest.

There was also a music salon, with a piano for small concerts. It was the only piano in this wing, if he recalled correctly, and therefore perhaps that room was utilized more often.

Pulling Huxley along with him, he went straight for the fifth door on the left and pushed on the latch.

It gave — just as the door at the top of the stairwell also opened. They tumbled inside and shut the door behind them.

The salon was dark. Voices echoed down the corridor.

Huxley got down and looked through the keyhole.

"What are they doing?" Carthage asked as he leaned on his stick.

"Just talking," Huxley whispered back. "They've stopped in the hallway. What do we do now?"

Carthage turned, squinting in the dark. This was an octagonal interior room, and the only window was a skylight that offered a little lesser light through the drifts of snow piling up on the roof.

He could barely make out sofas, bookcases along the

octagonal walls, a fireplace at the far end, and a grand piano in the middle.

"All of these rooms are connected by passageways," he said. "There should be some kind of lever somewhere on the wall. Help me find it."

They started at opposite sides of the room and began to grope the walls and the bookcases through the dark.

Carthage, feeling around the molding of the fireplace, grasped what felt like a switch carved into the mouth of a plaster lion. Hoping for the best, he pressed it, and the bookcase Huxley was standing near gave a click and then swung inward with a mechanical groan.

A vase on its lower shelf wobbled, then tipped. Carthage lurched for it, but he was too far away. Huxley dove and caught it just inches from smashing on the floor.

They paused, both audibly panting, and listened.

On the other side of the salon door, the voices grew louder.

"What is it?"

"I thought I heard something behind one of these doors."

Carthage slipped into the passageway and motioned to Huxley. *Hurry!*

Huxley replaced the vase — in a slightly less precarious position — and snuck into the passageway behind him. Together, they pushed the heavy door shut. It gave a weighty click again as it closed.

Inside the salon, there was the turning of a latch and the creak of hinges. From behind the bookcases, the voices were muffled.

"Is anyone staying on this wing?"

"The baron and the baroness are down the hall. What did you hear?"

"I'm not sure." The heels of boots tapped closer.

Carthage and Huxley, not daring to move, crouched instead inside the passageway. Carthage held his breath, sure the protectorates could hear his heartbeat.

"Oy. It's getting nasty out there."

"Aye." The footsteps receded. *"That ungodly wind has me chasing ghosts."*

Only when the salon door closed again and the voices faded behind it did Carthage and Huxley feel the safety to stand up and keep moving. The passageway was almost too dark to navigate, but then Huxley located a box on the wall which had electric torches stored inside it. They each took one and set off down the passage.

Although the passage had obviously been maintained, it was clear that it had also not been used very recently. There was a layer of dust on the floor, which they created rather incriminating tracks through as they went, and cobwebs glittered occasionally in the corners.

As they navigated the palace from between its walls, they passed what had to be hidden doors into other rooms. Sounds echoed oddly off the stones, curving around the corners and junctions of the corridors in peculiar ways.

Behind one wall came the gentle whine of a violin. Behind another, a lady said something and some others laughed. From another, the crash of falling china, and then a sharp retort from the servant that dropped it.

Sometimes, there was the rumble of water through

pipes, or the hiss of gas overhead, or the suddenly warm air of a nearby fireplace.

The passage walls, which were stone, had yellowing canvases hanging on them, paintings of religious scenes and calligraphy prayers.

"What is this?" Huxley asked, shining his torch around the passage. It landed on a haloed portrait of the Messiah.

"That's The Lord, Huxley, perhaps you should become acquainted."

Huxley blared his light in Carthage's eyes. "You know what I meant."

"This palace was built during the Second Age," Carthage answered, pausing at a junction. "After the regicides and the burning of the first castle, Alexander the First ordered the new palace be built with passageways for escape." He turned left. "He feared a coup, so the passages were kept secret from everyone except the family and their personal guards. They say not even the King's brother knew the passages existed. But they've never been used in a crisis, and they haven't been secret for a hundred years."

"How do you know all this?"

Carthage felt around the threshold of a doorway for a latch. "Because I read."

Huxley detected the implicit accusation. "I *read*," he answered.

"The star sagas don't count," Carthage said as he triggered the latch. "Here. Unless I've gotten us totally lost, the theater should be just across the hall. It's a new addition — this passageway won't connect."

They emerged into an empty but large and well-lit room which was decorated with tapestries and had a plush patterned rug on the floor.

Huxley took the lead, but Carthage looked up and caught him by the sleeve.

"Huxley," he said. "Look."

Mounted to every inch of space on the walls were swords. Engraved medieval broadswords, two-handed longswords, sabers decorated with military tassels, scimitars curved and gleaming, a pair of fencing foils crossed over the fireplace, ornate rapiers, cutlasses, falchions, a katana, and even a few daggers mounted to plaques. There had to be at least two hundred blades displayed around the room, along with military tapestries, flags, and two battered shields that had obviously been through a war.

"A whole room of nowt but swords," Carthage remembered, looking around in awe at the gleaming walls.

He was *here*.

This wasn't a dream anymore. He'd been to the palace. He'd seen the things he once could only read about. And it was everything he thought it would be.

The air was weighted with the dust of ancient battles and the tang of metal. He breathed it and tried to memorize the way the moment felt.

You were right, he told his younger self. *You weren't foolish. You were right to hope.*

"If only my mother could see me now," he said aloud.

"If *my* mother could see me now," said Huxley, "I'd

be legally disowned." A grandfather clock chimed as it reached the bottom of the hour. Huxley looked at it with alarm. "We have to go. The show's already started."

They emerged from the sword room into an atrium. The atrium was empty, but muffled sound hummed from doors that had to lead to the backstage of the palace theater.

Through these doors, they entered the auditorium.

20

A GRAND FINALE

Huxley stepped backstage. It was very dark compared to the atrium they'd just been in, and his eyes took a moment to adjust.

They were standing in the wings on stage left, surrounded by some old and unused pieces of scenery, like trees and castle walls. Past the stage's grand proscenium arch, and the blood-red curtains that concealed Huxley and Carthage in the wings, Miss Andromeda Skyhawke — or, the woman who called herself that — stood on the apron of the stage, wearing white and faintly glowing in a halo of stage light.

That old theater smell of sawdust and many layers of paint had a smoky texture laid over it. Perhaps they'd already detonated some pyrotechnics, because what lay beyond the stage looked not only dark but hazy. Huxley could just barely discern the glint of opera glasses that suggested the auditorium, including the balconies and boxes, were full.

He assessed the backstage. Spiral stairwells ran up to three different tiers of catwalks. On both sides of the stage, on the third and topmost tier, were small balconies — fly galleries, for controlling sandbags and rigging. The second tier had a catwalk that ran all the way across stage left to stage right. It looked to be a catwalk for a spotlight operator, and there was someone standing on it.

Huxley elbowed Carthage and pointed. Sergei.

What was he doing?

He was standing on the catwalk, directly overhead Andromeda, unseen by the audience and unmoving. He seemed to grasp something small in one hand.

Carthage said something, but he was drowned out by music. There was a full orchestra in the pit. He pointed instead, looking urgent, and drew a finger across his throat.

Huxley wasn't exactly sure what Carthage was saying, but he understood well enough. Whatever Sergei was doing up on that catwalk was a matter of life and death.

Sergei was bigger than either of them. Stars, maybe both of them *combined*. He had broad shoulders, stout limbs, and large fists. If they were going to take him down, it would require teamwork — and perhaps the element of surprise.

Huxley gestured to indicate they should split up, and Carthage nodded in agreement. As Carthage went for the spiral stairs on stage left, Huxley darted behind a curtain into the darkened crossover and went for the staircase on stage right. He climbed to the second tier, then checked Carthage.

Carthage had just reached the second tier on his end, and they made eye contact. Sergei, intent on the show beneath him, didn't see either of them moving in the dark. Huxley, holding Carthage's gaze, pointed up. He was going to go up one more tier.

Carthage looked to have his teeth on edge, even from a distance, but he grasped his stick as a ready weapon and advanced onto the spotlight catwalk with a sure stride that all but concealed the limp.

Huxley marveled at the things he now understood. How often did Sylvester Carthage walk through pain with a high head?

Sergei, perhaps feeling the weight of another man on the catwalk with him, turned.

Huxley scrambled up the next flight of stairs, and reached the fly gallery just in time to see Carthage rush Sergei, aiming the heavy brass end of the expensive walking stick in a mean uppercut that cracked Sergei in the jaw and sent the big man reeling back.

On the offense, Carthage chased Sergei backwards across the catwalk with another vicious blow, closer to Huxley.

Huxley climbed up the railing of the fly gallery and crouched at the top rail, readying himself. Below, there was a wave of earnest applause as Andromeda welcomed a volunteer onstage.

Huxley's heart leapt as light caught the glimmer of a silver crown in the girl's hair. That was no ordinary volunteer. Now the princess was standing onstage alongside Andromeda as the men grappled overhead.

Sergei, overcoming the element of surprise, redoubled and punched Carthage in the face.

As Carthage staggered back, Huxley sprang from the fly gallery and tackled Sergei, the impact of his landing knocking them to the metal grating with a hard bang.

Sergei's arm flailed, fingers loosening. A small remote flew from his grip and to the floor below, bouncing once then landing in the wings on stage left.

"An incredible wonder..." Andromeda said.

Huxley, straddling Sergei, scrambled to land a punch, but Sergei grunted and kicked him off. Carthage, intentions plainly set on reaching the remote, turned and moved for the staircase. But Sergei caught Carthage by an ankle and yanked him down.

As Sergei climbed over Carthage on his way toward the staircase, Huxley rushed him from behind, slamming them both into a railing. But the big man turned, throwing him, and rammed him backwards into the opposite railing.

The top rail bit the small of Huxley's back, feeling suddenly insubstantial as the ground loomed beneath. Sergei threw an elbow at Huxley's face, which Huxley blocked, but then tackled again at the waist and this time lifted, tipping their combined weight over the railing.

He was trying to throw Huxley over.

Panicking as his equilibrium turned upside-down, Huxley lifted a leg and tried to kick Sergei.

It was the worst thing he could have done. Sergei seized that leg and leveraged it to tip Huxley's center of gravity over the edge. The ground pulled, and Huxley went over as Sergei gave him a last shove.

His hands shot out as he flipped over the railing,

and only one found purchase on a metal bar. Catching himself with just one hand, he dangled over the stage in the darkness of the wings.

Sergei stomped toward the staircase, shimmying the catwalk and threatening Huxley's failing grip. Carthage was getting up, and moved along the railing toward Huxley to rescue him.

If he could just take hold of the bar with both hands, he could pull himself up and back onto the catwalk. He reached with his free hand and felt his grasp slip as Sergei moved from the catwalk onto the staircase.

He was going to fall.

VANISHMENT

Huxley was going to fall.

Carthage dove to pull him back up, seizing desperately at Huxley's failing hand.

He was too late.

The drop was not insignificant. Huxley fell from the catwalk to the darkened wings and rolled on impact. He was lying just feet from the discarded remote, but he didn't get up.

For a moment Carthage could only grip the railing as sickness washed over him in waves. A fall like that might kill a man — or it might paralyze him. He willed Huxley to get up.

Huxley's head moved. His hands opened and closed against the floor.

Not dead.

Huxley, coming around, began to crawl for the remote. Sergei, coming down the staircase, thrust a hand into his coat. Carthage's nausea intensified. The orchestra swelled, and it felt physically painful. He turned and looked up at the fly gallery.

Come on, Sylvester.

As Sergei reached the bottom of the staircase, Carthage raced to ascend. Pain lanced him as he took the stairs two at a time and reached the fly gallery gasping.

Here was the pin rail, where all the heavy things hidden overhead in the fly loft were tied off with nautical knots. Which one? He followed the ropes, craning his neck to look.

In the wings, Huxley dragged himself nearer to the remote. He was within grasping distance of it, and outstretched a dazed hand.

Sergei pulled a revolver from his coat and raised it at the back of Huxley's head.

Carthage seized the end of a hemp line and pulled the knot free of the belaying pin.

Violently loosed as its rope flew, a sandbag plummeted from the fly loft and crashed into Sergei from below. The gun flew out of his hand as he fell crushed under its weight.

With perfect timing, the audience applauded.

Carthage scrambled down the stairs and reached Huxley as the music swelled again. Onstage, Andromeda pulled a sheet off of a large prop standing center stage: a golden cage.

Huxley, remarkably, seemed in no way permanently injured. There was something to be said about being twenty-five and having soft bones. Or maybe just being Huxley and having dumb luck.

As Carthage helped him up, Andromeda offered the princess a hand, and the princess stepped up into the golden cage. She sat down in the chair, grinning, and Andromeda wordlessly flourished.

As trumpets blared from the pit, Andromeda half-turned toward the wings.

She must have been looking for Sergei. When she saw them, her face changed. Paling, she could only stare. Carthage felt Huxley draw a breath, ready to call her name.

The sudden bang of pyrotechnics never gave him a chance. Startled, Carthage and Huxley staggered back together, shielding their eyes.

When the smoke cleared, Andromeda was gone.

So was the princess.

The golden cage was empty except for the chair she'd been sitting in just seconds before. The audience gasped, and then murmured, unsure if this was part of the act. But when several long moments passed, and nothing reappeared, shrieks began to echo across the auditorium.

Of course — one final trick. The gambit had been this all along. It was why the Terraformists had groomed a magician for the ruse, not an actor or an opera singer.

Miss Skyhawke's last and greatest act was to make the Future Celestial Queen disappear.

Protectorates began to blow whistles as regents and guards ran onstage. There was a trap door open on the stage floor, and palace protectorates plunged under the stage in pursuit of the performer and the princess.

Screams volleyed across the room as the doors all opened and people were ushered out. Carthage, worried about being caught lurking backstage, pulled Huxley back out the door into the atrium from which they'd entered.

They laid low for the next ten or fifteen minutes as chaos echoed through the halls of the palace.

"She got away," said Huxley. "I don't believe it."

Carthage rubbed his tired eyes, thinking. "I don't believe it either," he said.

"What do you mean?"

Something about this wasn't right. Andromeda Skyhawke was admittedly athletic, but he doubted she could overpower and kidnap the preteen princess, at least not handily. And how was she supposed to escape the palace now that the protectorates were searching for her? There was some final component to this plot they were overlooking.

"Misdirection," Carthage said suddenly.

"What?"

"*Misdirection*," Carthage repeated, straightening. "We're both idiots."

"Speak for yourself," said Huxley, but followed him back through the stage door.

Inside, they were alone. Carthage walked around the quiet stage, studying the tape marking the apron and considering.

The auditorium had been evacuated and the grand doors locked. From some service tunnel that ran under the stage echoed shouts. The protectorates were pursuing Andromeda Skyhawke and the stolen princess through the tunnel, hoping to intercept the pair before they reached the exterior of the palace.

They would never catch her.

The answer was dawning on him, and despite the terrible circumstance, his aches evaporated under the heat of the lights and the familiar sanctity of the stage. The wheels of his mind turned quicker, accelerating his pulse.

"Where do you think they went, Huxley? In a closed room — with sixteen hundred people watching?"

"Not down," said Huxley. Carthage was pleased to see him catching on. "That was the misdirection."

"Very good. If the open trap door was where she *wanted* us to look, where were we *not* supposed to look?"

Huxley searched the auditorium with his gaze. "Into the audience," he said, "and they were evacuated with the crowd."

Carthage nodded along. That was a good solution, but it presented some issues. "How did they escape unnoticed in the crowd?"

"The lady wears a mask, which she might have removed, and perhaps the princess was disguised."

"And she didn't cry out as she was escorted through the crowd?"

Huxley's brow furrowed. "But they *did* disappear," he said. "We saw it."

"But *did* we actually see them disappear?"

"Well, no," said Huxley. "We didn't actually *see* them disappear — you never do. You only see where something is, and then there's a flash, and then you see where it isn't."

"And why is that?"

"Because…" Huxley turned with him toward the golden cage. "Because nothing actually disappears—"

"Because it's still hidden in the hand," Carthage finished. He looked down and followed a black electrical cable, snaking from the bottom of the cage, to its socket in the wall. Seizing it, he yanked it out of the plug.

The golden cage flickered as the hologram of its empty inside winked away.

Inside, Andromeda Skyhawke stood watching them with a silver derringer in one hand. The Future Queen slumped over at her feet, unconscious.

"The last place anyone would look is an empty box," Carthage said, approaching her.

"Projectors and one-way glass?" Huxley asked, as he grasped the way the effect was done. "You stole our trick!"

"Made it better, I'd say," Carthage acknowledged. "And actually, I believe *I* got the idea from a wee girl on Carpathia."

Andromeda looked terrified. She stepped out of the cage, training the gun on them.

Carthage stopped in front of her. "Sergei was ready to kill you if things went wrong," he said. "He was standing overhead with a radio detonator. You ought not to sneeze, as I think you'll find he's wired your costume in some deadly way."

Andromeda's eyes widened.

"In fact," said Huxley, and raised the remote out of his pocket. "You ought to lay down your gun."

Carthage, startled, moved away from them both. He remembered now that Huxley had clasped the remote in the last moment before Sergei was struck down. But he'd forgotten about it, and was surprised to see Huxley wield it now. Then again, he'd not realized, until a few days ago, that Huxley had already crossed that barrier of violent resolve it took to carry a loaded gun.

He felt suddenly unsure. She had betrayed them both, but for Huxley it was personal. His trust had been violated and turned against him.

Was he only bluffing? Or would he really hit the switch?

Carthage wavered between interrupting this confrontation or aiding the princess. Worried by the way the girl was slumped and unresponsive in the golden cage, instinct carried him over to the Future Queen's side. He pulled her carefully out of the cage and laid her on the stage floor to look for a pulse.

"She's alright," Andromeda said as she and Huxley circled each other. "Only sleeping. I would never hurt a child. I'm a victim in all this, the same as either of you."

"You must be joking," Huxley answered, and came boldly closer despite the gun trained on him. "I knew you lied to me, but have you really lied so completely to yourself? You were quite frank on the train. What you wanted was the illusion of your character to continue — even if it cost us our lives."

"I thought only of what they promised me. By the time I saw what I was an accessory to, I was too afraid of Sergei to escape." Perhaps she was acting, but if she was, she was good. Her voice choked, and her accent slipped, and her gaze glistened with gaining tears. "Surely, Huxley, you read that in my eyes? He controlled every waking minute of my false life. Yes, I was a puppet — and a puppet has no power to cut its own strings. You'll never know the bitter tears I wept for both of you. I've been eaten alive for days, imagining you falling through the clouds."

"Andromeda," said Huxley, and raised the remote. "Put down the gun."

She looked at him for a moment, visibly pained.

"You're bluffing," she said at last.

"I'm not. I don't know what might happen when I hit this switch, but I will do it."

"I've seen you truthful," she said. "I know what it looks like."

"Andromeda!"

"I'll be shot for treason if they catch me," she answered as she stood over the open hatch of the trap door. The voices underneath the stage had faded, but still — where was there to run?

Her voice fell to a whisper. "Please, just let me go. I will vanish back into obscurity. As of tonight, Andromeda Skyhawke — I swear to you — is no more."

She was right. Huxley did not have the resolve — or perhaps it was cruelty — to hit the switch. Instead, he stood and watched her as she disappeared into the hatch and vanished one final time.

Carthage did not think they should let her get away, and started to go after her. But the princess stirred, drawing him back to his knees.

She grasped her head and sat up. There was a lingering odor of chloroform on her.

"Your Majesty," Carthage said. "Are you alright?"

"I just—" started the princess, seeming confused.

It was overwhelming to be sitting on the floor with her, and he was afraid to touch her now that she was conscious. His hands hovered, unsure. What was the royal courtesy in this case?

"Will you?" she asked, and held out her hand. Glad to be asked, which removed any confusion, he got to his feet and helped her to hers.

She looked just like her portraits — the high cheekbones and keen eyes that made her strongly resemble her late father. Her green dress was radiant against her black skin, and a diamond tiara sparkled in her dark curls. One hand wore a long white glove, and the other was hidden in a sling that matched the color of her dress.

Remembering she was only turning thirteen, something unexpectedly sad knifed him. She looked just like a very small and composed lady. Perhaps growing up in a castle was its own confinement.

"There was something wrong with the magician," she said, bewildered. "She was crying as she climbed into the box!"

"There was an attempted abduction," he told her. "But we thwarted the plot."

The Future Queen's eyes widened, and she collected herself enough to curtsy. "I'm so thankful, Protectorates."

Mortified that she was showing them deference, he remembered only then how they were both dressed.

"No," he said, unwilling to deceive a monarch. He

stood back from her and took a knee, lowering his head. "These are only disguises. Sylvester Carthage, ma'am. And Mr. Arbrook Huxley." A sideways glance confirmed that Huxley had adopted the same position. "We aren't protectorates — we're entertainers."

"How confusing," she said to herself. "Why are you dressed like protectorates?"

"I'm afraid it's a very long story, ma'am."

"I am called Lily for now," she introduced herself. "But don't get used to it. Tomorrow, after my birthday, I'll have a new name. I just haven't been able to decide. It's such a big decision." She tapped them both on the shoulders, prompting them to get up.

Carthage wrapped his fingers around his walking stick, clinging to it as he stood up.

Her brow furrowed, and she bit her lip. "Is there something wrong with you?"

"No," he said, remembering the charge he received in the judges' tent. *Can you fulfill your obligation without impediment?* "I..."

But his breath caught as he looked at her. She'd taken her left arm from its sling when she reached to touch them, and now held it close to her chest as if she wasn't used to having it. The arm was twisted and malformed, with only three fingers on that hand.

Perhaps this was why she'd only ever been painted, and never photographed. Surely the regents feared the kingdom might reject a monarch with a crippled hand. A person with apparent defect, called upon to become an icon that represented a nation. They would hide her away, keeping her out of photographs and wrapping her arm up in a sling, casting coins with a perfect profile and molding this young girl into the person that her subjects thought she should be.

She was doomed to a life of illusion.

"There's nothing wrong with me," he answered. "I've just got bad legs."

"I think I shall call you Protectorates anyway," she decided, after looking at them for a moment. "For, to me, that is what you seem like. And what would you think if I called myself *Celeste*?"

"I think that is what *you* seem like," he answered.

She smiled at him, a strained and lonely smile with a furrowed brow.

"I suppose," he said, and bent slightly at the waist. "Today has been a sorry birthday. You were promised a magic trick, and you've been cheated." He was standing onstage in the palace at Celestia, but he had nothing with him. No props, no hat, no cards or flash paper, and just one item down in his pocket.

He reached behind her ear and pulled the brass jail key from behind it, holding it up to her.

The sadness fell away, the furrowed brow yielding to a bright and genuine smile. The first trick he had ever learned, the simplest one he knew. But as she took the key, she looked at him like nobody had ever done anything so amazing.

She made him remember, suddenly, that wee girl who had lingered after his show on Carpathia. A poor little farm girl, or the Future Queen — maybe there was no fundamental difference between them. An audience of one, countenance transformed by his humblest efforts to elicit a smile.

She laughed, a better sound than a hundred people clapping, and he laughed too.

Perhaps, as Dominic's last words suggested, there *was* a fallacy to imaginary friends; an inadequacy to fictional adventures. This wasn't exactly what Sylvester had dreamed, but maybe there was something even better than dreams. Perhaps imagination and reality needed each other. Life so often didn't do dreams justice, but — maybe — the opposite could also be true.

"Your Majesty!" It was Vicewar, bursting through the grand doors of the theater. A few other protectorates followed closely on his heels.

As the Future Queen turned away from Carthage, he was startled to feel her press something into his palm.

"Lord Protectorate!" she cried with obvious affection. "I've had a terrible adventure, but I'm alright!"

Vicewar heaved an audible breath of relief as he mounted the stage with them.

As the others greeted the Future Queen and inspected her for harm, Vicewar pulled Carthage and Huxley quietly away — backwards, so that they didn't have to turn their backs on the Future Queen — escorting them out of the theater.

His voice was low. "I am ever in your favor," he told them. "I'm sorry for the ruse earlier. I will explain in depth at some later date. For now, know that we have arrested Sergei, and that you have done more good tonight than you realize. I have already covered for your jailbreak, and I will see you off the grounds and to an inn for the night. Tomorrow, you may announce that you have survived, and I will confirm your identities and make sure you are promptly issued new identification."

"I understand you must have trusted us to intervene in the plot," said Carthage, "but what gave you such great faith in us? We're only entertainers."

"Exactly," answered Vicewar. "Who would even attempt thwarting a Terraformist plot single-handedly? No sane person would try it. I thought it required the audacity, arrogance, and stupidity only two people in show business could have."

THE LORD PROTECTORATE made good on his promise. He escorted them off the premises without further incident, then sent them down the road to Starborough's most lavish hotel, which they were checked into on the Crown's dime.

Vicewar's final request — although it rang more like a command — was that they tell no one what happened. Only the Lord Protectorate knew that they had infiltrated the grounds, impersonated the palace guard, and conversed with the Future Queen.

Carthage felt embarrassed about all of it, and gladly agreed, while Huxley seemed less enthused about sweeping their act of heroism under the rug.

As they bid farewell to Vicewar and headed upstairs to their rooms, Huxley gave a long and pained sigh.

"What's wrong with you now?" Carthage asked. They'd

survived an attempted murder, escaped the frozen wilderness, broken out of jail, thwarted a revolution, and befriended a monarch. He was exhausted and pained, but buzzing with victory. Vicewar had even made sure they were fed before he parted.

What could Huxley's problem possibly be?

"I was just thinking about our finances," Huxley said.

"What about them?"

"In case you forgot, we staked our train to the bank. The same train that is now littered in pieces on a mountainside."

"Oh, Huxley," said Carthage. "There's more to life than material things."

"You won't be so holier-than-thou when you and I are both carted off for our debts. It'll take thirty years on a chain gang to repay what we owe!"

"I think that's hyperbole," said Carthage.

"Well, it will *feel* like thirty years on a diet of bread and water. We'll both turn old and haggard in weeks. That's if we aren't jumped and killed by gang bosses in the first few days!"

At the top of the staircase, Carthage leaned on the banister and started to laugh.

"It's not funny!" Huxley shouted. "I've got the rest of my life ahead of me! Our show is destroyed and so are we!"

"Huxley," said Carthage, and pulled the ring from his pocket. "We'll be just fine."

"What— what is *that*?" Huxley snatched it out of

Carthage's hand and held it to the light, like it might be fake.

"A token of gratitude from Our Celestial Lady," Carthage answered.

"She *gave* it to you?"

"No, Huxley, I wrested it off her hand. Yes, she *gave* it to me!"

Huxley didn't look amused. "How long were you going to wait until you told me?"

Carthage, still laughing, turned away for his room. "Until you got hysterical."

22

THE PRODUCER

Mr. Stratton Pierce met Huxley at a patio table outside the Oakley boarding house in Queens Junction twenty-one minutes after noon.

Pierce wasn't very old, but his temples were white-washed by stress, and he had the slowness of a man unaccustomed to physical activity. He wore a patterned waistcoat with a bolo tie and a charming smile, and used a lacy handkerchief to mop sweat from his wide brow as he apologized for being late.

Huxley had taken his coat off and hung it over the back of his chair, enjoying that pleasant comfort of being just slightly hot in the yellow gaze of the Principal Star.

After the ordeal on the mountain, it seemed at first he would never defrost. He'd been in Fallsbright now for almost three weeks, re-discovering the forgotten joys of walking barefoot, having lunch outdoors, and leaving the windows open while he slept. He was pleased to find himself almost sweating now as he supped on this patio in full daylight.

It was a lazy heat, and from Huxley's vantage at the

sidewalk cafe, Queens Junction seemed to move slowly. The town, which had sprung up around the train depot, was still unpaved, although Huxley was surprised to see that they had recently replaced the gas lamps with electric ones. It was still rare to see electricity on Fallsbright.

There was a different attitude here, which carried horses and wagons at a comfortable and polite trot instead of the breakneck crush of traffic always constant on the mainlands. People tipped hats on the sidewalks, and a few workers loading hay at the livery across the street paused to swap stories and laugh at jokes. Even the clouds seemed to be unhurried as they drawled across in an impossibly wide sky.

Huxley inhaled. The dry air was high and bright with mowed grass, and the eucalyptus blooming along the roads, and the hay the stablehands carried off in forkfuls.

At a nearby table, somebody sliced an orange — almost certainly a Huxley orange — bleeding a fragrance that was intoxicating with memories.

Pierce was still talking, and Huxley forced himself to listen.

"We've bought the old Edgewood and renovated it," Pierce said. "Are you familiar?"

"I know the place," Huxley answered as he wiped his plate with a bit of cornbread. He had ordered lunch and started eating while he waited on Pierce.

When he arrived home, he felt as endlessly hungry as he did ceaselessly cold. Three squares of hot food a day warmed a different part of him, something deeper. This was what lunch was *supposed* to be. Cornbread and succotash, hominy grits, pork chops and red-eye gravy, fresh butter and strong coffee.

"We've just installed electric lighting," Pierce went on. "New paint, and we also added two new dressing rooms."

"When does the show open?" Huxley asked.

"In two weeks," Pierce answered. "Previews are glowing — you can read it in the papers."

"I have, in fact. Congratulations."

Pierce gave a wide smile. "Thank you." Then the smile faded. "Of course, then my stage manager went and got himself bucked off a green horse. Broke half the bones in his body. Laid up in traction for the next six months."

Huxley winced as he washed his meal down with a slug of coffee.

"I understand you grew up just a few miles down the road." Pierce fanned himself with his wide-brimmed hat. "The Revue ain't for the faint of heart. We'll be doing two shows a day, six days a week. But there's a refurbished garret upstairs for you to live, and there's Sundays off for supper at home."

Abigail Oakley, her hair done in a braid and her gingham apron specked with flour, interrupted to take Pierce's order. He waved her off and helped himself to the pot of coffee that was already on the table.

Abigail turned to clear Huxley's plate, which he'd picked clean down to the marrow of the bones. "Mr. Huxley, how will Ma Oakley feel when she sees you barely touched her food?"

"Tell her it was worse than usual," he said.

She snickered. "You got any room left in that bottomless pit for dessert?"

"What do you have in the way of whole pies?"

"It doesn't sound very gentlemanly to sit and eat a whole pie all by yourself, Mr. Huxley."

"I could be persuaded to share," he answered.

Pierce cleared his throat.

"Put a ribbon on it," Huxley told Abigail. "I'll take it home." Then he turned back to Pierce. "Room and board included, you said?"

"Yes, and a very handsome salary."

"Beauty's in the eye, Mr. Pierce — perhaps you could name an exact figure."

Pierce ran a finger around the rim of his coffee cup, a ghost of a grin. "Why don't *you* name a figure?" he said. "Tell me what would be a handsome salary for a man like you."

Huxley considered that for a moment. It was a good question.

What was it he *wanted*?

He finished his coffee and laughed. "We seem to have some crossed wires, Mr. Pierce. Thank you for the generous offer — but I'm afraid I couldn't leave my company."

Pierce's easygoing look faded. "I was under the impression that your company was bankrupt."

"Your impression was wrong. As was mine — when you requested a meeting, I thought you might be looking to invest in us. I'm afraid that I have wasted your time, and you have wasted mine."

Pierce's hand formed a fist on the tabletop. "Make a wise decision for once in your life, *boy*. You and your gimp are already awash in scandal. An offer like this won't come around again."

Huxley rose from the table and put on his hat, pausing to leave his payment and a gratuity. "Here's to hoping."

"That's the last time I do any favors for your father," Pierce spat, also rising from the table. "And the last time I show any respect to you. You're just as foolish and ungrateful as he warned me you'd be."

It made more sense now. Huxley thought he was supposed to be angry, but was somehow touched instead.

Many nights, lying awake in his dormitory bed at school, he had wondered if his parents regretted him entirely. Backstage manipulation of his life and his career was not what he wanted from them, but it did suggest that they cared.

Abigail returned with his pie, and he kissed her on the cheek, the Fallsbright way.

"Best of luck with the Revue," he told Pierce. Tipped his hat and winked before he walked away. "Break a leg."

23

VERIS & VYSKANDER

Jasper the electrical sprawled on the table under the window, wiring harnesses lying exposed like the guts of a patient on a gurney, and Carthage squinted through his reading glasses, trying to file the teeth of two cogs so that they would evenly meet.

He was sleeping in a boarding house in Queens Junction, in a top-floor room that offered a bed, its own stove, and ample room to spread his tools. The only impediment to his work was that the building didn't have electricity, which he'd quickly come to learn was still a rare commodity on Fallsbright.

It was his first time on the isle, and there were some things he didn't think he'd get used to. Firstly, the downright dreadful amount of kissing involved in saying hello and goodbye — although Carthage was relieved that his alien status seemed to generally exclude him from the custom.

Secondly, the swarms of biting insects that came out in the early evening. Huxley called them mosquitoes and seemed unconcerned by them, even though they could bite you through your clothes and suck the blood out of your body, which seemed to Carthage like something to be concerned about.

Thirdly, the temperature.

He worked now with the windows open and his coat off, sleeves rolled past the elbow, no waistcoat and no tie, but he was still sweating through his shirt.

He'd taken some time off, which he mostly spent reading, but now was glad to have something to do with his hands again.

Huxley had sold the ring (by what dubious broker, Carthage chose not to ask), and with part of that money they paid a salvager to go up on the mountain and haul the wreck back down.

They recovered a few more of their personal belongings, which was comforting, and they sold the train itself for the price of its weight in scrap.

This turned out to be fairly lucrative, as the cars all had copper wiring in the walls, and for the copper alone the salvage operation turned a profit that put them back in good graces with the bank — although it would take a few more payments to square the loan completely.

They also recovered the equipment and electricals that were in the freight car. The electricals had all sustained cosmetic damage, and some of them had physical damage as well. But none of them were broken beyond repair. Carthage had already restored Marietta, Blackjack the fiddling electrical, and some of the others, although they would need new paint before they returned to performance.

• 300
★ ∗ •

Now, he worked to repair Jasper, and felt the irony of that act they had done so many times together. If only bringing the electricals to life were as easy as tossing a sheet over them and waving a magic hand.

His reading glasses weren't getting the job done. Squinting was straining his eyes.

"Have you seen my...?" he started aloud before realizing he was alone.

It wasn't entirely true that none of them were broken beyond repair. The absence of Dominic still ached. Soon, Carthage would have to start thinking about building a new butler, but that was still hard to fathom.

He got up to look for his loupes himself, and was still ransacking the room for them five minutes later when there was a gentle knock on his door.

He sat up from where he was searching under the bed. "Aye?"

"Mr. Carthage?" He recognized the voice of Abigail, the landlady's daughter. "There's somebody downstairs to see you."

"Thank you," he said, and got up. His braces were down, and he pulled them over his shoulders and buttoned the top buttons of his shirt before putting his coat back on. He didn't feel entirely decent going out without a vest or a tie, but he'd seen from the locals that it was acceptable, and he was simply too hot to overdress.

Taking a moment to wipe the grease off his hands, he reached for his cane and went downstairs. Who would call on him in Fallsbright?

The boarding house was a narrow three stories, with

a parlor at the bottom and a restaurant adjacent. As he reached the parlor, he found a woman sitting on the edge of the sofa, gaze fixed on the high street beyond the windowpane.

She was so out of place here that he stopped in the doorway and said nothing. Sensing his presence, she turned and stood up quickly, as if startled.

"Elys?" He said it like a question.

She took him in, and her eyes darted to the cane. "Sylvester?" His name was also a question.

He crossed the threshold into the parlor. "What are you doing here?"

"I was..." She hesitated, as if she were about to say she was in the area. Fallsbright was a week by rail from the Central Isles, which made that a dubious excuse. "I wanted to see you," she said instead, closing the distance. "After I got your letter, I wanted to make sure you were alright. You *are* alright?"

"Aye," he said. "Reports of my death were greatly exaggerated."

She didn't laugh. Her eyes were bright with fear, and perhaps tears she was refusing to spend. He hadn't seen her that way many times, but it was a look still seared in his memory.

It was the way she looked at him after the house burned down.

He realized that Abigail lingered in the foyer, eavesdropping. She was a kindly girl, but an irascible gossip, so he held his arm out to Elys. "Will you walk with me?"

★

I̶T WAS EARLY evening, and the Principal Star was falling under the horizon of the isle. A warm and purple twilight swathed Queens Junction like velvet drapes.

Carthage walked with his sister down the sidewalk, in the long shadows of trees with limbs burdened by red-and-pink flowers.

They didn't talk about his near-death experience.

They talked about the things he'd seen on Helios, and how things went with Elys's business on Atlas. She mentioned the surprising turn that the Future Queen had taken the royal title *Celeste*, a name which boldly embodied the spirit of the Empire itself, promising the people a strong and unified reign. And the even more surprising turn that Celeste had been photographed for the first time and revealed to have a crippled hand.

At this, Elys stopped walking, unlinked her arm from his and turned to scrutinize him. "Are you alright?"

"Yes," he said.

"It's unlike you to walk with a cane. The papers were saying sommat about suffering a fall."

He looked at the cane for a moment. "I was determined to live an illusion," he said finally. "I think that I have exaggerated my own pain by trying to conceal it."

He didn't just mean the pain in his legs.

"I do stumble. Now and again, I even fall. There is no reason for me to pretend otherwise, except for arrogance." He ran his tongue over his teeth as the clattering of a stagecoach in the road filled the silence between them.

"I'm to blame," he confessed as the coach drew

away. "Everything that has happened to us... the end of the Cannongates. There's no excuse for me to pretend otherwise about that, either. The fire was my fault. An accident — but entirely my fault."

She looked down and smoothed her skirts, although she looked just fine. It occurred to him then — for the first time — how similar they were. He'd almost never seen his sister cry. Perhaps he was grasping some lesson she had yet to learn.

"It must have hurt you," he said knowingly, "that I've never said it."

She looked up, her eyes dry and her brow pulled tight. "I suppose," she said, as if only just now entertaining the thought. But her voice was heavy. "Perhaps it did."

"I'm sorry," he said. "You have no idea how much I regret what happened."

"I only ever wanted to protect our family," she answered, keeping a steady voice. "For so many years, I've been so afraid — afraid that everything I love might vanish like a wick. I told myself I only wanted what was best for you. But perhaps — maybe — I was also angry. And perhaps I have let fear and anger cloud me for too long. I thought that all I ever wanted was an apology. But it occurs to me now, hearing you apologize, that what my spirit truly longed for was to finally *forgive.*" She swallowed, and then steeled herself, as if drawing up the courage for it. "It was an accident, Sylvester. It was only a mistake."

He exhaled some weight he didn't know he was carrying.

They both shuffled for a moment, looking away. Not exactly certain what to say next. Cicadas in the trees chirruped with blistering decibel. Elys dabbed one corner of her eye with a handkerchief, in a manner like she'd gotten a speck of dust in it.

"Will you perform again?"

"Yes," he said. "I'll be well enough to go back onstage in a few weeks."

"Will you visit Atlas?"

He felt a smile tug the corner of his mouth. "That could be arranged."

"Good," she said. "You ought to visit your nieces and nephews. Adelaide will have had the new bairn by the time you drop in. And it would do mother well to see you. On her better days, she asks after you."

"Alright," he promised. "I will."

"I would also like to see your show," Elys said, putting her handkerchief away.

That tug of a smile gave way to a grin. "I'll send you tickets."

"Alright then." She fussed with her reticule for a moment. "I'm going to visit a sick friend here on Fallsbright. I have an eight o'clock coach into Halpertsdown. I just thought I ought to stop by and see you first."

"It was very agreeable to see you."

"Yes... it was." After a moment of clear indecision, she pulled him into a sudden and startling hug.

Shuddering a breath into his shirtfront, she said something he didn't hear but fully understood.

I'm glad you lived.

Overcoming his shock, he wrapped his arms around her and buried himself face-down in her hair to hide his expression.

After a moment, she released him and stepped back, curt again. "I'll tell the girls to expect you."

She had him feeling overly sentimental. "Tell them I love them."

She nodded, a small smile, then she left.

He stood in the dim and milky shade of evening, watching his own regrets leave with her. Feeling rested.

Somebody whistled. It was Huxley, who was eating an apple as he approached. He, too, looked after Elys.

"Well, well, look at you," he said. "Who was that sublime vision of feminine—"

"My little sister."

Huxley coughed up an apple seed. "—chastity?" He had several parcels bundled under one arm, and procured an envelope now, as if to change the subject. "I have the post."

Carthage took it, squinting at the delicate handwriting on the envelope. It was addressed to both of them, and it had no return address.

He opened the envelope and took out a folded letter, but the handwriting proved to be too fine. Patting his interior pocket, he remembered he'd taken his reading glasses off, and left them... well, somewhere... while he was looking for his loupes.

"Have you seen my—"

Huxley pointed, wordlessly.

Carthage put a hand to his head and discovered his

missing loupes. "*Ah*," he said. "I looked everywhere for these!"

The letter was written on good paper in a reserved dark blue ink and a careful hand. They read it as they walked across the street to the train depot.

My two friends,
I hope this letter finds you well and recovering from your
ordeal. I must begin by begging your forgiveness for my part in
the declaration of your death. At the time, I did believe you had
both perished, and I was mortified when I saw you again in the
flesh.

At the beginning of the competition, I discovered the identity of
Andromeda Skyhawke to be a charade, but I had already been
marked as a pawn by the conspirators. A collaborator working
within the palace revealed himself to me, informed me of an
incendiary device planted somewhere within those walls, and
threatened to detonate it if I told anyone what I knew. I am
almost too galled to write these words, but said collaborator
was a corrupt protectorate from my own ranks.

This startling revelation left me with little idea of whom to
trust, and therefore, despite a great protest of conscience, I was
coerced to rule Abernathy's death accidental and to play part in
the ongoing ruse.

The night you were apprehended, I have never been more
relieved. That you had learned of the treachery afoot and had

come to thwart it allowed me the opportunity to locate the explosive device and eliminate the corrupt protectorate.

We later learned this traitor was charged with transporting the trick cage containing Skyhawke and Our Celestial Lady out of the castle. You may not disclose this to anyone, but we also learned the plot was to hold the Future Queen as leverage over the Empire. In preventing the abduction of HM Celeste, you also prevented what I must believe would have been the beginning of a Terraformist revolution.

The collaborators have all been arrested and face capital charges — except, of course, for the lady-at-large. Although we have succeeded in keeping the public in the dark about this thwarted disaster, I believed that I owed the two of you a private explanation.

I love Our Celestial Lady more than life itself, and I have sworn myself to sacrifice anything in Her name. Truly, I owe you more than just an explanation, and if you are ever in trouble, know that you have a friend in high places.

Sincerely,
Miles.

PS: As a thank you for what you have done, I've sent you something, which should arrive on the train with this letter.

"What a character," said Huxley when they finished reading the letter.

Carthage considered the outcomes of all the players. "What do you think happened to the woman?"

Huxley frowned. "I'd rather not think on her, frankly. But I doubt we'll ever see the charlatan again..." His frown faded as he changed the subject to something more curious. "What do you suppose Vicewar sent us?"

Curious, they walked down the platform to where the cargo was being unloaded. Huxley identified himself, and the railman pushed his cap away from his eyes. "Oh," he said, "the *big* one."

They were shown to the end of the platform, where a gigantic wooden crate showed stamps from a half-dozen rail depots. It had their names on it, alright, but they were perplexed. The crate was so large it towered overhead.

"Just pull that," the railman said, pointing to a pull cord on the crate. Other freight workers stopped working and gathered to see what was inside.

Carthage pulled the cord, and the sides of the crate collapsed and fell away with a loud clatter and a gust of air.

The railman took a step back. "What in all the depths is *that*?"

"*Endeavour!*" Carthage and Huxley cried simultaneously.

Their elephant was none the worse for wear, despite his long journey. Carthage found the switch and turned Endeavour on, discovering the beast still had some power left. Endeavour trumpeted smoke, eyes burning with life, and fanned his ears.

Huxley crowed, pumping his fist. "Attaboy!"

Endeavour trumpeted again in answer, and Carthage laughed.

Huxley pulled a rolled-up poster from under his arm. "We might have to add him to the poster." He unfurled the paper and gave it a sharp flick to activate the advertisement.

SEE THE DEATH-DEFYING SYLVESTER CARTHAGE AND HIS ELECTRICAL MENAGERIE, read titling underneath an illustration of a train plummeting through the clouds.

"What do you think?" Huxley asked.

Carthage felt embarrassed just looking at it.

He wasn't shy about seeing his name in print, but this was different. This was not an act — it was a *real* and unscripted thing that they had done, cheating death. Using it to sell tickets seemed rather much. "Isn't it..." He hesitated. "Sensational?"

"Oh," said Huxley, and looked at the poster for a moment. "You have a good point there. Well, I'll have it amended."

He took a pen out of his coat and scrawled on the paper so that it now read SEE THE *SENSATIONAL,* DEATH-DEFYING SYLVESTER CARTHAGE AND HIS ELECTRICAL MENAGERIE.

"You're right," he said. "That's much better!"

"That's..." Not what he meant, but... "Excellent work, Mr. Huxley."

"It's time for the comeback tour, my friend!" Huxley rolled up the poster with a proud look. "Wait until you see what else I've done."

They both turned toward the platform as the freight

engine hissed and rolled away to reveal a bright blue train on the other side.

Scraping every last cent they had from the salvage and the sale of the ring, they bought this new train, which Carthage found comfortably similar to the last one. It was still being painted and furnished, and now there was a drop cloth draped over one side of it.

Huxley raised an arm and whistled to the workers on the tracks. They yanked the cloth, revealing a mural on the cargo car underneath: gold-leaf lettering on a bright blue backdrop, shaded so that it seemed to jump three-dimensionally off the side of the train.

Carthage's heart leapt.

The Electrical Menagerie.

It was real again, and so was his name at the bottom: *proprietors Carthage & Huxley.*

Huxley crowed again, as if delighted by his own name, and slapped Carthage on the back.

Carthage felt the same. After everything, here they were on the other side. Even their show was now reborn.

Darkness was falling fast, and the Lesser Lights glimmered overhead. He looked beyond them, toward Heaven, overwhelmed with gratitude.

Huxley glanced up, too.

"He isn't falling," Huxley interjected suddenly.

"Who?"

"Veris. The royal astronomers say he was only moving to a new position."

Carthage looked for Veris and found it. Fixed and shimmering in the night sky. "Good," he said with a smile.

Huxley observed him, curious. "You like Veris?" He pointed proudly across the sky. "My favorite is Vyskander."

Vyskander, the star that crashed into Veris?

Carthage laughed aloud. Fitting.

They turned to each other on the platform. Huxley spat in his hand and stuck it out.

Seeing Carthage draw back, he laughed. "You're on Fallsbright now. This is how we seal deals on *my* isle."

When on Fallsbright... as long as Carthage didn't have to kiss anybody. He spat into his own hand and shook with Huxley.

"You sure about this?" Huxley asked, holding him there.

It was a bit late to be asking that, since they'd already bought a train and had it painted. But Carthage understood what Huxley meant.

They were back to where they began — setting off with no more than a train between them. This time, they didn't even have anonymity to slink back into. Now, for better or worse, people were watching.

Was he sure it would work? Of course not. This was show business. Nothing was sure.

Was he sure he wanted to do it anyway?

"You know what they say," he answered, pumped Huxley's hand and winked. "The show must go on."

★

My New Friend,
I hope you enjoyed this book. It is a mostly accurate account. (We are of the opinion that the author did a fairly adequate job).

Would you like to read more about me? (A rhetorical question, of course). I am starring in a story which you can read for that magical price of absolutely FREE!

Also, seeing as we are starving artists, perhaps you would be inclined to write a review for *The Electrical Menagerie* on **Amazon** or **Goodreads**?

Each and every review is a slice of bread on our table (not meant lightly... I live with a man who can eat his weight in bread). It also greatly consoles our fragile egos to read your positive reviews. (The negative ones we use for tinder in the stove, which is also useful).

As always, if you'd like to correspond with me, you can reach me via electronic mail at this address:
AQHuxley@writeratops.com

Although we are very busy, I love to read your letters and will do my best to reply.

Ever yours,
A.Q. Huxley

FREE eBOOK!

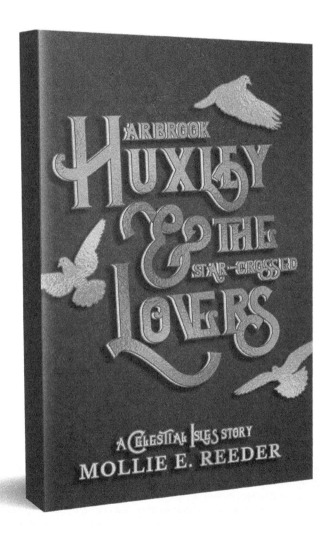

ACKNOWLEDGMENTS

Thank you, person reading this, for spending your time with me in my world.

Thank you Sarah, Gillian, & Kyle for supporting me, editing me, and answering my plethora of questions throughout the publishing process. Your loyal friendships are truly a gift.

Thank you Laura A. Grace for your unending enthusiasm, passion, and labor to illuminate others. You are a (Unicorn) Queen.

Thank you, Melody, my sister, for shaping my imagination. Thank you JJ, Mallory, Meagan, Leslie, and Laura for being my first and greatest fans.

Thank you Mom & Dad for always supporting my dreams — even when they were hard to understand.

Thank you Nate, D'Lytha, Brian, Jason, and Danielle for recognizing something in me and trusting me enough to call me a co-producer and a partner.

Thank you all my ARC readers, reviewers, and supporters — there are too many of you to list, but you know who you are!

And all gratitude to my "Father of Lights", Jesus Christ, through whom all things were made; who hung the Stars, and who holds me aloft as I reach for them.

ABOUT THE AUTHOR | MOLLIE E. REEDER
Mollie's first job was with a major theme park, where
she operated a roller coaster, fixed parade floats, and
helped Scooby-Doo put on his head. Now, Mollie is a
movie producer and the author of character-driven
science fiction/fantasy novels for adults who never
outgrew imagination. Her favorite things include Jesus,
dinosaurs, and telling cinematic stories that blend glitter
and grit. Follow her on Twitter @writeratops.

*Miss Reeder is thrilled that Messrs. Carthage & Huxley
permitted her to recount their adventures to you, and thanks
them for their cooperation throughout the publication process.*